TURN TO DUST AND ASHES

Fall Far from the Tree Book Two

AMY MCNULTY

Snowy Wings
PUBLISHING

ﷺ I ﷺ

TOMIKO

I missed my brother.

I missed both my brothers. Elder Brother Nobutada might not have shown me as much kindness, but he hadn't always been the ruthless reflection of our parents that he had been in the days—months, years—leading to his and Father's deaths.

But I could not let this grief—this hesitation, this regret—show in Mother's presence. Not for one single solitary moment.

"You act as if I should care, Yeoman," she said. "Enough with the excuses. I will not stand for anything that is simply an excuse for why I should not have my men lop your head off from your shoulders where you kneel."

"No!" The man—one of the land-holding lesser yeoman farmers who oversaw the cultivation of crops somewhere outside the capital—prostrated himself once more on the ground, grinding his nose into the *tatami* mat, as if he thought that with just a little more effort, he might eventually sink into the surface beneath him.

"Rise!" snapped Mother, losing some of her composure. She stood, her handmaidens scrambling from beside the dais to step in so she wouldn't trip over any of the long, flowing layers of her imperial *kimono*. "I told you to rise already. I will not stand for endless groveling when it does nothing but waste my time and delay the inevitable."

I had to stop my mask from cracking. If Elder Brother Kojiro were here, we'd have discussed this later, huddled beneath the safety of lantern light in one of our chambers. Mother insisted on shows of fealty, on prostrations of obedience, even if they irked her. It was hard enough for her own family to find the right balance, let alone the poor layperson whose one chance to have an audience with her might also be their final one.

I had little hope for this thin, shirking farmer yeoman.

"The rains," he spat, reluctantly sitting up on his legs again, the threadbare hat in his hands surely ripping even more as he twisted it between both fists. "They flooded our crops. You can ask Lord Nakamura; his crops fared no better—"

"I am not speaking to Yeoman Nakamura right now, am I?" Mother's smile was sweet. Welcoming. But let your eyes wander a short distance above those fire-red lips, and those black eyes—so dark amidst the painted snow of her face—could never let anyone mistake something as simple as a smile for kindness.

"No, Your Majesty." The man went to prostrate himself again but flinched halfway, squeezing his hat tighter and rising back into a sitting position.

Mother raised an eyebrow. "And is that how you apologize to your empress?"

"No, Your Majesty!" The man flung himself forward, his nose back on the mat. "I apologize profusely for my offense. I spoke out of turn."

Mother's smile was genuine this time. She paced back and forth, ignoring the handmaidens struggling to keep her train straight despite her sharp movements, stepping between them as if they were mere spirits she could not see. Her eyes brightened as she looked down at the farmer. There was no mistaking that she genuinely enjoyed this—her conflicting moods, her confusing message, her refusal to let anyone do anything but displease her.

Few would dare to look her in the face to fully understand that she knew precisely what she was doing, that it was no mere accident that her moods shifted with the direction of the wind.

But I did. I could.

"I believe I just told you, Yeoman, that such prostrations are a waste of my time." She stopped moving suddenly. "And wasting your empress' time must be one of the highest forms of insults."

"No!" The man scrambled to sit up again. There was no missing the pallid tone his skin had taken, the moisture that clung to his forehead and dripped down his cheeks. "I apologize, Your Majesty," he said, inclining his head slightly. If he twisted his hat any harder, I was certain he would tear it in two.

Mother turned her back on him, her gaze settling on me seated on the dais behind her—beside where her own cushion lay in the center. There were empty cushions on either side of the imperial seat. One for Mother—for she sat in Father's seat now, just until the heir was ready, she claimed—one for Imperial Prince and Heir Nobutada and one for Imperial Prince Kojiro. I refused to sit anywhere but the seat for Imperial Princess Tomiko, at the farthest reaches from the center. I would not move into the heir's seat.

"What do you think, Princess?" She never gave Kojiro a title when she spoke to him. She never gave him an ounce of respect. "Has the yeoman wasted enough of my time?"

I took in the scene of the man on his knees, the guards standing silently flanking him on either side. The handmaidens stood with Mother's train between their delicate fingers. Other servants stood by, in the shadows, perhaps grateful to retreat from sight. They needn't have bothered. In this room, only Mother existed, only Mother mattered, and for a brief moment, she'd allowed this man to pretend he did. Now she asked me to step up. To speak. To be.

"Honorable Mother," I began, fighting every urge I had to swallow, to appear anything but the perfect heir and princess, "I am not sure there is someone who can take his place. If we are ever to get the crops back to the numbers we need, we will need experts to guide the process."

Mother's face fell as she waved a hand—slightly, almost imperceptibly—in my direction, turning back to face the man. "There is always another man. Always another farmer. And this one is clearly no expert."

"Your Majesty, please. I have a wife. Children. Grandchildren.

We serve Your Majesty and the Great Empire of Hanaobi with all of our hearts, with all of our spirits, with all of our beings—"

Mother stepped forward, gracefully with small steps, although she was at his side before he could speak another word. For the briefest of seconds, his eyes raked over her face and whatever he saw there caused him to grow paler still before he remembered to stare instead at the floor in front of him.

"Do you know how many men and women have told me the exact same story?"

The man shook his head.

"How many have told me they have wives and husbands and children and grandchildren…" She sneered and began to pace back and forth in front of him, her billowing *kimono* making it seem as if she were gliding without the assistance of feet.

The man shook his head again. His hands were trembling as they clung to his hat for dear life.

"If I only executed those without families for insolence and failure, I would have to exempt all but the barren and widowed and those poor wretched souls have suffered enough, wouldn't you say?"

The man nodded, his throat bobbing.

Mother stopped in front of him again. "I am a widow, Yeoman."

The man struggled to speak. "Of-Of course, Your Majesty. I apologize. I never meant to imply—"

Mother turned again. "I have lost two sons."

She had no proof of Elder Brother Kojiro's death. No reason to assume he'd done anything but run away. She couldn't have possibly imagined where to. She never would have thought him brave enough, bold enough. But she could never have understood the well of courage she buried and suffocated and stifled in him with just a nod of her head.

"I am so sorry, Your Majesty."

She walked closer to me, pointing toward me as she turned back again to face the man, her eyes never once traveling to acknowledge the women bending and scrambling to get her train out of her way. "Were it not for my dear daughter, the final heir, my joy in this world"—she smiled toward me as she said this, but the kindness never reached her eyes—"my last remaining family, I should just die, is that what you are saying, Yeoman?"

"No!" The man straightened his back. "No, never, Your Majesty! Never! I never meant such an offense. I only asked that you give me another chance so that I may be sent home to my family one last time."

"Yes, to your wife and children and grandchildren and all the rest." Mother fluffed her hand toward him as she sat back down on her cushion, the handmaidens crossing in front of and behind her to arrange her train like a bright red river of blood cascading through the pale brown of the *tatami* mats. "It sounds to me as if there are plenty of hands at your farm. I will give your family another chance." She nodded toward one of her guards. "But I will not give you the chance to see them once more." The guards grabbed the man by the armpits, his legs kicking as he floated above the floor and he was dragged out of the room. "From the sounds of it, your goodbyes alone would take half a day, and you do know how I hate wasted time."

"Your Majesty! I—" But the man's words were cut short as one of the guards hit him atop the head with the hilt of his sword. The actual execution would take place outside, where the mess would simply return to the soil, where the sun spirit could reclaim what she had once given.

He'd lived a long life at least. A good life from the sound of it. I knew he must be grateful. If his farm did not produce more within the year, his son would live a far shorter one.

"Sougo," snapped Mother. From where I sat, I could see the slight color of her own skin at the back of her neck, the flush of perspiration that dotted it from her trek around the room.

"Yes, Your Majesty?" Sougo, one of her trusted attendants, stepped forward from the shadows. He turned to one of the servant girls. "Fetch Her Majesty her tea."

"Thank you, Sougo." Mother looked satisfied. Despite everything, she was not above rewarding behavior that pleased her with common courtesy should the mood strike her. She did not say anything more until the servant girl returned with a tray on which sat a tea pot and two cups. With a slight tremble to her hands, she put the tray down between Mother and me and went to grab the teapot.

"Let Princess Tomiko do it," said Mother, sweetness and iciness coating her words all at once. She was in a good mood after sentencing the farmer and she would not strike at the girl for her momentary relapse.

The girl nodded and I stood, my own handmaidens rushing to take hold of my train. It was shorter than Mother's but still plenty longer than anyone else's in the room. The pale pink of the material stood out against the brown *tatami* as I took my small, measured steps forward to the tray. I set to task scooping the matcha into each cup before taking careful hold of the pot and pouring the water over the powder.

Mother turned to Sougo. "Who is this Nakamura he mentioned?"

Sougo's stiff lips grew thinner as I picked up the whisk and set to the task of making the froth appear from the tea. "His neighboring farmer, I suppose."

"You suppose?"

I stopped mid-whisk of my mother's tea.

"I will check with the records at once," said Sougo. "I apologize most profusely for my rudeness."

I let the whisk move again.

"Do not bother." Mother smiled at me—graciously, genuinely— as I cradled her tea with both hands and handed it to her. I did not complete the proper tea ceremony, but Mother was in need of refreshment, and she could only stand such a halfhearted attempt from her own family. The insult otherwise would have been too great.

Thus her desire for me to make the tea.

"Thank you, Princess," she said, sipping the tea. I returned to the tray to make my own cup, although I had no need to quench my thirst. "I am sure he has failed to produce as well. Find him and bring him to me for a chance to explain himself." Her eyes danced almost gleefully as she brought the cup back to her lips.

"At once, Your Majesty." Sougo bowed and went to exit, never once showing his back to his empress. Guards could when called to, the handmaidens had to at times to keep the train from tripping my mother, but Sougo would not dare.

"Come sit with me," said Mother after a moment, motioning to the cushion beside her. Elder Brother Kojiro's cushion.

I tapped the whisk against the side of my cup and left it on its stand, cradling the cup as I shuffled to sit beside her, my handmaidens trailing behind and then in front of me as they arranged my *kimono*.

"How go your studies, my dear?"

"Well, thank you," I said. Mother's kindness in these moments was not lost on me, but I had long since noticed the difference in how she treated me—compared to my poor oaf of an older brother, who ought to have been my equal, my superior even, and to those around us. Those invisible, visible people around us.

"Master Kondo speaks most highly of your progress." She laughed before taking another sip. "I can see how grateful he is to teach you instead of the heir before you."

I cradled my cup of tea in both hands. The tutors to the "heir before me" all wound up dead. Other than the barbarian foreigner with the golden hair. The one I hoped had safely stolen my brother away.

Mother did not notice my solemn mood. "He tells me you are quite skilled in the tongue of the barbarians."

"I am," I said, in that very tongue. It sounded coarse and sharp.

Mother laughed again. "You are lovely," she said, holding her cup out in the air until a servant scrambled to take it from her. She tucked her hands back into the billows of her sleeves. "You understand that being the ruler of Hanaobi involves intelligence and discipline. That there is reason to take pride in your accomplishments, so long as you defer to those who deserve your deference and loyalty." She reached toward me, running a soft finger across my cheek. The intimate gesture seemed so out of place in this room. "You were meant to be heir. I am sure of it. All we have been through… The spirits ordained it to see you on the throne."

I said nothing, not sure the spirits would rejoice in the deaths of my father and eldest brother, nor in the banishment of my elder brother and closest friend. But then again, it was they who'd put my family on the throne in the first place. They who'd allowed my disgraced aunt to abandon her people and lie with a barbarian beyond the sea.

"As much as it pained me to lose Prince Nobutada, I am so glad the spirits saw fit to put you next in line."

She did not say *his* name, did not mention how it might be that I'd be next in line.

She did not mention the weapon Father had had crafted for Elder Brother Nobutada, the one I'd given to Elder Brother Kojiro before I'd bade him to run far, far away. I wondered if she even imagined it unaccounted for. Doubtful.

When had Mother decided that Elder Brother Kojiro disappointed her? When had she looked at me and decided I was the one who ought to follow Father on the throne?

If Mother ever gave up her grip on it.

"Honorable Mother," I began, almost ready to defend my brother for the insult by omission, almost ready to speak up, "you flatter me."

I ran my thumbs over the warm clay cup, the unevenness digging into my skin. I could not stand up for him. I knew how hard life had been for him here—knew Mother would have killed him and thought nothing of it—and yet, the most I could do was support him from the shadows and tell him to run away. I hoped he was happier in the duchy. Part of me wanted him to have shown our mother how wrong she was about him. The rest hoped he didn't stop there and had ridden boat after boat until he was far, far away —away from Hanaobi, away from the duchy, away from any place our mother's grasp might reach.

"I do not flatter," replied Mother after a moment's thought. "I only reward fealty and talent."

"Your Majesty." Sogo returned, a strange look of triumph on his usually-taciturn features.

It didn't go unnoticed. Mother raised her eyebrows. "You have news of this other farmer so quickly?" She waved a hand at him. "You need not bother me with the details. Just summon him to me."

"Yes, of course, Your Majesty, but that isn't it." He held a parchment up that he'd kept tucked beneath his arm as he'd entered. "The trade ship arrived from the duchy just now. The captain sent a messenger from the docks with the letter he received at sea. He's on his way himself as soon as he's finished unloading."

My heart thudded wildly against my breastbone. Had Elder Brother Kojiro been found? What kind of news might make Sougo—who lived to please his empress—so uncharacteristically happy?

He's dead. He has to be dead.

The cup slipped from my fingers, but no one else noticed as the liquid soaked into my *kimono*. Even the handmaidens were mesmerized by the sight of Sougo unhinged.

"Sougo," said Mother, "if you do not start sharing the reasons for your mirth with me immediately, I shall be quite disappointed with you."

"Of course!" Sougo prostrated himself on the floor, bowing—but quickly—in apology. He shook the letter above him. "He is dead," he said, confirming my every fear. "The barbarian duke who kidnapped your sister-in-law, our empress, is dead at long last!"

A wash of relief flooded over me. He did not speak of Elder Brother Kojiro. He had run, he'd hidden, the secret weapon I'd gifted him always there to protect him.

Mother did not seem as joyful as the news ought to have made her. She looked... wounded. "Sougo," she said, recovering and intertwining her fingers. "My husband was emperor before me."

The smile slipped from Sougo's lips like a cascading waterfall had wiped all hope from his face. "Of course, Your Majesty," he said, bowing slightly, likely unable to imagine his offense.

But I knew it now. Depending on Mother's mood, she might not get over it and we might not get the rest of the story until the captain made it to the palace. And there was poor Sougo to consider. His loyalty ought to be rewarded. Mother herself had said she'd valued fealty.

"What Master Sougo surely meant to say," I said, almost surprised at my own boldness, "is the duke who has been our country's sworn enemy for nearly two decades, the one who took the disgraced princess away from our lands and turned her into a traitor to all the spirits hold dear, is dead." I widened my eyes at Sougo, letting him take the reins. *Mother could be assuaged if you knew how.*

"Yes, of course!" Sougo swallowed, his misstep in his exuberance now clear to him. "Leave it to the elegant Princess Tomiko to voice my thoughts more eloquently than I could ever hope to."

Mother let one eyebrow raise, but her curiosity seemed to have won over the slight. "How?" she asked simply, and I prayed Sougo would be savvy enough to know what she meant.

"Slain in battle," said Sougo, poring over the letter once more. His eyes darted madly up and down over the page. "During a confrontation with"—he gulped, and I knew he was about to say something Mother would not like to hear—"our own Hanaobi people, those runaways, those traitors," he spat, adding the latter part for Mother's appeasement, no doubt.

My heart fluttered hopefully. The expats had risen against the duke? After sneaking into the land and managing to escape their barbaric guards? Who but... Who but their prince, their heir, could motivate them so?

"Farmers," said Mother. "A band of farmers killed a ruler with the might of an army." She did not sound pleased at all that her sworn enemy had fallen. Then again, the war between them was a silent one, hidden beneath treaties and platitudes, even as we traded crops and goods with one another, Hanaobi always getting the raw end of the deal—but it did not matter, as Mother allowed some of her people to escape to the duchy for just this reason. She should not have been surprised that they'd risen up.

She had put the idea into Father's head that he and Elder Brother Nobutada should head to the duchy in secret, should command the runaways to step up and do their duty by fighting the duke in his own territory.

It was the result she had wanted. So why was she disappointed? Surely, even she could see that the invasion she'd planned to arrange one day soon was not preferable to the problem taking care of itself. There was no loss of life or resources on our side this way.

"Well, yes, the expats were the target of a raid the duke and his men made," said Sougo, consulting the parchment again. "But they were led by..." He drifted off, his eyes darting wildly, his lips turning into a sneer. "The duke's heir, Rohesia," he said, puzzling me to no end. He left it unsaid that she was Empress Momoko's heir as well. That, by all rights of succession, she was the true heir to Hanaobi.

He was not finished. "And a young man from a band of thieves," he continued, "a man claiming to be the duke's true heir."

Mother was surprised at that one. Her features barely moved, but I noticed the slight twitch of her lips.

But he was still not finished yet. "And," he said, swallowing as he looked up toward us on the dais, "Prince Kojiro and the Captain Tierny who was his tutor at his side. Your Majesty, this letter..." His face suddenly more sullen, he would not say more.

Mother's hands wrung together and her lip twitch grew more pronounced. Sougo opened his mouth but shut it again as Mother stood and the handmaidens shuffled in quickly to remove her train from her path.

"Who sent this letter the tradesmen carried?" asked Mother stiffly.

Sougo's eyes pored over the words. "I don't know whether or not to trust what it says." He stepped forward and handed the letter to Mother with both hands. Sweat glistened on his brow.

She snatched it from him and he stepped back, bowing as she began to read. Mother's eyes widened. "Get me this messenger who handed it to you," said Mother, gliding past Sougo as fast as her measured steps would allow, "immediately." She stopped and turned to stare at Sougo, who shirked back from her glare. "And prepare for the execution of the ship's captain after I am done with him. I will not suffer the insult that he would send such an important message ahead on nothing but a piece of parchment instead of coming to my side to tell me in person the moment his ship landed." Her voice grew louder as she spoke and a pinch of red appeared at her temples, where the white makeup ended as it met up with her hairline. "It is time," she said, looking more composed. "We have been preparing for this moment. Our assault can begin."

She strode forward, gliding from the room, her handmaidens trailing after her, the guards in line behind them.

I understood at last. She could not let this go. She had to have her invasion. The duke's death was but a small part of her objective.

Perhaps it was Elder Brother Kojiro's fate that mostly concerned her.

Sougo turned toward me, his face ashen, and he bowed his head. "Thank you, Your Highness." He left the rest unsaid.

2

FASTELLO

Every time. Every single time.
I found myself reaching for things with my right hand, I'd see the bandages wrapped tightly around and through the remaining fingers, and I'd pause.

It wasn't just that I no longer had my index and middle fingers there—destroyed more than halfway down, later cut more cleanly by the duke's physician, insisting it was the best way to stave off fever and pus. As if I cared about such things in those first few days after she'd died. But more than one person had insisted I'd put it off long enough and I'd let them make me do it. Took a long swig of ale, grit my teeth on a piece of bark, and let that butcher have at me. I didn't care. I'd laid her to rest—proper-like. All the best resources at my command. I'd made a speech about how we all had to join together, to accept one another in the days ahead... But I didn't actually feel as confident as my words might have made me seem.

"Fastello?" Luana stared at my hand with me, as if all the answers I needed to lead this isle could be found beneath those red-soaked linens. She took a step forward and grabbed my left hand from my side, placing the parchment there. I felt like a child who had to be taught how to do the most basic of things.

She'd lived like this every day—nearly her whole life.

She'd had no fingers on her hand. On this hand. Yet I was damaged—a husk—just by losing two of them. And I'd only lived that way for a couple of weeks.

Had it been a couple of weeks? The days had blurred together in the aftermath of it all. Luana held tight to my injured extremity, taking it with both hands to her chest, almost leaning her ample bosom into it. That did nothing for me. No woman had since I'd lost Cateline—but especially not this woman.

"Fastello," she said, no attempts to disguise the concern in her voice, "the physician did say to rest after the operation."

"I rested yesterday."

"One day isn't enough."

A sharp pain echoed from my missing fingers—the physician insisted that was normal, that the other injured soldiers he'd dealt with with missing body parts also complained of an intense pain where the parts had once been—but that made me think again of her. Had the ghosts of her fingers hurt her, even years after she'd lost them? She'd told me once she'd been born that way, but I'd seen the scars, the burns to seal the wounds—I just hadn't asked.

I hadn't asked a lot of things. There was so much I'd never gotten to say. Come to think of it, I'd hardly known her. She'd just floated into my life—or more accurately, I'd hopped on her horse and ridden us away—and she'd taken my breath away.

"What's wrong?" asked Luana, taking me into a half-embrace.

I bit through the pain and shrugged out of her grasp. "Don't coddle me, woman."

Cateline used to not like when I did that. I hadn't meant to coddle her, really, it had just seemed like she'd needed help…

Luana pinched her lips, barely even flinching as a couple of nomad boys and a girl wove around her, one taking advantage of the wide stance of her legs to crawl beneath her skirts and pop out from the other side, shouting at the others and sending them running and screaming away. "I know you're hurting. We all are in a—"

"Don't speak to *me* of hurting."

Luana turned on her heel, not sparing a word more to try to comfort me.

So be it. There was nothing she of all people could say that would comfort me. I'd not forgotten how she'd left me for my father —a man old enough to be her own father, a man already sharing his bed with multiple other women—for a few more jewels to adorn those delicate fingers and ample breasts.

She smiled and laughed as a member of the clan called out to her while doing her laundry in a washbasin set up in front of one of the tents. Luana spun to maneuver around another of my people carrying a barrel over one shoulder, laughing as he nodded his head at her, his wink hard to miss. Light of foot and graceful with her arms aloft above her head, she looked as if she were dancing.

There was a time when I'd thought her a goddess on land, a being from the skies above whose feet never quite touched the dirt beneath her.

But remembering what I'd once thought of Luana just made me think of Cateline and her Stargazer goddess—of the old bat who'd tricked her and hurt her and murdered countless women and children. The old bat who was my grandmother.

If her goddess was real, why had She let so many suffer, even among Her worshippers?

I didn't know how long I stood there in the midst of the tents pitched inside the grand entryway of this overly large castle. Some of the families had claimed rooms upstairs and many more pitched their tents inside for a semblance of privacy among the crowd. Still even more spilled out into the surprisingly small courtyard. I supposed the duke had no need for fresh air and exercise, as pasty as the man had been.

Someone bumped into me and I lurched forward. Gilia—one of father's other mistresses, albeit one slightly closer to his age— jumped in place, almost dropping the armful of veggies she'd scrounged up from somewhere. "Sir… Fastello. Apologies."

I nodded blankly at her. Whenever I saw her, I thought of Rento —my half-brother, her son. He was a wretched lad, but he'd been family nonetheless. And now, like so many others, he was gone.

She didn't seem to ever want to talk about it, though I caught her wiping tears away from her swollen eyes more than once as of late. Her attention flicked to the parchment I'd forgotten was still in my hand. "Do you need help with that?"

I swallowed and stared at the rolled-up parchment. I had no idea why everyone seemed so insistent I couldn't do anything for myself, yet also expected me to do more than anyone in the duchy had ever done before.

Were you any more confident in Cateline's abilities? I shuddered at the realization of how she must have felt.

"I've got it," I said, grabbing at the paper with the remaining fingers on my right hand. They poked through the bandages, a trickle of caked-on blood from the nearby wounds hard to miss along my ring finger.

Gilia watched me clumsily paw at the seal and unfurl the scrawl, as if expecting me to give up at any moment, when she'd need to drop her basket to swoop in and rescue me.

I stared at her over the parchment, waiting for her to leave me be. "Where'd you get those?" I asked, instead of asking her to be on her way. I wasn't happy with my people and the way they'd followed my conniving father without asking questions, but I wasn't going to win hearts—or manipulate them to follow me blindly if needs must—if I snapped at all of them. (Luana would be an exception, of course. She definitely deserved it.)

Gilia smiled and nodded her head behind her. "Down in the cellars of the kitchens." Her eyes widened. "This place is packed to the brim—this was just the stuff the cooks were determined to throw out, saying it was rotten." She shifted her arms to paw through one of the leaves on a head of lettuce. The edges were brown, but the majority of the leaf was green and luscious. "Some people," she said, shaking her head, and she seemed to remember where she'd been heading and stepped away. "Wouldn't know we were in a famine by the looks of the garbage pile in this castle here."

I'd thought perhaps the remaining servants—I'd had no desire to force anyone to stay, although most had cited a lack of anywhere else to earn their keep and hadn't budged from their posts—were just eager to run through the duke's seemingly-infinite stores as quickly as possible. They'd made clear they had no love for cooking for several hundred new residents. To be fair, the duke hadn't employed many cooks and servers. But where else would I take my people? Our forests had burned, and although the caves and some trees remained, our days of hiding were over.

Besides, the duchy needed someone to lead it. And the duke's daughter had made it clear she had no desire to stake a claim.

Not that I completely trusted that in the long term. I barely knew the girl, and there were stories about her, what she'd done… Even if under the orders of her father.

Then again, who was I to judge on the basis of one's father? Though he'd never successfully convinced me to go that far.

Still, she'd proven herself an ally. She'd killed her own father—with intent, unlike me, who'd…

I swallowed.

My eyes drifted back to the parchment. It was a message from the guards stationed at the docks. I read the words in haste, crumpling the parchment when I finished.

I strode forward, weaving amongst the tents with purpose, jogging when possible to get to the stairs.

"Cheers!" said Nico, already in his cups. He nodded and raised his mug toward me as I passed.

I smiled, even though the action brought a sharp pain to my chest. "Enjoying the wine cellar's stock, I see?"

"You know it!" He laughed and brought the mug to his lips. He seemed happy. Strange, considering his talents—of the roughing-up-people variety—no longer saw much use these days. Perhaps enough drink was all he'd needed all along.

"Just pace yourself," I said. "Let's not blow through it all in a month." And we needed to save some for the rest of the duchy's citizens. There was so much to consider, to plan, and finding something for these restless gadabouts had to be among the first tasks to consider. There'd been more than one brawl in the confined space of the castle, and the guards had long since grown weary of breaking them up—and of me staying their hand when it came to the violence they were accustomed to using on the nomads, of which, I reminded them, their new duke was one. Then there was the food, how my people always seemed to be celebrating. Even the duke's massive hoarding of goods couldn't sustain itself long at this pace.

There were nomads in the long hallways, nomads spilling out of this room and that. There were even some women playing a game of chance with knuckle bones that rolled down one of the sets of steps.

The sight of the bones made my own ghostly knuckles ache.

At last I arrived at an area devoid of nomads, a darkened part of the hallway lit by a single torch on the wall's edge. Almost without saying, my people knew to steer clear of it—the library where Tierny had set up his quarters. That and one of the rooms, made apparently to look like a room from Hanaobi, the land across the sea that Rohesia intended to claim for herself and her cousin from beyond the waters. Even her father's quarters had been seized —by myself—and she hadn't batted an eyelash. But the moment the hand of one of my people had reached for that Hanaobi room door, she'd withdrawn her sword and needed to say nothing to get her feelings on that room across.

My people stayed away, though Rohesia had let Jiro claim it. Not without some unspoken reluctance.

If the nomads seemed a little more distant from the library than usual, the reason became clear enough as I approached. Rohesia— Lady Rohesia by rights, but she wouldn't hear of me addressing her as such—leaned against the wall beside the doorway in shadow, one foot flat against the stone behind her, her arms crossed.

She watched me as I approached but betrayed little movement otherwise. Even devoid of the armor I'd first met her in, she looked more soldier than lady, a simple white tunic tucked into plain brown pants. She was skinnier than the armor had made her seem. It was a wonder she could even move when she had the chainmail shirt on, let alone the full regalia.

I lifted the parchment up, as if I needed it to gain entry. "Are Tierny and Jiro inside?"

She nodded slowly.

I put a hand on the handle and hesitated. She didn't move. "You'll want to hear this, too."

She shifted from her position and stepped in behind me,

although there was no mistaking the glaze that covered her eyes for anything resembling genuine interest.

"...have to gauge the empress' reaction once we make land before I even bother to head for the palace." Captain Tierny leaned over a large map on a central table that he and Jiro had been working on for the past few weeks.

"She knows," I said, holding the parchment out in front of me. "And word is instead of being grateful that we've wrested control of this duchy from her enemy"—my gaze shifted nervously over Rohesia, but she settled against the fireplace in much the same position she'd been standing in the hallway, ignoring me—"she's merely thinking of the opportunity it presents."

Jiro and Tierny both turned to stare at me, their expressions as different from one another's as they could possibly be. Tierny grinned, stepping around the table and extending an arm toward me. "You have news?"

Jiro frowned and stared at the map on the table again, although he still turned an ear my way.

I brandished the parchment again. "From the docks. The empress knows the duke is dead and she... prepares to launch an assault on the duchy."

Now Tierny's grimace better resembled Jiro's expression. "That's... disappointing."

"Is it so?" Jiro said, so quietly, you could almost doubt you'd heard him. "It is not... unexpected."

Tierny rubbed his chin, weaving his fingers through his golden beard. "So there was never any hope of peace, was there?"

"Mother would never let a..." Jiro struggled to find the word. He spoke our language quite well, but there were still times I caught his eyes glazed over, certain he wasn't following along but for whatever reason wouldn't interrupt us to say as much. "She would never forgive. She will be angry it was not she the one who killed him."

"But in a way, this doesn't have to be a bad thing," said Tierny. "If she'd wanted peace, I'd have had a harder time reconciling planning our own quiet revolt against her. Now it just means war."

"Yes, and now she will be more alert and expecting." Jiro glanced toward me for a moment but looked away. I didn't imagine the darkness shading his cheeks. Ever since the incident in which he'd blown my fingers off—unintentionally, of course, and with an unbelievable little cannon he showed me later when everything had settled down—he'd had trouble looking at me. I might not have been ready to forget I'd lost two fingers, but I held no anger toward him. To me, it was more a reminder of what—and whom—I'd lost. A punishment, a marker.

"Good or bad—whatever you think this is, I don't want to fight," I said, tossing the parchment onto the table in front of Jiro and Tierny. "How do we avoid this?"

"We don't," said Rohesia. She leaned away from the wall and joined us at the table. "War doesn't wait to be invited." There was a flicker of life in her usually-cold eyes, which I noticed only at the most inopportune times. As far as I was concerned, the sooner she and the others were off on their quest to free Hanaobi of its tyranny, the better. I could use Tierny's help here, but whatever it took to get the duke's daughter out of this city. My only concern was that she'd come back the rightful empress of Hanaobi—that was something Jiro had enlightened us all about in the chaos of the past few weeks—and pick up the war against the duchy where her predecessor had left off.

But I'd chosen to trust her. I *would* trust her.

I'd offered her the chance to at least challenge my claim to the duchy. We'd discovered my mother, the only good person in my entire bloodline, had also been the daughter of the duke and, since she'd been older than Rohesia, being her child then granted me better claim to the title because the bloodthirsty, evil duke had been my grandfather. It had all been enough to make me dizzy with confusion. But the duchy needed a leader and so did my people, now that the cocksure "king" of the nomads had fallen at the blade of his own son. And while I didn't relish the job, the only thing I relished less was having this coldhearted woman step in as duchess. I knew she was on our side now, but even so. Those eyes of hers…

Fortunately, she'd claimed no interest in the title. But perhaps she was just waiting for me to do all the hard parts of getting this mess of a duchy back up and running again, then she'd step in to rule the patchworked pieces.

So, war didn't wait to be invited? "Then you need to bring it to the empress fast—and preferably over there." I threw back my shoulders, doing my best to appear more confident than I felt. "I need strategies for defense should the war start here sooner or should… your plans fail."

"Of course," said Tierny. He glanced back and forth between Jiro and Rohesia, as if asking for their blessing to say more. I detected a slight nod from Rohesia, though Jiro ignored him. "Our mission is more of a covert one," he said at last. "Small scale. My ship alone should do it. The rest of the fleet will remain stationed here. I'll speak with the other captains, tell them how to handle the first round of assault by sea, and the guards will have to man the cannons with even greater fervency."

So they planned not a grand battle but a covert mission? I liked the idea. Fewer casualties, fewer men needed when I couldn't spare them here. Although a couple of sticking points gnawed at me. "But what about trade?" I asked. "I don't know how long the duchy will last without Hanaobi's crops."

"Mother knows that," said Jiro. "You can count on nothing more from her."

My stomach soured. We'd have to work with what we had. We had farmers of our own—hell, even Hanaobians were among them —but the crops had been impacted by drought and blight a few years back and the land still hadn't fully recovered. But I couldn't count on these three to assist me. They had monumental problems of their own to deal with—and should they succeed, the duchy would benefit far more than it would from having them here in this room at all hours, offering me advice and suggestions for doing what I needed to figure out how to do myself.

"Besides," said Tierny, "trade will be our cover. If the empress has issued no formal end to our trading agreement, no official announcement of war, she'd have no reason to deny us entry to her borders. In fact, she might welcome it." He nodded at the two others involved in this scheme. "We'll need to go soon. We hoped to present the news ourselves." He swallowed. "Now we'll have to pretend as if we didn't know she was told already and see how far that takes us."

How they'd last beyond the docks was something they'd have to worry about themselves. Rohesia certainly knew a thing or two about a band of slaughterers waiting at the dock for a ship, from what I heard tell.

"The tide," said Rohesia, crossing her arms. "It's going to delay us at least a week."

"I know. We'll just have to leave the first day we're able." Tierny shuffled papers together and tapped them against the table in a pile. "At the very least that keeps Hanaobi ships from approaching as well. We should be safe for the next week."

"That's another thing," I said, tapping my remaining index finger on the parchment. "No ships have launched since the duke's defeat. The records say there was a Hanaobi merchant ship, but they left days before. How did the empress come to know? And how did we get word back for that matter?"

Tierny, Rohesia, and Jiro all shared a glance. Tierny was the only one to speak. "Have you ever sent word by bird, Lord Fastello?"

It looked like I was never going to get back to worrying about food shortages tonight.

3

ROHESIA

I left Tierny and Kojiro to their endless explanations, their education of the boy laying claim to the title of duke. This was the state my father's death had left the duchy in. To be overrun by raiders and left on the shoulders of a boy barely intelligent enough to grasp the idea of war, let alone figure out that there were always traitors around every corner. To sit on the duke's seat was to never have another peaceful night's sleep again. Those who seemed loyal might only be so until your back was turned for one moment. It wasn't even safe to trust blood to have your back for you—as Father found out.

As I would never forget.

I did not mind the foolish boy claiming the duke's seat—the nephew I'd had no idea I had, the nephew who'd been born the year after I had. I had no interest in sitting on that seat, in ruling through fear and not the respect from his own people that dolt seemed born with without even having to try.

I would bring peace from the shadows. I would do what needed to be done—what these men who plotted and held hope for the future could not bring themselves to do. I would claim another throne across the sea if my cousin would not—but only to depose the woman sitting there. I would rid these lands of despots and let the people's suffering end. I trusted my nephew to have the best interests of those in the duchy at heart. He could stay here. But I did not trust him to have the strength and the courage to do what needed to be done.

He'd been so lost, so confused when he'd plunged a dagger into his worthless father's heart.

I'd been in pain when I'd killed mine. But I'd known exactly what I was doing—and why it needed to be done.

Just as I knew that messages sent by bird across the sea were no point of interest. But who would dare send them was. Not the one who'd messaged us—Father and even Captain Tierny had their spies in Hanaobi. The ones who'd send a message out.

But I couldn't be sure who Hanaobi's spies in the duchy were. Even though there were only a handful of people who were let near the creatures.

The men posted outside the aviary at the docks could not have seemed less alert—they were playing a game of cards under torchlight, a barrel turned over to act as a table, several more barrels on their sides to act as chairs—but to be fair, they noticed me as I approached. And I did not make it easy for them.

"Lady Rohesia." One stood and the other followed suit, their hands going to the hilts of their swords.

At my approach.

I wrapped my fingers around my own sword hilt. I hadn't worn my armor, hadn't thought it necessary. Not because I hadn't thought things might come to this, but because I hadn't expected to uncover enough traitors to need the protection.

If it turned out to be just this many, I could still handle it.

"Who's been in here?" I asked, jutting my chin toward the aviary. The sounds of the rushing waters and the rising tide were especially loud from where we stood just a short distance from the docks. The boisterous laughter of the sailors stationed to guard their ships while they remained docked echoed over the crashing waves to break the silence that hung over us.

The man who'd said my name looked over his shoulder at his two companions and nodded, letting go of his hilt. The other two followed suit, although the fingers on one of the men's hands kept hovering and twitching over it. "No one, my lady," spoke the man in front. "None but us and our day shift, tending to the creatures who land." He nodded upward. The aviary tower was thin and tall, its turret extending far above any of the surrounding buildings to attract the birds sent along with the ships and call them home when they had a message to share.

It was more difficult to send birds to a ship—let alone to the land across the sea—than it was to simply stick them in the ship cargo and let them follow their instincts to return home.

But no ships had left port since Father's death, so there could be no other way a message would have reached across the waters. And Father had had some that heard the call of individual ships more than they did this tower, using whatever homing instinct lay within them to scour the waters for their intended recipients. There was less chance of success that way, but… In any case, there were no ships unaccounted for, which made this all the more perplexing.

There was the possibility of Hanaobian birds themselves. But where would they have been drawn to in the duchy?

These men would not admit to sending any messages, whether they had or not. But someone had to have received one. "Who received the message earlier this evening for Fastello?"

Their eyes were blank, their expressions illegible. True, I was not used to things like joy and affability pointed in my direction. But I was used to fear, obedience. Not this utter lack of anything. I let my own hands fall from my sword, only remembering too late that my wrists were not adorned with their daggers because I'd worn nothing but a shirt and pants on this mission. Still, I could reach the sword in a moment if need be.

The man nearest strode forward, his hand resting casually atop his sword as if it were merely an armrest. "We cannot comment on any messages sent by or received for the young duke."

I don't know what was more troubling. The fact that he implied the duke sent messages I was unaware of or the fact that he called him the duke at all. Few of Father's men seemed eager to recognize the upstart as their new liege.

"I am here on his behalf," I said through gritted teeth.

He looked around, as if baffled. "And where is his letter granting you the right to inquire on his behalf? I see no parchment in your hands, no seal."

"I will thank you not to impede the requests of my nephew."

"Yes, your long-lost nephew." The man looked over his shoulder and laughed. His companions echoed, the man with the twitchy fingers far less easily. "Half a nomad. I wouldn't find the humility in me to bow a knee to him were it not for the fact that a cold, heartless bitch were the only other known alternative."

My wrists ached at the absence of the daggers I'd have gladly aimed at this throat just then. Instead, I drew my sword, holding the blade with both hands. It was the first time I'd drawn it outside of practice in weeks. It felt strangely heavy in my hands, even though my arms were missing the metal plates that would have weighed me down.

The man laughed and looked back at his companions. "The gal has balls still, I see," he said. But he didn't finish his thought as I drove the blade through the gap between his chest plate and shoulder blades.

And here I'd thought I'd decided to minimize the bloodshed. I stared down at the crumpled heap. Blood spurted out from between his lips, spotting my shins with red.

There was a chance he'd live. I hadn't been entirely ruthless.

Then again, I wasn't sure which of these men I'd need alive to talk—or if any one of them alone would do.

I could hear the other men draw their swords and I spun away from the heap of a man just as another sword slashed clumsily where I'd been standing. The man—not the twitchy one—stumbled forward. He'd put all his strength into a swing he hadn't known for certain would connect. The fool.

I was lighter on my feet without my armor and chainmail. I spun and caught him on the back with the metal-coated heel of my thick leather boot and he fell face-forward, screaming as he sliced a gash into his arm with his own sword.

I stomped on him harder, pushing him all the way down. He caught the blade just right so the sharp edge dug harder into his arm instead of flattening it and ending the torment. I'd have laughed if I didn't know now how entirely unfunny such suffering ought to be.

The thought that this was funny shouldn't have even crossed my mind.

I'd rarely laughed before. I'd rarely taken what one might call "pleasure" from it all. But there was something in it—some kind of meaning—that had made it all so full of purpose and sense. I didn't like thinking about it so hard now. I didn't like that the veil had been lifted.

"Raise the alarm, you ba-bastard," sputtered the man beneath me, no doubt to his twitchy companion, who stood some distance away, the barrel they'd been using for their game of chance knocked over at his feet. There were two cards—aces from what I saw of them—sticking out from the top of the twitchy man's boot. They'd no doubt been there even before the makeshift table had fallen over. No love between cheats and thieves. I couldn't stop myself this time as I laughed. Long and hard, louder than the waves and the distant chatter and the bird calls and everything.

"You disgusting… monster," said the man beneath my feet. I looked down at him, raised my foot half an inch, and ground it into his back harder, twisting my heel for good measure against his spine. He screamed.

"I thought… I thought it might be your father," said the twitchy man, causing me to stop grinding. The heap below me panted.

"What about my father?" I asked, all semblance of humor sucked out of me.

"I knew your man," he said, and I certainly knew he could not have possibly been referring to any suitors. Father had had no interest in finding any for me, and there was nothing but his own encouragement of such things that could induce me to find one on my own. I'd never understood… Why the men had always been so eager to do so. I'd thought it the difference between men and women, but I'd never met a woman like me either. Then again, I'd never spent more than a moment's time with any of them.

"We wasn't close or nothin'," the man continued, "but we had a pint or two together when we'd be fresh from…" He swallowed, as if what he had to say next could make the blood pooling at my feet less offensive in comparison. "After spending some time with the ladies," he said, no doubt referring to the houses of the night that offered young women like cattle to men regardless of rank or station, so long as they had the coins for the pleasure. "He was a good man. In his own way."

"The… alarm!!" sputtered the man beneath me. I rolled my eyes and kicked once at his head. I tried not to hit him with too much force. His eyes shut. Whether from death or unconsciousness, I'd have to find out later. This one was talkative enough that it wouldn't matter.

"I know so few good men," I said, pointing my sword toward the twitchy man. "You'll have to get to the point—sooner rather than later."

"Sherrod," he sputtered. "Your… man. Your attendant. When in his cups on more than one occasion, he told me how much he loved you."

I froze, a chill I'd never felt before rising up my spine.

The man mistook the reaction. "As a daughter," he qualified. "He had a girl at the… There was someone else who caught his fancy like that."

I sighed. "Yes, I know. He married her." I'd only seen his widow once since that day. At his funeral. She hadn't cried. She hadn't trembled. I hadn't known she'd existed, hadn't been privy to that side of the man who had been so often at my side… But I recognized coldness—indifference—when I saw it, and there had been no emotion in the eyes of that supposedly bereaved widow.

"Well," said the man, swallowing loudly, "thing is, he felt bad for you. Said your father had sucked out your heart when you was just a bairn and he'd stomped on it for good measure, tearing all light and empathy out of ye. But he loved you even so, said he knew there was some kindling of good in you. Said your mother had been kind to him and that you'd been a cute thing when you'd clung to her calves like she were the land and you were a ship lost at sea."

There must have been something in my expression because the twitchy man backed away. "Not to say you're cute at all anymore, my lady." I raised an eyebrow at his use of the title when his cohort had so brazenly made a mockery of it. "Terrifying and unbeatable —you live up to your reputation."

I chuckled and found myself lowering my sword. I laughed again, feeling the mirth bubble up from my stomach and out through my mouth, even as I splashed through some of the sea water that stained the stones, dyed red from the blood of the two men beside me. "Sherrod talked too much," I said, drawing up next to the man, the tip of my sword at his throat. He didn't even try to fight back, letting his own blade clatter to the stones at our feet. I cocked my head and strained my ears, listening. Behind the roar of the waves and the distant chatter, I could almost hear it. Hear his voice calling my name, fraught with tension, always a shaky lilt to his objections. Sherrod… "But I do find I miss the sound of his voice." It was the first time I'd admitted such a thing out loud. And to this cheating, coward of a stranger.

His legs shook now, his eyes shut tight. He leaned his head back against the wall to the aviary behind him, his lips whispering what might have been a prayer. Father had banished all mention of Ytoile and that Stargazing religion, but I supposed the man had found he'd had nothing to lose at the end of his life.

Besides, Fastello was duke now. I couldn't see him telling anyone who they could and couldn't believe awaited them in the great hereafter.

I took a step back and sheathed my sword. "You needn't be so frightened," I said. I looked behind me at the pile of dead or unconscious men and I shuddered. I didn't expect my next task to be bloodless, but I'd made a vow to shed as little as possible. "I only defended myself—and my honor," I added, knowing the first man hadn't struck first. "The duke will know I'm here—I'll tell him. I want to find out more about the message he received tonight—and who might have sent one in the past few weeks against the duke's orders."

The man opened one eye and then the other, staring at me with a glaze of water over his irises, almost as if not believing what stood before him. He looked like Sherrod. He'd been the only one who could look at me with such a mixture of fear and amazement, the only one who'd ever been constantly concerned with my comfort and my health.

He'd been like a father to me. My true father. I knew I'd treated him terribly, but… He'd loved me.

I'd never doubted my own father had loved me. But I'd been the only one he had since my mother had passed. And that hadn't been enough. He'd lost sight of what it meant to rob other parents of their children, to love any other of his daughters.

They were dead now, along with their mothers, the other wives my father had taken for himself before he'd met my mother. Burned to nothingness—along with innocent orphans and other devout women—by a madwoman who'd have pinned the act of cruelty at my feet.

And no one would have doubted I'd done it. Not even Sherrod, who'd loved me. Who'd seen something like good buried deep down inside me.

"Have you bitten your tongue?" I asked, exasperated.

Shaking his head, he pointed behind me at the two discombobulated bodies. Which man specifically he meant, I couldn't be sure.

"He took the message this evening," said the twitchy man. "Sent it to the castle right quick." He pulled his hand back quickly as if slapped. "But I know nothing about anyone sending any messages. I swear it. On my life."

A stain grew at his groin, traveling down his leg to form a puddle at his feet.

I'd have to speak to Fastello about looking for sturdier guards for the aviary.

4
KOJIRO

We could not leave for five more days. Tierny explained—in his own barbaric tongue and what he could in Hanaobian—that it had to do with the height and speed of the waters. I hadn't realized captains had to take such things into consideration.

I also didn't care. Every day we hesitated was another day Mother had to mount her strategy for attack.

They said her men couldn't come here any more than we could go there until the tides changed. But that did little to calm me.

"Relax," Tierny had told me, my anxiety apparently clear on my face. He'd patted me on the back then in his rough, barbaric way. "Worrying won't help anything."

That may have been true, but that didn't mean I could stop worrying. These past few weeks… I'd seen so much. I hadn't done anything, not anything of import, but I'd seen those around me bring a society crashing down and then start picking up the pieces. I knew it could be done in Hanaobi. Only I… I wasn't sure that my society needed to be so drastically torn to bits.

I did not dare share those thoughts with these barbarians. They wouldn't understand. They couldn't understand the beauty that existed in Hanaobi.

There was one thing we could all agree on, though. Mother's reign had to end.

What would happen after that… Well, there was no better place to be to decide that than by my cousin's side, in the shadows, useless and weak—underestimated and overlooked.

Mother had never foreseen my foibles could be my strengths. I would make sure she knew before she fell.

Even so, I felt no ill will toward Fastello, who somehow managed not to irritate me to the extent that Tierny and others like him often did. Fastello recognized the need for seriousness at times. And he'd taken the brunt of my foolishness and seemed to bear me no ill will.

Not that I'd hold him to that. Mother was the model of showing one face while hiding another. I could not entirely dismiss the possibility of Fastello hiding his true feelings, even if I'd found no reason to doubt him.

"Ask them what they need, then, to start living more comfortably." Fastello paced in front of the group of Hanaobians gathered in front of a barbarian farmer's house. The farmer had taken them in—had recognized their superior skills—and they were just one of several groups of Hanaobian refugees who'd snuck aboard trading ships to start a new life in the duchy.

As if life in our beautiful land was worth the risk they took to come here—the life of hiding in the shadows, away from the spirits of the sun and the day. They'd risked death since the previous duke had forbidden all Hanaobians—other than his daughter, strangely —from setting foot in his lands. Mother alone was all that inspired such fear in them, I was sure of it. Be rid of her and I'd make my homeland a place that people flocked to, not ran away from.

I translated Fastello's question to the farmerwomen and men who'd approached us from the group, acting as their mouthpieces. They talked amongst themselves and Fastello followed their conversation with his eyes, even if I was sure he couldn't truly follow a word of it. He absentmindedly scratched at his ear with his bandaged hand. He'd recently had surgery, I'd noticed, to smooth out the haphazard job my weapon had done to destroy two of his fingers.

"They want their own homes," I said when they'd finally

stopped talking and come to a consensus. I glanced at the pale barbarian farmer and his wife on the porch of their home, passing a pitcher of water along from one worker to the next. "Their own land."

"I understand," said Fastello, sighing as he began to pace, the dirt beneath his feet sending out small dust clouds. "Of course that's what they'd want—it's what they deserve." He frowned. "But there's no spare land to farm… I'd have to convince the existing owners to sell at least portions of it, and there's already that one farm that was damaged by the fire…"

He spoke so quickly, I felt my mind go blank. He stopped and stared at me, reading my confusion on my face. "I'm sorry," he said, and he repeated himself, slower and more concisely, so I could tell the farmers in our own tongue.

They'd already gotten the gist of it from what limited barbarian tongue they could speak and their disappointment was palpable.

"Still, there's no question—they need better homes. Real homes. I won't have them crowding together in barns." Fastello waved at the barn where they'd been sleeping amongst the cows and the horses. He scratched his cheek with his bandaged hand again, grimaced, and then switched to his other hand. "And they should have options. Not just be farmers if they don't want to be— although we do sorely need their help and guidance." He sighed and sat down on a tree stump, partially eaten away by termites. His sleeve had specks of blood on it, no doubt from his bandages, and his dark hair hung limply over his dirt-stained cheeks. This was not the type of person I pictured when I thought of a country's leader.

I translated what he'd said. The farmers stared at him as if he were a mad man, less for the content of his dialogue and more for the lack of care he put into his appearance before them.

Seeing they had no response, Fastello looked back up. "We can build homes here—I'll have to talk to the farmers about that. There are some homes in the heart of the duchy, although not many. Right now my own people are just living in tents, scattered throughout the castle…" He stood, tapping his chin as if something had occurred to him. "There are those rich people," he said. "The ones with large houses. They have enough room to spare. Surely, if I ask them to let these people in, at least until more permanent homes can be established…”

One of the farmer women cocked her head to me in question and I translated best I could. She shook her head and spoke before I finished.

“They hate us,” I translated for her.

Fastello dropped his hand from his face. “Who? The rich people?”

“Everyone,” I said for them without waiting to translate. “All the people.”

He strode nearer, shaking his head. “The nomads have nothing against your people.” This word “nomad” I didn’t understand, but I knew that was what he called the free-spirited, happy, dancing people who followed him. I did not think they worked. I’d only seen them eating and dancing and drinking. I supposed the closest they got to any real use was the women who cleaned their clothes and sometimes cooked their food—but it wasn’t like they shared that with anyone else, either.

“Maybe,” I said, interpreting to the farmers again, “but they have no homes to share—and besides, the farmers aren’t… They don’t want to walk back and forth from the city to the farms every day,” I said, looking to the farmers for confirmation. They nodded and spoke amongst themselves, providing a unified answer. “They would like the homes built here. They will stay in the barns until then.”

“But—” began Fastello.

I still listened to the farmerwoman who spoke. “And they will tell the others they have the choice of going back and living with these… rich people… and doing other work or staying here. I am sure most will want to stay,” I added myself.

Fastello actually looked relieved. “I’ll talk to the farmers and guards and figure out how to get these homes built as soon as possible. Perhaps my people can make some more tents, so they’re not all trapped inside among the animals.”

I had an idea. Unlike with my mother, I was not scared at all of sharing it with this country’s ruler. “Your people… The nomans?”

He smiled. “Nomads.”

"Yes. I am sorry, but… They do nothing. They are a happy people, but they are a do-nothing people."

One of Fastello's eyebrows shot up. I froze, but he shook his head. "Go on."

"Get them to help build. Get them to help farm. They will earn their food—and help feed others. They can travel from the castle and back; they will probably not mind."

Fastello stared at me blankly and then launched his unwounded hand at me and I flinched, despite all my efforts not to. But he wrapped an arm around me and squeezed, just as Tierny would have done.

"You are brilliant, Jiro!" He even pressed his filthy cheek against mine in what might have been the most bizarre form of touch I'd ever experienced. "Those layabouts need to learn a new way of life in a new duchy, stop depleting our reserves and do what's right, what's needed. Although I don't think we had the worst idea, er, *convincing* the rich to share resources with the poor…" He stared off and let go, and I felt my face flush as the farmers stared at me, as taken aback by Fastello's weird gestures as I'd been. "I'm so stupid. So dumb," said Fastello, and I didn't know what to translate anymore. "The solution to several problems right there in front of my face and I…" He'd held up both hands in front of him as he'd spoken and he stared at the bandaged hand as if it had slapped him. He often did that. Acted as if nothing were different and then looked at his hand and froze. I felt guilty every time.

Mother might have rewarded me for weakening the duchy's new leader. But I'd had no idea he'd become that when I'd done that. He'd been nothing but kind and welcoming to me, if always a bit noisy, if always a bit strange. The only reason I'd had at all to dislike him even a little bit had been…

Hair like fire, skin like snow. Spots of sun scattered all over her complexion. She'd danced, too, and in my mind, I kept seeing her dancing in a silver dress, a young woman blessed by stars.

She'd danced right into the fire. She had welcomed death, so long as she could take an evil soul with her.

I'd been nothing to her. She'd even looked at me as if she were going to spit in my face for the first few days I'd known her. But I couldn't stop staring, couldn't stop imagining my hands running through those sunset-colored curls.

She'd loved Fastello, I thought. He'd certainly taken her loss hard, harder than I had. The injured hand might have reminded him of her because she'd had no fingers on the very same hand.

I said a silent prayer to the sun and the other guiding spirits in her honor, even if I knew she'd been a spirit of the night, of the stars.

Fastello patted my arm and nodded his head toward the farmers. "Update them and I'll go speak to the farmer who owns this land, let him know what I can offer him in exchange for a small slice of land to house everyone. We'll head back when we're finished." He smiled at the small group of farmers, looking at them even as he spoke to me instead. "I sure am going to miss you. We could use a skilled translator, especially to teach them enough of our tongue to communicate the basics."

I laughed. I actually laughed. Fastello eyed me warily and stepped away. But he'd called me a "skilled translator." How my mother would have found that funny. Tomiko—she was the skilled one. But I could no more picture her here among the dirt and the disheveled young duke than I could Mother. She had the heart for it, though—but she was too clean, too auspicious. She shouldn't be dragged down to the dirt like I'd been.

I spoke with the farmers and they seemed satisfied, walking back toward the rest of our people. We'd have to talk with the rest of the farms harboring Hanaobians before I left with my cousin and Tierny for home. I wasn't sure Fastello could communicate his plans effectively without me.

I found myself startled at the compliment I'd given myself, even if only in my thoughts.

I walked back toward the horse I'd used to arrive here, patting down its haunches and smoothing its mane as I waited for Fastello to join me. He was taking a while speaking to the barbarian farmer and his wife, who both seemed concerned but not angry or upset with our ideas. Not that I cared if they were. They owed my people. They were lucky they didn't revolt and kick them off the land to reap the profits of their own work for themselves alone.

Hooves pounded the dirt from the direction of the main road and I turned to watch one of Fastello's people—his nomads—approaching, the air billowing her dark, voluminous hair behind her, the only thing seeming to keep it on her head the colorful scarf she used to tie the top of it all down. She was there with him that day when I had… destroyed Fastello's fingers. She'd been angry with me at that moment, though she hadn't spoken to me since. I'd seen her a lot around Fastello in the past few weeks. He'd lost his smile around her more than once, but she'd persisted in speaking with him.

Fastello frowned as he turned to see who approached. I sighed. We had no time to spare for frivolities. I wished she'd stayed back at the castle and waited to seduce him upon his return. I knew she'd had reason to be upset at the time, but I did not forget she'd once called me a "filthy outsider."

"Hey, Jiro," she said as she pulled on the reins of her horse and eased it into a trot. She smiled, and I shivered as I turned away because I'd pictured Cateline in her place for a moment, saw her pale face smiling down at me instead of this darker one. There was no question that this woman was actually more beautiful—but that only made me more uneasy. And I had no idea how she'd found out and bothered to remember my name. We hadn't been introduced before.

I nodded and rifled through the saddle bag on my horse for want of anything better to do.

She swung her leg to slide off her saddle and I was ashamed to say I watched her out of the corner of my eye, saw the slender, lovely leg that popped out from beneath her long skirts as she did.

She grinned even more widely as she approached. "I caught you looking," she said, reaching over and tapping my nose with her long, elegant finger. I startled and jumped back.

She laughed. "It's all right. All the men look."

My shoulders tensed.

She clasped both hands behind her back and leaned sideways, forcing her startlingly night-sky eyes into my view as she blinked up at me. "Fastello told me you spoke our tongue."

"I do." I coughed and stepped back, putting more distance between us. "I try to."

She ran her fingers through my horse's mane and turned to glance at me over her shoulder, a powerful intensity in her look. "Then you were just ignoring me. That's a little hurtful."

My coughing became a full-on spasm then. I bent over, clutching my abdomen.

Chuckling, she stepped forward, bending over so we could see each other face-to-face. "I'm only teasing. You're so handsome, and you're so adorable when you're nervous." Her bosom—uncovered at the top, far greater in size than I'd ever seen before—brushed against my shoulder and I looked down into the cavern between her breasts out of instinct more than anything.

I jumped up and stepped backward, covering my mouth to try to control the spasms, spinning around so she'd no longer be in my view. I'd only caught some of her meaning through the raging of my heartbeat and the coughing, but it was clear enough.

I didn't know how Fastello managed to spend more than a moment around her. Her laugh was angelic, far more befitting one of the silver dancers of the night than these fire dancers of the night and day.

"You thought…" I said, struggling to think of the words. "You said I was filthy. Filthy outsider."

"I did?" She frowned. Then she seemed to remember. "Oh. Yes, well… That was a terrible day in so many ways." She shuffled a foot in the dirt. "Fastello told me you were his friend. That it was an accident. So if he forgives you, then so do I."

"Luana, leave him alone." Fastello walked up beside us. I hadn't noticed him leave the farmers' sides. He grabbed hold of his saddle and pulled himself up alongside it. "We have so many more farms to visit and limited time to do so. Say what you came to say and be on your way."

Luana pouted, and I couldn't tell if she was genuinely hurt or of this was another of her games to make men uncomfortable. "Good morning to you as well, Fastello."

He grabbed the reins and turned his horse around. "Jiro," he said, ignoring her, "let's go."

I stared between him and Luana uneasily, then quickly strode to my horse and launched myself into the saddle.

"You were gone before I woke up this morning," said Luana, stepping in front of Fastello's horse. "I had to ask half a dozen people where you'd gone before that captain finally told me."

"Perhaps you should consider that intentional," he said. He stared above her head. He probably found it difficult to look at her, too, especially from this angle, where her bosom begged my eyes for attention even more readily.

"That hurts, Fastello," she said, and her lip trembled. "You finally let me back into your bed—"

Fastello's face flashed with fury. "You barged in there. While I was asleep."

"You wanted me there!" she said. I felt very uncomfortable. I wondered if Fastello had ever lain with Cateline as he'd lain with this woman, and for some reason, that sent a sharp pain to my stomach. Even though I'd known I'd never have had a chance to lay with her. I wasn't sure I'd wanted to do that—to drag her down from her lofty beauty.

"I never said I wanted you."

Luana scoffed. "Oh, you've said that plenty of times, honey. You used to *beg* me."

"That was before!" Fastello waved his injured hand around and freed it from the loop he'd made around his wrist to better steer the horse. "What you did last night… was unforgivable."

"You gave as good as you got," she said, tossing her head back.

"Only because I was delirious… I thought I was dreaming. I thought you were…" He looked away, his face marred by pain.

"Cateline," she finished for him. She sneered the name more than she said it, and it felt dirty that she spoke that name at all. She shrugged and gazed at her feet. "I let you think whatever you want. Whatever you needed to snap out of this, this…" She waved her hands around, exasperated. "Feeling sorry for yourself."

"Let's go," said Fastello to me again, guiding his horse with one hand to step around Luana.

"You wanted me!" she said, not moving back to make room for the steed. "You knew—maybe not at first, but at least halfway through—and you kept going! You didn't kick me out. You just let me lie there on top of you, made me feel like you'd forgiven me."

Fastello's horse drew short. "I don't need to forgive you," he said. "I just don't need you."

He guided his horse past her and around the horse she'd ridden on, leaving her behind without another word.

Her lips trembled and a light seemed to die out from her eyes. She rubbed one wrist against each cheek in turn and sniffled, looking up at me. "Well?" she snapped. "Don't you have somewhere to be?"

I scrambled to weave my hands through the horse's reins and to set after Fastello.

I left the crying beauty behind me, unsure what else to say.

I stopped. I'd felt like that often and I'd simply wanted someone to say… "There are people who want you," I told her. "Do not waste the tears on people who would treat you poorly."

I didn't wait to hear what she might have to say.

❀ *5* ❀

TOMIKO

Mother did not approve of the turns I took around the garden when the sun was shining this brightly. Though the sun spirit was the most valued among the spirits in our land—she'd created the land long ago, which had given birth to the other spirits —Mother still insisted it was best for royalty not to be kissed by the spirit's light.

It was why she and I wore white makeup, even though we were certainly pale beneath it all. It showed the people that we were spirits alive on earth, that we had equal power and deserved equal respect from them because we didn't need to nourish ourselves from the light of the sun.

Or so the royal family has said for ages immemorial. I found the makeup stifling, especially on so warm a day.

I took my turn around the gardens with my handmaidens, who moved silently in my wake, my train in hand, one a little behind me holding a parasol to shade me. They said nothing. I could only faintly hear them breathing.

Part of me wanted to speak to them. Without Elder Brother Kojiro here, I had virtually no one to talk to. My teacher. My mother. But neither could I really pour my heart out to.

But to speak to anyone else—to speak freely at all—would upset

41

Mother. And though my feelings for her were strained in light of the danger she posed to my brother, I could not bring myself to disappoint her. I'm not sure it would do any good for anyone even if I did.

A low-hanging branch of cherry blossoms brushed the top of the parasol as we passed and the handmaiden carrying it—Ayako—went pale as it lightly grazed the top of my head. She bowed as she pulled the parasol back up, apologizing.

I smiled and tapped a hand to my hair, feeling that the jade ornament tucked into my bun had shifted slightly. "It is no bother," I told her, doing my best to affix it back in place.

Ayako exchanged a look with someone behind her and I turned to see my other handmaidens—Emiko and Yukiko—staring at her with horror on their faces, their fingers still holding gently to my train.

"It is all right," I said. I shook my head slightly as they stared blankly, plucking the ornament from my head entirely. "There. Now it is not crooked. It is not in the way. Can we continue our walk?" I smiled again, hoping to put them at ease.

Yukiko let go of my train to step forward, both palms extended. "I will carry that for you, Your Highness."

I placed the ornament in her hand, waited for her to return to her place, and continued our walk.

Though we returned to silence, it felt uneasy. I felt alone, even surrounded by others. I remembered Elder Brother Kojiro and how we'd often spoken of feeling that way, how we'd clung to our late-night visits to one another's bedrooms simply to talk and enjoy each other's company.

I knew I'd saved him by sending him away with Elder Brother Nobutada's weapon. But I could not help but regret it in part.

Though I was so happy to hear that he'd not only lived and survived—he'd thrived, doing what Father and Elder Brother Nobutada could not. Doing what Mother would have never expected of him. Despite her often-pinched face, Mother clearly had found the news distasteful.

I tried to push down the spark of hope that sprung in my chest at the thought of seeing Elder Brother Kojiro again. Never mind that he stood between me and the crown. I would support him from the shadows, as I had no need for the seat myself.

Yet I knew Mother would never allow that.

She already spoke of war with the duchy, even though the foul man who'd stolen my aunt lay rotting. The duchy would be in ashes, she'd said, adrift without a skilled and educated leader. She'd bristled to hear that the duke's favored daughter—my cousin, though I could not speak that aloud, could not remind anyone in the court of that relationship, though I was sure no one had forgotten—had stepped aside for an unknown nephew, the duke's grandson no one knew about, who probably had no proof of his claim. It irritated her to think that we wouldn't be facing off against this Lady Rohesia, that she wouldn't have an excuse to kill her before she made any claims to the Hanaobian throne.

And her reluctance to step in as duchess of the duchy—was that a good or a bad sign regarding her intentions for our own country?

Mother did not ask my opinion, but I was sure it was not a good one. While being duchess might have meant she could have commanded a force our way to seize control of both countries, I considered the possibility that she came to an agreement with her nephew to work together to seek rule of both countries, to split the burden and support one another when need be.

As if a barbarian-raised princess could ever hope to understand the graces and civility of our country.

But there was Elder Brother Kojiro as well. If he'd worked with this new duke and our cousin together, then perhaps they'd made a truce and there could be hope for peace yet—despite what that letter may have said. I knew my brother and I knew what he thought of Mother. I could not see them working together so easily.

As we passed close by the fence enclosing the garden from outside the palace, my foot stopped as I encountered resistance from behind me, as if someone were pulling me backward. As they were usually so skilled at walking undetected, I'd nearly forgotten that there were handmaidens behind me for a few minutes. I heard a harsh whisper and I turned to see Emiko a few steps behind Yukiko, my train tugged tightly in her hands.

"Go," she whispered. She said more, but I couldn't hear above the call of a swallow as it swooped overhead.

"What is it?" I asked.

Emiko turned to me and paled. It was then that I looked behind her to see a space in the fence between the stalks of bamboo used to create the posts—a space large enough for a small person to fit through, which was precisely what a little boy was attempting to do. My hands flew to my mouth as the boy froze, as if suddenly remaining still would make the half of him protruding into the garden vanish from my eyes.

"Please forgive him," said Ayako at my side. "He is Emiko's younger brother… He knows he should not be here. He will go."

I looked at the faces of each of my handmaidens in turn, and all three averted their gazes sheepishly. "What's wrong?" I asked them. I looked at the boy again and saw the lump in the front of his *kimono*. "What have you got there?" I walked toward him, weaving around my long train to reach him.

Panicked, he started moving again, flailing widely and attempting to shove himself through. He kept slamming that inconspicuous lump against the post. He must have slipped in just fine but loaded his shirt with so much, he could not slip out as easily.

"Your Highness, please. I beg you—" It was Emiko, my train dropped to the dirt, attempting to step between me and the boy.

I grabbed him by the wrist just as a leaf-bound packet of *mochi* tumbled from between the folds of his shirt. "Did you take that from the palace kitchens?" I asked, perhaps a little more sternness in my voice than I'd intended.

Emiko threw herself into the dirt, her hands folded together beneath her face, her nose grazing the stones beneath us. "Please," she said. "Please spare him. I have no excuse, but please!"

I tugged on the boy and he fell forward, nearly grazing his sister's head. His shirt caught on the post and opened wide, revealing more leaf-bound packets of food. Enough to feed a whole family.

Yukiko and Ayako appeared at Emiko's side, exchanged a look, and Yukiko handed Ayako my hair ornament to hold alongside the parasol—the parasol I'd managed to evade in my rush to catch the boy—and then Yukiko threw herself on the ground beside Emiko. The boy looked at the prostrating women and a glisten of sweat dotted his dirt-stained face. He might have joined them had I not still clutched tightly to his wrist. "What is going on here?" I asked.

"They are starving," said Ayako, her lip trembling. "Their families—my family—all farm for the same lord and he is stingy. They work from dawn to dusk and then some, and they farm so much food, yet the lord spares so little for them. We send our wages home, but it is not enough. There is little food to buy in the streets and…" She looked lost, as if she wanted nothing more than to prostrate herself beside her companions, but she gazed at the ornament and parasol, as if she didn't dare to get them dirty. "Bunji takes food back for all of them—when he can. Not very often. Not any amount that could be missed. It's old and dry, and the chefs would let the three of us eat it without protest, but they tend to frown on sending any home…" She bowed her head contritely. "If you must punish anyone, let it be us. Not the boy."

I stared at each of them in turn, unbelieving that this seemed to have been going on behind my back for some time. Was life for a farmer really so dire? Even the ones who worked for lords, who were tasked with looking over and providing for our people? Mother had had little problems with the lords, just the lesser-born yeoman farmers, the ones who bought their own lands and couldn't manage to keep it, to pay the tithe and make a profit…

Was it the tithe to the crown that caused this? Mother had used those crops not only to feed the household, but also to trade with the duchy. Less and less of the duchy's crops made it here in recent years, but still Mother had insisted on sending our rice, opium, and vegetables, had kept up the route of trade.

She'd known some of our poorest fled to the duchy in those ships. It was a well-known secret, even if it was a crime. Mother had overlooked it, hoping they could serve as a hidden army in the duchy. If we had any use for that now.

But sending more food than we could spare seemed folly for such a plan. If there was one good thing about Mother's insistence on war, it would at least close the trade routes indefinitely.

I wondered if one last spurt of farmers would flee before the way closed forever.

And I had an idea. A bold and crazy idea. I stared at the slit between the posts and realized I wasn't that much taller or larger than this boy.

"Take me there," I said and all of their heads lifted and turned toward me. "Take me to see your families."

I dropped the boy's hand and started untying my *obi* to the shock of all four of them.

I slipped out of the grand robes, only my plain, white silk under-robes left to cover me. I smiled and picked up the packet of *mochi* the boy had dropped before slipping out between the post. When they didn't follow, I peeked back inside.

"Come," I said. "Unless you would like to be here when Mother notices I am missing."

That caused them all to burst into movement.

FASTELLO

I collapsed into the chair in front of the fire in what was once the duke's room, using a heel and then a big toe to kick my mud-caked boots off. This was the third day Jiro and I had spent meeting with farmers, but we'd finally met with them all. Some had actually taken more cajoling than others, much to my frustration. These farmers were content to use the Hanaobi people's labor but balked at the idea of sparing a small amount of land to build them shelter? The selfishness of people continued to astonish me.

Of course, I recognized the farmers themselves had little to give. But they would give what they could if they hoped to retain the Hanaobian farmers. And they would start paying them more than food to do it, too, and a portion of their proceeds—though I'd have to decide things like market prices and taxes and how to get the farmers paid fairly for their products without starving the people who lived in the town with prices they couldn't afford.

I massaged my forehead as I stared blankly into the flickering flames. And how many days were left with Jiro before he, Rohesia, and Tierny left on their probable-suicide mission, taking all guidance and input I'd come to trust along with them?

A sharp pain shot across my hand where my fingers had been and I pulled my hand away, realizing I'd instinctively relied on that hand again. The bandage was off now—the physician had wanted me to wear it longer, but its stiffness was irritating and it made my skin itch, and my two knuckles were covered in thick scabs. The casual movement had opened a hairline crack in one of them and I stared, watching the blood trickle, my thoughts drifting to Cateline once more. I'd kept so busy, I hadn't thought of her enough. There was the other night when Luana had snuck into my bed and I'd thought, just for a moment… I'd let myself keep pretending, let her just do whatever she wanted.

I took a sharp breath and squeezed my hand tight into a fist, not caring about the pain. She hadn't shown her face in front of me since, though I'd seen her around the tents. I'd been working with Gilia and Mina and some of the others to try to convince the nomads to prepare for a life of farming. Bit by bit, we were changing minds.

And I was just exhausted.

There was a knock on the door and I realized I'd closed my eyes and must have been drifting off for some time.

"Come in," I said, my eyes still closed. At this point it could be the empress herself with a dagger in hand and I wouldn't even budge.

Fortunately for me and the duchy, it wasn't the reigning empress. Instead, it was a woman as quiet as a mouse, who spoke from mere inches at my side before I even realized the door had opened. "That woman is here to see you."

I jumped and screamed, my eyes widening. Rohesia. Of course.

She didn't even blink at my reaction.

"What woman?" I asked, rubbing my hand over my face.

"I forget her name," said Rohesia.

"Well, that's helpful." I felt like I was speaking a foreign language with her. It must have been all those days of hearing Hanaobian.

She lifted her hand and I actually leaned back in my seat out of instinct. I'd seen her flick those daggers out of her wrists the past few days during the training she'd been doing with the guards. But she simply pointed at me.

"There's blood on your face," she said. "A small streak of it."

I stared down at my hand, the crack in the scab grown wide, the blood oozing out once more. I sighed. "I'm sure. And dirt and exhaustion too." I stood and snatched a pile of clean bandages I'd refused to use to wrap my hands this morning, reluctantly spinning it around my hand and weaving it through my fingers. "Lead the way," I said, not caring about the blood on my face. Not even caring to know whom I was dealing with before facing her down.

I met Rohesia at the door and she stared at me blankly. I raised an eyebrow. "I'm ready as I'll ever be," I said.

Her shoulders twitched slightly in what might have been the closest thing to a shrug I'd ever seen her give. Then she led me down the hallway, weaving between and around nomads—though I noticed those who took note of her gave her a wide berth whenever possible. At the bottom of the last staircase, I saw the woman in question—no doubt about it, she looked this way and that all around her as if afraid a nomad might look up from talking and dining and scrubbing to reveal a knife they'd hold at her throat.

Then I realized this woman *had* seen a nomad holding a knife before. Had seen him killing her companions right in front of her.

"Agnes," I breathed quietly, recognizing her more from her body language than her appearance. Rohesia looked me over as if surprised to hear me speak and I stepped up beside her in front of the disheveled, blonde woman.

She stopped fidgeting as she took a look at me. She jumped back —I'd forgotten the blood on my face, the dirt, the unkempt hair— but then her eyes narrowed and she steeled herself, shaking a finger at me. "You!"

"None other," I said, grinning despite myself. I knew I ought not to find any pleasure in this moment—not after everything I'd been through, not after what my brother had put this poor woman through—but she was easy to tease. My face soured. She'd been there, hadn't she? At that final confrontation with the duke. My memory of that time was shaky, but…

"This woman is a traitor," said Rohesia simply.

"That's rich," spat Agnes. "Coming from you."

One of the nearby women stared at us over her shoulder as she gathered some wooden plates stacked in front of her tent.

I put a hand toward Rohesia's shoulder and she spun out of my reach. Left grasping at nothing, I grimaced and nodded toward a darkened corner of the castle entryway. "Let's speak somewhere a little quieter, shall we?" I went to put my other arm around Agnes to direct her at least, but she recoiled, whether at the sight of my bloody bandages or the thought of me touching her, either was a fair guess. I nodded and kept my hands to myself, leading the way. When I parked my shoulder against the wall and turned around, I found both women glaring at one another. Agnes might have been the only one brave enough to attempt such a feat with the previous duke's daughter.

"She should be in the cells," said Rohesia at last.

"You should rot in—"

I whipped a hand out between the two of them. "All right. Enough." I looked Agnes up and down. "Where have you been?" I wouldn't have been surprised if she said she'd been sleeping amongst the pigs from the state of her dress.

She sniffled mightily unladylike and gave Rohesia the onceover.

"Agnes," I said, prodding her.

She folded her arms and shrugged. "The tavern. Meggy's new place."

I nodded, remembering the tavern mistress who had helped us when we'd all been in hiding. Rohesia didn't betray her reaction to the words. I doubted she could have known about the underground —at least, she couldn't have known about it before the duke's demise. Surely she would have told the duke then. But apparently her little lord wet nurse had had his ear to the ground… And I had no idea when Rohesia had decided to turn traitor toward her father. Frankly, I had no idea whether to trust her entirely now, as much as I wanted to.

I nodded, deciding not to speak more of it. We shouldn't need an underground anymore—not when I'd outlawed any poor treatment of Hanaobians, nomads, Stargazers (what few remained)—of anyone. But I couldn't be sure things would stay that way.

"After that day," said Agnes, "the guards, well, they forgot about me. I knew I couldn't go home—not just because they might find me there, but because I had no home to go back to." She sniffled. "Meggy had always been kind to me."

I waved a hand to cut her off, even as I lifted my eyebrows at her rosy vision of her experience hiding at the tavern. She sure hadn't shown her gratitude before when I'd hidden at Meggy's tavern with her. I was glad to hear the tavern mistress had found a new place to operate. I'd forgotten her tavern had been vandalized on the duke's orders.

"Then why are you here now?" I asked.

She gave me a sideways glance and sniffled again. "They said the new young duke was looking to be speak with the rich of this city," she said. "I didn't realize that man was you."

My lips soured. Extending a hand to the aristocrats in the duchy was one of the endless tasks on my to-do list. I needed their funds, the space in their homes… I didn't expect convincing them to share would be easy.

A thought struck me. Even if she was devoid of a fortune, she knew these people. She might be just the person I needed to talk to them.

"I'll work with anyone who can help me. Are you going to get our homes back?" asked Agnes. "For those of us whose stuff was stolen?"

I'd forgotten to ask what had inspired her to leave her refuge at the tavern. Personal gain. Of course. Not that I or anyone I knew had any room to criticize.

I nodded, playing along—and besides, if she could prove an ally, I'd have no problems with her returning to her home and enjoying many of her shiny things. I just hoped she'd be open to sharing more of them.

I slipped an arm around her, more out of habit than anything else, and this time she didn't flinch away. "I have a proposition for you," I told her. "The duchy has greater need for the wealthy than ever."

I doubted she'd look as relieved as she did just now after I told her more about what I had in mind.

❦ 7 ❦

ROHESIA

Fastello assumed I had the wherewithal of a toddler, apparently, if he'd thought I wouldn't take note of the "tavern" that hysterical woman had mentioned. I had already posed questions at several taverns—every one I could remember Sherrod frequenting, not that he'd shared all of his favorite spots with me—looking for the source of the note sent to Hanaobi. Fastello been evasive when I'd brought up the results of my investigation of the aviary a few days prior—had been more concerned about the men I'd sent to the infirmary, but he'd failed to notice that I'd sent them to the infirmary and not the cemetery. I hadn't been entirely sure I had. Part of me was actually impressed that it had worked out that way.

I'd made a vow to approach everything from now on with less bloodshed. Although I had found that increasingly frustrating in recent days.

But feeling even frustrated—feeling anything—was something to behold in and of itself. I'd never let more than the smallest inklings of those types of feelings stir to the surface before.

I stood by in the corner of the room as Fastello tried to haggle some sort of agreement with the irritable blonde woman. Why he bothered to promise her a return of her riches in exchange for her pledge to help others was beyond me—she had nothing currently to give. It was as good as shared already. And isn't that what his people did—just snatched from those who had too much and doled it out to the rest of the duchy?

She left more disgruntled than she'd arrived, actually muttering to herself as she made her way through the cluttered town square and living spaces of the poorer parts of the city. I knew because I followed her. I didn't even tell Fastello of my intentions—I didn't know how much help he could be. I would have asked Tierny or Kojiro what they knew, but they were so preoccupied with what they planned to do once the tides lifted and we arrived in Hanaobi.

I felt uncomfortable every time they spoke of seizing the throne there. My long-lost cousin sent me a questioning look every time it was mentioned, as if waiting for me to ask if he'd dare challenge me.

I had little interest in power but for the fact that I was discovering it made so many more people eager to please you. The guards were withdrawing from me lately—training with me at times, but whispering amongst themselves, barely speaking a word to me. Not that we'd ever been close, but they had at least afforded me the respect I'd thought I deserved. Perhaps it had all been no more than the result of Father's hold over them.

The tavern the blonde woman entered—never once looking back, never once thinking she might be followed—was immediately familiar. I'd known Sherrod to frequent this place, and I'd been here a few days ago, asking about the elusive messenger. The owner had feigned ignorance of all of it, I was certain. I'd tried to casually steer the conversation and she'd claimed she wasn't even the original owner of the place, that her business and another one had had to combine following her tavern's vandalism—and then, her mouth had clamped shut the moment she'd gotten a better look at me.

This time I wouldn't ask questions. I'd sit and drink and listen. That was what the cloak was for. To avoid looks that lingered, whispers that sang across a sea of voices. I would not draw attention.

I chose the end seat at the bar, parked in the shadows, the nearest person three seats away, though the place was rather packed this late in the evening. Most people preferred the tables. They sat in groups—mostly men, but some women dressed up in fine attire among them. The ladies had an unpolished edge to their finery, as if it had all been tossed on slapdash. These were not the aristocrat women Fastello sought for his misguided if noble intentions.

A girl came over almost instantly. "What'll you have?"

"Ale," I said, though I couldn't care less about the stuff.

That wasn't enough to get her to go. "Spices or no?"

I stared at her blankly.

"Spices," she repeated. "Our tavern is known for them."

A few of the men sitting nearby spared me a glance. I'd made a mistake, exposed myself as anything but a regular.

I nodded. "Spice."

That seemed to satisfy the onlookers, who turned back to their conversations. I watched the kitchen into which the blonde woman had vanished almost the moment I'd stepped inside. After a few moments, a middle-aged woman came out, a trio of bowls cradled in her arms. Before I could see to whom she delivered the bowls, the serving girl returned and placed a mug in front of me. She lingered, staring down, as if checking to make sure I'd actually drink it.

I'd planned on only nursing it, but I took a sip. I had to swallow hard to get it down. I shouldn't have gone with the spices.

"Do you… remember me?"

I studied her a moment, the mug still in my hands. "Sherrod's widow." She was dressed so plainly—I'd seen her in more finery the few times I'd met her. She'd been in black the previous time.

"Malle," she said, but I knew the name would have come to me.

My cover utterly blown, I shifted the hood off my head. My eyes flitted to the kitchen behind her, and I noticed the middle-aged woman retreat back inside. There was nothing unusual about servers serving, no doubt, but I wanted to know what it was about this woman that made her welcome someone in hiding like that Agnes. Perhaps with Malle here, I wouldn't need to rely on stealth regardless. "Can we talk?" I asked.

"I'm working."

It was a curt answer to match the curt tone of my voice. "How… have you been?" I asked, trying my best.

Malle grabbed a rag from under the counter and started wiping at the empty space between me and the nearest other patron. "Not great," she said. She raised an eyebrow. "My husband didn't own much, did he?"

I thought back to Sherrod and had a hard time picturing him outside of the shadows he'd slunk into in my wake. He had a place of his own somewhere in the town, but he almost never spent a full night there. He'd had a room at the castle so he could be at our sides at a moment's notice. It was bare, but for some silken sheets from Hanaobi he'd admired in the marketplace one day. But those were long since taken over by nomads.

"Are you living in his home?" I asked. Maybe there was a clue to his connections there.

She sighed, the rag in her hand going suddenly still. "Yes, but… He just had a room over a tavern." She cocked her head and spoke quickly. "Not this one. When he proposed marriage, he said we'd be living in a room in the castle."

"The castle is rather crowded these days." I took a sip of the ale, forgetting the taste, and cringed a little. "Not sure you'd want to live there. Besides, his room's been taken over."

She grumbled something about no-good thieves. Then she spoke louder. "Did they take his things?"

"He didn't have much there," I said. "Just some satin sheets."

Her nose wrinkled. "I bet those would have been worth something, though."

"I'm sorry I didn't think to get them to you." Was that really what concerned her at this very moment? Then again, she was working here. I supposed that meant Sherrod couldn't have left her much. Had she married him in hopes of living a life of luxury? I actually didn't know how much or how often Father had paid him, now that I thought about it. I didn't even know how he'd worked his way up to being my attendant. He'd just sort of always been there.

"Hey!" shouted a man from down the bar. He held up his mug and pointed at it, the smile on his face vanishing. "Refill?"

She nodded at him and left a moment to take his mug, turning around to fill it from the tap. His gaze lingered on her backside the entire time her back was to him and he grinned again, even going so far as to nudge the man next to him and point her way. I rolled my eyes and took another sip of my drink, swallowing hard against the strange taste, as she placed the refill back in front of the man with a wide smile on her face.

The smile fell almost instantly the moment she turned back toward me. "Sorry about that," she said as she feigned interest in wiping the counter around me. The men laughed as they peered at her backside again over their drinks and I regretted lowering my hood. I wasn't used to men's attention myself—not like that, not that I'd noticed any directed toward myself. I wondered how she and other women put up with that all the time. The way her smile had slipped the moment she turned her back to him made the whole thing between men and women feel forced and false.

"What did... Sherrod mean to you?" I surprised myself by even asking. By even caring. I'd spent more time thinking about the man since his passing than I had in all the time before then. I felt guilty at that thought.

Malle took a deep breath and tossed her shoulders back. "If you're asking if I deserve his property..."

I shook my head. "No. He didn't have much, now that I think about it, but whatever he left for you you're welcome to."

She sighed at that, as if she'd been hoping I'd reveal a secret stash of gold he'd left behind.

"It's just... I took it for granted he'd always be there, and... I don't know who else even misses him."

She grimaced, then tucked a strand of hair behind her ear. "We weren't married long. And he wasn't an awful husband, nor even an awful customer... He could actually be... kind of sweet." She swallowed. "But I only married him because he promised me a chance to leave behind a life I detested." She wrung the cloth between her hands. "And then he died, barely making a difference at all. If it weren't for Meggy, I'm not sure I'd have been able to avoid going back to all that."

"Meggy?" I asked, bringing my cup to my lips casually. "The tavern owner?"

"Yeah," said Malle. "Sherrod first gave me her name and said to go to her if I ever needed help." She shrugged. "She offered me this job. It's something."

"Sherrod never told me about you. Or her. Or a lot of things," I admitted. "I just want to know more about him. I should have asked then, but I…" My insides were conflicted. I'd meant to interrogate her, maybe find out more about Sherrod's connections, see who might have sent that letter to Hanaobi, but there was genuinely something there in my voice, a flutter in my heart that activated as I spoke the words.

Malle threw the towel over her shoulder. "My shift is almost over," she said. "I was going to sell what I could of his, maybe find a better place to live. But I think he'd want you to have some things of his—the stuff that's more sentimental. If you want to come with me?"

I nodded, surprised by the way my throat closed up before I could answer. She nodded back and turned around, off to take another order. I felt a hot and wet tear trickle down my cheek.

❧ 8 ❧

KOJIRO

Captain Tierny was keeping something from me.

"I've picked the men from my crew—swapped out a few for those who could be trusted," he said, pacing in front of the window, a fading ray of amber sunlight breaking through a gray sky disrupted every few moments by his passing feet. "The ship is ready. There were some repairs that needed to be made, but the tides gave us the time to make sure it was all done with great care."

I stood straight at attention in front of him, though it was difficult for me to concentrate on his words when his demeanor belied something he wasn't saying. He squeezed his hands together. "Just a couple of days now."

He returned to the table, poring over the maps and the notes, the charts and the letters. Somewhere in all of that was his grand plan for "liberating" my country from its despot empress.

"Why do you care?" I asked, the numbness inside me making me wonder the same thing about myself. Distance away from Mother had hardened me, had soothed my disquieted soul. But in the face of returning there, plan or no, my throat constricted again.

Tierny turned, his hands still gripping one another tightly. "Do I care about the plight of your people? Of course I do."

I raised an eyebrow and stepped closer, still not sure the life of

58

the Hanaobian people compared in any way to a "plight," at least not in the face of the mess that was this barbarian land. But I'd spoken with so many Hanaobian refuges, had started to get a clearer picture of life outside the palace in Hanaobi. They worked their hardest, and sometimes, their hardest wasn't enough.

I, of all people, could understand how fear of my mother could drive people away. But there was hope for my land if only she weren't in it.

"But I'm also concerned about my own homeland." He sighed. "If I could hope for peace between our nations, perhaps we could leave it all be… Learn to grow a sustainable number of crops, learn not to rely on imports so heavily. But we've barely had a chance to breathe before there's news the empress is planning war, despite the fact that we're no longer her enemies." He tapped a letter on the table—the one Fastello had brought to us a few days earlier.

"You told Mother you were against the duke," I said, sidling up next to him and running a finger over the wrinkled parchment.

"I was," he said. "I'm against all despots who rule without concern for their people's comfort and wellbeing."

Though the words hurt to pore over—I recognized almost all, though my brain was slow to translate them coherently—my fingers stopped at my name, written in that simple and coarse barbaric alphabet. "What is this say about me?"

"What *does* this say," corrected Tierny, annoyingly never quite letting go of his role as my teacher. He snatched the letter and looked it over, his eyes flitting back and forth instead of up and down to read the lines. He crumpled it. "She knows you're alive now," he said. "She was told you helped lead the rebellion that led to the duke's downfall."

I laughed. I loved that Mother believed such a thing about me. My real role had been confined to blowing off two of Fastello's fingers, however helpful that must have been to the efforts.

He didn't say more, but he swallowed and looked busy as he shuffled the papers around the table.

"What more?" I asked, then remembering before he could correct me, I added, "What else is there you hide from me?"

He pinched his lips. "I didn't feel the need to tell you. I'm sure it didn't need to be said."

"What?" I demanded, surprising myself with the volume of my voice.

Tierny jumped and then turned around, leaning back on the table and smiling weakly at me. "The empress orders Rohesia's execution," he said, "should anyone on her side find her."

"Not surprise," I said, sighing as I added, "Not a surprise. She could take her seat from her."

"Yes, but... It's a quieter order, one not so publicly shared that... She's ordered your quiet execution too. Not to be done in a public manner, but to make it look as if you've fallen in battle. As if someone from the duchy—perhaps Lady Rohesia—were responsible."

That was also not at all surprising, but I bit down and did not speak more. "Who is telling you this?" I asked. "Who sent that letter? Why did Fastello not say...?"

"He didn't know," said Tierny. He pointed to parts of sentences. "The additional information is in code. I have men I trust there as well as here," said Tierny. "But I made sure the ones here knew not to send word across the waters after the duke's downfall. No replies at all. I'm sure it was none of my men." He tapped his chest as if that somehow lent credence to his statement.

He knew as well as I that Rohesia was searching for the person who'd warned Mother. There was no need to speculate what kind of fate awaited the person who found himself at the end of her sword—if he didn't strike first.

There was a knock at the door.

"Come in," said Tierny, shuffling the papers to pull a map without markings over the rest of the plans. He grabbed for a glimmering jade lion that Rohesia often kept between her hands during our meetings and used it as a paperweight. I didn't know what it meant to her, but I knew enough about my cousin to assume she'd find his cavalier treatment of the priceless ornament repugnant.

A nomad woman came in baring a couple of mugs in one hand. I recognized her almost immediately as Fastello's girl—Luana—the one with a beauty that was hard not to notice and a confident presence that demanded not to be missed.

"I thought you might be thirsty," she said, wandering near the table.

Tierny eyed her warily. "Thank you," he said, not passing up the mug she held out to him.

She thrust the other one toward me with one hand, laughing as I flinched and the mug sloshed a little at my feet. "Well?" she said after a minute.

I grabbed the mug with both hands, cringing at the moisture that traced a line down its side. She grinned, a light glistening in her dark eyes.

Tierny seemed to already be half-finished with his. A layer of foam coated the yellow and white whiskers around his mouth. He spared a quick glance at Luana as he took another sip. "Thanks, lass," he said, nodding and then plunking his mug down. He shifted the jade lion aside and rolled up the papers on the table into a long tube the size of a sword. "I guess it's time I visit the docks again. Get things settled once and for all for the voyage." He nodded, taking the papers with him.

Did he think Luana might be the spy? I wasn't aware it was even possible the nomad people of the duchy could think so far beyond their borders.

It wasn't until he'd closed the door behind him that I realized he was leaving me alone with Luana.

She clutched one hand behind her back and traced a long finger along the edge of the table. "Does all of this get boring?" she asked, gesturing to where the papers had been. "Poring over papers and planning and waging war and all that?"

I stared blankly at her. There was a lilt to her speech, a slight cadence I found in Fastello and other nomads that made her rapid speech slightly more difficult to follow. She stopped moving and cocked her head at me. "You're not drinking."

I stared down at the liquid in my mug. I'd had plenty of the stuff since arriving in the duchy. I was hardly eager to drink more of it. *Sake* was another thing I missed about home. Even if I was free of Mother here, this barbaric land could never equal it. I wondered how Tomiko was doing. She'd be sure to keep in Mother's good graces. Only I still worried what a war between these two lands might mean. Mother might deserve whatever the duchy threw at her, but Tomiko… I'd do whatever it took to spare her.

"Cat got your tongue?" Luana appeared at my side once more, both hands clasped behind her as she bent down to peer up at me.

She was fond of getting a little too close, this woman.

I turned around and placed the mug on the mantel above the fire.

"What's it like?" she asked, the smile slipping just slightly from her face. She ran a hand over the jade lion. "In Hanaobi?"

Her eyes lit up as she brought the lion closer to her face. I put a hand atop it. "Beautiful," I said, meeting her gaze when I did without meaning to. Her irises were almost the same shade as the ornament—not brown, like I expected—but they were deeper, darker, less clouded. I turned away, taking the lion with me. "Frightening," I added, not caring what she thought of me. I'd never see her again in a matter of days. "There's a quiet, natural wonder over all the ground, the sky. It's… clean." I didn't know how else to explain it.

Luana sidled up beside me, laying a hand on my shoulder. "Are we too dirty for you in the duchy, Jiro?"

I bristled—whether at her touch or the lack of formality, I couldn't be sure. "You don't know," I said. "You don't understand. I wish you could see." I held up the lion, letting a glimmer of sunlight dance off its edges.

"I can almost see it now," she said. "Through your eyes."

I turned my head to find her resting her chin on the back of her hand, which she kept on my shoulders. Though I couldn't help but feel there was something darker there about her, she seemed the most genuine I'd ever seen her. "Fastello says you're a prince," she said.

I swallowed, nodding.

"Is there a princess back home?"

It took me a second to figure out what she meant. Or so I thought. "My younger sister," I said.

She pulled back and pinched my upper arm slightly. "I meant a wife. A betrothed." She laughed. "Not that that stops all manner of men to be sure."

Something cold dropped down my sternum. I shook my head.

"No lover?" she asked, swirling away from me. "No servant girl you meet in the dark when the whole palace is sleeping?" Her movements were like a falling leaf floating on air before it made its final descent to the ground. She whirled back to me, grabbing both my biceps and pulling me to face her. "No servant boy?" Her voice had lowered, almost conspiratorially.

I shook my head, not even sure what she could possibly mean.

She touched a finger to the tip of my nose quickly. "Good," she said, then took me by the hand. The shoulder of her dress dipped as she tugged, the bunched-up material framing the smooth, even skin in an extremely alluring way. "What say we find somewhere to get a bit more comfortable?" She winked. "You can tell me more about the beauty of your country."

I just barely remembered to drop the jade lion on the table as we passed it, lest my cousin notice its absence.

❧ 9 ❧

TOMIKO

It'd been several days since the princess and heir of Hanaobi had gone missing, her handmaidens missing with her.

I hadn't meant to stay gone so long, had only meant to take a look for myself at the conditions of one of these farms. But then when I'd gotten there, after making the long walk through the capital, I hadn't wanted to go back.

It'd been odd—liberating in a way, but foreign—to walk with larger strides, free from the confines of my royal wardrobe. Certainly, I'd walked faster than usual in private when sneaking off to spend time with my brother, but I hadn't had to travel quite this distance. My legs were shaking before we'd even exited the capital surrounding the palace, my senses overwhelmed with the bustle of the people walking to and fro among the dirt paths, some with baskets on their heads. One pair brushed my shoulder with a long stick held between them that dangled dead pheasants as I squeezed through the crowd to follow Bunji. I screamed softly, causing the entire crowd around me to stop and stare.

Emiko swooped in beside me. "She thought she saw an insect," she said, smiling.

One of the men carrying the pheasants scowled at me. "Don't dishonor your mistress," he said to me, brushing past.

I looked at Emiko and then myself. She still wore her palace finery—not as resplendent as something I would wear, of course, but among the better outfits amidst those on these roads—and I was wearing my inner *kimono*, which had gotten dusty from these roads and resembled what the majority of people here were wearing, although the material was finer if anyone was paying close attention. I'd also wiped as much of the makeup off my face as I could manage as we made our way. Perspiring had left me no choice. So I'd looked like Emiko's servant instead of the other way around.

"We should go back," said Yukiko. "We may not have been missed yet." She looked over her shoulder, as if watching for palace guards heading after us.

Bunji was still just visible in the distance, and I didn't want to lose sight of him. I shook my head and pushed my blazing legs forward, making it through the crowd and bursting free at the edge of the village. The crowds thinned here and I moved my legs as fast as they'd take me, marveling at the speed and the way my heart accelerated.

"Your High…" Yukiko began calling me from behind me, but she cut herself short. "Bunji!" she resorted instead, causing the boy to stop. He leaned up against a tree and crossed one ankle in front of the other, waiting for us all to catch up.

I spun around, breathing deeply, harder than I'd ever breathed before. I laughed, almost dizzy. "I suppose I'll need a new name," I said, wondering at how they even managed to walk wrapped up so tightly. "If you call me 'Your Highness,' I think everyone will take note and either discover the truth or find you somewhat crazy." I tapped a finger to my lip. The air was cool and inviting on my skin. I closed my eyes and stuck my nose forward, as if trying to push my face against the breeze. "Shoko," I said.

"Pardon, Your Highness?" asked Ayako as I opened my eyes.

"Not 'Your Highness,'" I reiterated. "No 'Tomiko,' either. Just call me 'Shoko' while we're out here."

My three handmaidens exchanged a look that made me certain they all thought I was crazy. Perhaps I was. I laughed and picked my legs up again, running toward Bunji.

Partway to the farm, we convinced a passing trader to give us a ride in the back of his cart in exchange for Bunji helping pull it part of the way. He'd insisted on none of my handmaidens helping, but he hadn't seemed opposed to me stepping up—but the girls wouldn't hear of it. It was just as well since I was exhausted. I wouldn't have minded helping, but I didn't know if my limbs were capable of it. They were numb and almost shaking, but I'd felt so exhilarated, I'd hardly cared.

That had been my first adventure—my first exposure to the world beyond the palace. It had been invigorating, addicting... I loved being treated no differently than the people around me. Days had passed since we'd made our way here to a farm outside of the capital. It was quite a distance, though from the top of the tallest hill surrounding the paddies, you could see the capital and the curved roofs of the palace. Shirai, the farm foreman, didn't ever seem to let me linger very long, though.

"Do you want to eat or do you want to be back on the dirt road eating scraps and lice for dinner, eh?" Shirai chewed on a blade of grass, a scythe over his shoulder as he caught me staring.

I bowed my head and trailed after my handmaidens—or I supposed I was to think of them just as Emiko, Ayako, and Yukiko for now. They wore constant expressions of fear on their faces, their beauty marred by just a few days out in the sun. I wondered if my face looked just as haggard, but I found I barely cared, considering the pleasant burning I experienced in my legs and arms. Even the ache of my back, though obtrusive, was a new feeling. It wasn't like the stiffness I'd experienced from sitting too long in an upright position. This thoroughly ached, a pounding reminder that I was alive.

Emiko nudged me and handed me a basket, passing her own basket among the reeds, gathering rice grain. I followed suit.

The girls had left their fancier attire with their parents, had begged them to hide them from Shirai and the lord who ran the farm, whom I'd yet to meet. It seemed he rarely bothered to oversee the work, leaving it all in Shirai's hands. Emiko's parents had convinced Shirai that I was their niece, that I needed work after failing to find some in the capital. The girls—and even Bunji —kept my real identity hidden even from their parents, who were only partly in on the secret. I was just another handmaiden, they'd said, and they'd all needed to flee the palace because we'd made a mistake and we might be facing harsh punishment. That meant it would be harder for Bunji to sneak in for more food reserves, I knew, and that had depressed the mood of the girls' families considerably. I'd bitten my tongue then, knowing I wasn't going to keep up this charade forever, that things would be back to normal soon enough. I'd even reward them with more food when I could.

I'd just wanted to see what it was like for those beyond the palace. Perhaps with this knowledge, I could convince Mother to be more lenient.

The minutes rolled into hours and before long, even the thrill of feeling the ache in my back and limbs began to be too much. After two days of this labor, my limbs didn't shake so, but still, the burn was getting deeper—almost too much to bear. As I put my latest basket down in the cart at the edge of the field, I wiped my arm against my brow and surveyed the landscape, wondering how they all managed day after day, year after year.

I winced when I caught sight of the flush on Ayako's cheeks, the way the effort of the work marred her careful beauty. Shirai yelled at her as she paused to stretch and catch her breath, and my stomach roiled as I surveyed the fields and saw so many hard at work. How could Mother have doubted the farmers' productivity? They hardly paused in their efforts.

It was new to me—freeing, even—but these people had experienced it day after day, month after month, year after year with no end in sight.

I was struck numb with the sudden realization of the foolishness of it all, of the danger I'd put my handmaidens in. Would Mother understand what I had done—and if she proved understanding to me, would the handmaidens receive similar leniency?

Mother often expected more than she ought to from even those doing their best. I'd known that much. And yet I'd run off and put these women in danger with me.

What had she done when she'd noticed me gone? Had someone —a guard, my tutor—already paid a price?

"You like to stare off a lot, don't you?"

I turned to see one of the farmhands staring down at me as he dropped his own basket off. It was Goro, Ayako's older brother.

"I apologize," I said, bowing slightly.

He laughed. "You speak so formally." He leaned one arm atop his basket and ran a hand over his forehead to flick the bangs out of his eyes. "Just like Ayako. I suppose that's necessary if you plan to work at the palace."

I winced. I'd known that there was a way of speaking that most of the people used—it slipped out sometimes even when they tried to speak formally to Mother or me, and I often heard it down corridors when they didn't know I was listening—and I thought I grasped the basics of it, but it was difficult to remember to speak in shortened words here. I tried not to speak too much at all, period. But our unconventional arrival and the mistakes I kept making made it impossible for me to avoid the stares for very long.

"Thank you for your efforts!" called Shirai from the edge of the nearest paddy. "The sun is down and our work is done."

I moved aside to make way for the others bringing their baskets to the cart.

These people worked from sunrise to sunset with few breaks between. If only Mother knew that they were already doing their best, that there wasn't much even executing a loved one could do to change things.

It struck me then that this was why I had ventured out here. To confirm what I'd already felt to be true in my heart—that Mother was unfair to these people, just as she'd been unfair to Elder Brother Kojiro.

"Don't be offended," said Goro from behind me as I made my way back to the small home where Emiko's family ate and slept. They'd offered me shelter when we'd explained our version of the truth. Ayako's family lived next door, so I supposed it only made sense that Goro would join me on my walk back.

"I am not offended," I said.

He grinned. "You're speaking so formally again."

"It is a difficult habit to break," I said quietly. I wouldn't need to even try to break it soon enough. I had to tell them who I was. Soon.

"Fair enough." He smirked as he looked down at me, pushing his bangs again and leaving a smudge of dirt behind.

I fought the urge to reach up and wipe it off him.

"So, were you raised in the capital? Ayako's never mentioned you before…" He trailed off, letting a simple nod speak for the rest.

"Yes," I said. It was certainly true enough.

He winced, his shoulders rolling forward slightly. I'd never met a person so "loose," I supposed was the right word. So free and limber and careless of social expectations. Was this how all farmers were— the ones not too exhausted at the end of the day? Goro was youthful, probably only a few years older than me, and the work didn't seem to tire him like it did the others.

"Why do you make that face?" I asked, emboldened by his own levity.

He smirked. "I just feel sorry for you is all."

I stopped in my tracks. "Sorry for me?" A few other farmers walked around us, dragging their weary feet forward to their small huts.

"I didn't mean to insult you," Goro said, gesturing for us to keep moving. I matched his leisurely pace. "You can't help where you were born."

"But what would be wrong with being born in the capital at all?"

He shrugged. "It's just… confining there, wouldn't you say?"

He stopped and looked up at the sky, at the blue and purple edge creeping over the last ember glow of twilight on the horizon. I stood beside him and looked at the stars with him. "I suppose it is," I said. I'd seen the stars—studied them even—at home, but I had to admit they looked so much grander where I stood now.

"Ayako isn't how I remember her," said Goro softly. "She used to be… less weary." He glanced over his shoulder, but his sister was some ways behind us. "She looks like all the rest of them now. Worse. The capital life does that to them."

I observed the parade of farmers fanning out to their homes and I wasn't sure that I agreed. It seemed like this life was hard, that there was little room for the joviality I saw in Goro. I wondered why that still existed in him.

He leaned in closer toward me, his breath warm against my temple. "Can you keep a secret?" he asked.

Thinking of Elder Brother Kojiro, I nodded.

He leaned back again, but he kept his voice low. "I'm leaving this place."

"You plan to work for another farm?" I asked. Proposing he planned to move to the capital seemed less likely after how he'd disparaged it.

He shook his head. "I'm leaving this country. The rumor is that war is coming, and if I don't leave now, I may never have the chance —or worse, I might be conscripted into an army to fight a battle I have no desire to participate in." He stared toward the capital, where I knew the fleets were assembling. "There's a single trading ship left still headed to the duchy," he said, "and I plan to be on it."

The thought of losing the company of this solitary light I'd found in this weary, if beautiful, place concerned me. Was that the type of person who'd fled all these years? Our most lively citizens?

I needed to know more. What prompted someone to risk everything to cross the seas to a barbaric land? I wasn't ready to return home quite yet.

❧ 10 ❧

FASTELLO

Rohesia was acting strangely. I couldn't quite put my finger on it—looking at my right hand, the joke of that thought was not lost on me—but she was *here*. She was with us both in body and mind. She was present.

And that was odd behavior for her.

"I don't like it," she said, lacing her fingers together on the table. I winced. I hadn't known her father—I still couldn't think of him as my grandfather, no matter if I'd used that tenuous connection to step into her spot here—but there was something in her manner that reminded me disturbingly of the cold-hearted duke by his reputation alone. "I don't like all this sneaking and secrecy."

Tierny laughed, although not unkindly. "You'll have to get used to it, my lady." He didn't seem to notice her wince at the title. "Just because you were formerly on the side of brash and bold action doesn't mean you can continue that way now." He pointed to Kojiro and then thumped his chest. "The prince and I, we're more used to this sort of thing. It can work. It will work. And frankly, we're running out of time. We launch on the morrow."

I didn't feel at all that they were ready, even with the extra week the tides had afforded them. Then again, my part in all of this was limited. I had the duchy and its people to protect.

However, while Rohesia found the cover of the shadows so distasteful, I was not so comfortable on the front lines. But that's where I'd be.

"You cannot win against my mother in my homeland with an attack," said Jiro. "Cannot. She is… protect."

"Protected," corrected Tierny.

"And we have so few soldiers to spare," I added. "We'll need as many men as possible to defend us all here."

"That's why I've recommended we leave them all here," said Tierny. "My men and I will have to do for support. We won't be going with you once we land anyway."

"The best defense is a well-coordinated offense," said Rohesia, the corner of her mouth twitching.

"In many situations, that may be so, but in this one, I'm afraid you're outnumbered, dear," said Tierny, slapping her on the back. She recoiled slightly.

Crossing her arms across her chest, she pouted just a bit. "I've had enough of spies and the underground," she said.

"You never reported if you found anything," I said. When she didn't respond, I added, "About who may have alerted the empress to the duke's… downfall."

She scowled. Yes, her having emotions—even negative ones—made her seem like a different person to me. Studying her now, in the glow of a new morning, I was surprised to find she actually had quite a pretty face, now that I could bring myself to stare at it for more than a few seconds. She'd let her hair—usually cropped quite short—start growing and pinned the somewhat longer parts back at the nape of her neck with a long pin. The sun glimmered off a tiny cloudy green ornament. "I never found a promising lead," she said, her voice clipped.

I wondered if there was more to the story.

"It does not matter," said Jiro, straightening his shoulders. Was it just the sunlight on his back, or was he acting differently too? "It was no one here. We are the only ones to know what will be."

Tierny cocked his head at that. "I think he means we're the only ones who know these plans, so there's no danger of anyone warning her. That's all that matters at this point."

Jiro frowned. Whether at Tierny correcting him or the content of what Tierny was saying, who knew?

"She'll know we're sending one last ship," I said. "In fact, I'm worried about what you all might do if you encounter her entire fleet along the way. You might never…" I swallowed. "You might never make it all the way." Though these three were far from my bosom companions, I shuddered at the thought of their loss, of the helplessness I'd feel left to combat the tension between two nations all on my own.

Tierny tapped his temple. "Don't you worry there, son." He never addressed me with a title, but it'd admittedly feel odd if he did. "I know how to get around the expected route a fleet might take. We'll get there. I guarantee it."

"I only mean, so long as she already knows you're coming, you might be bolder about it." I noticed Rohesia's eyebrow arch as I spoke, her gaze studying me with interest. "Don't let her fleet attack you. Raise a flag to indicate you're on a diplomatic mission." I turned to Jiro. "She can't honorably attack your ship before she's even formally declared war. Even if she had, it's custom to allow for an envoy, isn't it? To at least pretend to be negotiating for peace?"

Jiro seemed to be thinking over what I was saying. Then he shook his head. "If there is no way we can… avoid. But if we can, shadow is better."

"So if you're caught on the way there, you'll reveal yourselves?" I asked. "Jiro, you're the prince—the heir. Surely, you can boldly enter the front door of the palace."

Jiro's lips soured. He asked Tierny something in his language and Tierny looked grim, nodding as he replied.

"I only mean," I said, once it was clear they weren't going to let me—or Rohesia, I supposed—into the conversation, "I know Rohesia is the heir." It was Rohesia's turn to glare at me now. "But what if you strengthened your claim. Both your claims. What if… you wed?"

Rohesia's eyes widened, and I might have seen her shoulders flinch slightly. Tierny stroked his beard while Jiro just looked confused.

Tierny must have translated what I'd said to Jiro because as soon as he was finished speaking, Jiro shook his head, jumping up from his seat. "No."

"I know you're first cousins," I said, grimacing, "but there's precedent for such a match, particularly among ruling classes—"

"No," repeated Jiro. He looked across the table at Rohesia. "Cousin, I am sorry, but I cannot."

Rohesia turned away. "I didn't say I had any interest in marrying you, either."

The room descended into an uncomfortable silence. Tierny was actually struggling to hide a smile, I could tell, but he cleared his throat and walked toward the fireplace, his arms crossed tightly behind his back.

I lay my hands upon the table, biting back the sting from the image of red hair that flashed through my mind. "I meant it purely as a political marriage," I added, in case either thought I meant they might be in love. Still, the strong reaction made me wonder—did either have someone else they were in love with?

I swallowed at the realization of where the conversation might naturally go next.

"And what of you, son?" asked Tierny. "Have you given a thought to marriage, political or not?"

My phantom fingers stung. "No," I said. "I'll not marry for love. But I would marry for peace, if it came to that."

Jiro nodded toward Rohesia. "You marry with her."

Rohesia stared at him, her tightened facial muscles saying all.

"She's my aunt," I said.

"She is my cousin," he said.

"She is not getting married," Rohesia added.

"My," said Tierny, clapping his hands and approaching the table, "aren't we one big happy family?"

I shook my head. "My marriage to Rohesia would do nothing. It's Hanaobi and the duchy that need uniting, not the duchy with itself."

"I won't marry," said Rohesia.

I stared at her. "But you'll need to at some point," I said. "What's the point of all of this"—I pointed to the piles of maps and papers that were a result of the planning—"for you to claim a throne and then for you to have no heir?"

Rohesia stood up from the table. "I'm not a pawn," she said. "If you need me to help bring peace to Hanaobi, and thus to the duchy, I will." One of her hands grazed the small jade ornament at the back of her hair. "I will leave the matter of my heirs to those who survive me."

She stormed from the room.

Jiro looked ashamed—why, I couldn't be sure—and Tierny watched her go. "One step at a time," he said, a flittering smile appearing on his face when he looked at me. "Although I can't help but feel you're not entirely wrong." He looked at Jiro, as if about to say something more, but he didn't. "In any case, the empress would just view a marriage alliance as a threat, a reason to turn against her son officially."

I grimaced, remembering how both Tierny and Jiro were confident the empress had no interest in keeping her son alive.

"All right," I said, sighing as I pushed my chair back from the table. I held my right hand out toward Jiro, then, looking at it closer, held my left one out instead. "In case I don't see you before tomorrow. Good luck. May all that is good be with you and bring peace to both our lands."

Jiro studied my hand, his nose wrinkling slightly, as if it were a knife instead I held toward him and he was wondering why I'd do such a thing.

Still, he took it and shook it. "You are a good man," he said, slowly. "Good fortune to you and your plans. Take care of my people who make this place a home."

Gulping, I squeezed his hand harder. Somehow, although I'd be terrified in his position, I felt as if I might have the more difficult job being left behind.

ROHESIA

Before I left for what could be the last time—whether it was my death or a throne that awaited me, or both—I found myself staring at the door that led to the small apartment above a seedy tavern. The place Sherrod had tried to make a home, although I doubted he made much use of it, considering he had a room at the castle.

I wondered what reason he could have had for such a place regardless. I knew that he lay with women—I was not naïve, and Father was no different, even though he'd had the instinct to marry all of his and he'd stayed celibate after losing my mother—but there were places that provided both the company and the bed. Malle had come from one of them.

But it was Malle, then, I supposed, that had made him see the need for having a place of his own. I wondered that he had not just asked Father's permission to move her in with him to the castle—Malle seemed to think he would have—though I actually did not think Father would have responded kindly. But perhaps he would have surprised me had they both survived.

I knocked on the door, loudly but not so loudly as to attract attention. A man deep in his bottle staggered in the receding light at the end of the alleyway.

The door opened after a minute and Malle stared down at me from the narrow stairway behind the door. "You're back," she said.

Nodding, I removed my hood, snagging it on the hair ornament Malle had given me in exchange for some coins the first time she'd taken me here.

Malle frowned, but she looked both ways over my head and motioned for me to follow her. "Come in then."

I remembered to crouch when I reached the landing, avoiding the beam that hung haphazardly—dangerously—at the top of the stairs. My hand dipped into my pocket, where I wore my fingers over my jade lion, which I'd taken to keeping on me ever since I'd found smudges on it and was certain it'd been moved in the library. It was a silly thing to be concerned about, but it was among the few things I still cared about.

"Tea?" asked Malle, grabbing her kettle and hanging it from the bar over her fire.

I shook my head and looked around. The place needed a thorough scrubbing. Even the curtains over the one window seemed to be moldy. Then again, I knew Malle had her hands full with her work.

Besides, I had never cleaned in my life. Who was I to complain? I swallowed, reminding myself not to think so negatively of others.

"So," she said, putting her hands on her hips, "did you change your mind about buying more of the old man's things? Or find a buyer?" She jutted her chin toward a corner of the small, one-room apartment, where a small collection of miscellaneous junk remained haphazardly stacked on and around a chair.

I approached the pile even as my fingers grazed the ornament in my hair. It'd been so long since I'd engaged in battle—unless you counted that skirmish with a handful of buffoons—so there hadn't been a need to cut it. "I don't need anything else," I said, taking note of the threadbare clothes, the cracked mugs, the worn-down leather-bound book. I picked up the book, studying it carefully. "Are you sure you don't want to keep any of it? He was your husband."

"Husband?" Malle snorted. "We were married for a matter of hours."

I flipped open the book. It was largely blank, although it was almost half-full of short entries written in entirely too-small hand-writing. "You didn't love him," I said. It was a fact. I'd ascertained as much during my last visit, but I hadn't been sure. What was the point of marriage, then, if not to unite two people who wanted to stay with one another? I looked around me. This was the reason, I supposed, this "home," despite its poor condition. Sherrod had offered this young woman a way to escape the life she'd found herself thrust into.

Malle didn't answer, instead grabbing the kettle with a mitt and pouring it into a dirty mug she kept on the table. Opening a silver pot beside the mug, she dumped loose leaves into the steaming water, shaking the pot out entirely. She held the pot up, staring at it. "I wonder if this will fetch anything."

I sighed and removed a small pouch from my cloak pocket. "I don't need to buy any more of Sherrod's things, but I thought it fitting… Here. His salary."

The pot forgotten, Malle eagerly stepped forward to snatch the pouch from me. Her eyes widened as she rifled inside. "He was paid this much?"

I grimaced. "I don't know, actually. Father"—Malle's brows knitted together when I said that—"My father paid him." I tossed my shoulders back. Her expression felt like the jab of a dagger to what good memories I did have of Father. Not that there were many. I couldn't blame her for her feelings toward the former duke, but… This instinct, this feeling, wasn't rational. I held my arms out to indicate the apartment. "But I figured he didn't pay him enough. And Sherrod… I bet he would have liked you to have this."

Malle hesitated for a moment but then pulled the drawstring closed, dropping the pouch down the front of her shirt. She grabbed a strand of hair and ran it between her fingers nervously. "You think that?" she asked. "Even though he never told you about me?"

I bit my lip and nodded.

Malle reached over behind my head and on instinct, I flinched away, lifting my wrists out to block her, journal still in one hand. She jumped back, then laughed. "Sorry," she said. "I should know better than to sneak up on a soldier." She pointed to the back of my head instead. "I only meant to show you that again."

I dropped the journal in my lap and reached to the nape of my neck, removing the Hanaobian ornament Malle had exchanged for my entire pouch of silvers the first time she'd brought me here. The ornament was the same cloudy green color as my lion and even had a lion carved onto the small, round stone. I'd marveled at how delicately the tradesman must have worked to have made such a thing without a single error. I would have never had the patience, whether or not I possessed the skill.

"I shouldn't have taken your money for that," she said. "Not really. I'm sure it was meant for you. The fact that it was the only thing that really drew you amongst his belongings made that even clearer."

"What do you mean?" I asked, turning it over. It didn't reflect the flicker of the fireplace like a clearer jewel might.

Malle returned to her mug and brought it to her lips. "He showed it to me," she said. "Shortly before we were even wed. I thought he was showing me some gift he intended for me to wear during our nuptials, but he snatched it back almost as soon as I reached for it." She put the mug down and crossed her arms. "It was a gift for someone else, he said. A reminder of home, something to complement the only belonging he knew 'she' held dear."

I pulled my jade lion out of my pocket and held it up beside the ornament. Malle laughed. "See? Who else could it have been, really?" She cocked her head. For a flash, I could see what had drawn Sherrod to her as a soft smile illuminated dimples that appeared in her cheeks. "He loved you." She shrugged. "In a different way than he might have loved—or thought he loved—me." She turned back to her mug, picking it up and taking a sip while facing away from me. "He didn't speak to me much of you, either, but from what little he had to say… Well, he made me believe that all of the horror stories about you weren't necessarily true. You were a daughter to him, and he had to find something in there to hold on to, even when frightened of what you—and your father—might do."

She was about to drink again, but she paused, placing the mug back down and instead walking around the table to her bed. She lifted the mattress, sending a flurry of dust mites scurrying through the air as she reached for something hiding underneath. The mattress fell back down with a thunk as she stood upright, a journal identical to the one in my lap in her hand.

"I don't know what this all means," she said, "and I don't know how much he told you—if anything. But I do know that what you did—ending the duke's reign, taking revenge for Sherrod's life—was something he alone thought you capable of." She held the book out to me. "So… I'll trust whatever it is he hoped to do with you. I think he would have wanted you to have that."

First putting the lion back into my pocket and the ornament back into my hair, I took the journal from her. Opening it, I found what could only be described as a cipher.

12

KOJIRO

Would I have objected so strongly to marrying my cousin—for political purposes—before these past few nights with Luana here in this sanctuary, in this sole room made to resemble Hanaobi in all of this wretched land?

I could not be certain.

I would not have agreed to be married before we sailed at least. There would have been something ominous about carrying out that marriage before confronting Mother. Before seeing who it was who survived that confrontation.

"I don't understand." Luana peered down the barrel of the weapon with which I'd absconded when I'd fled my homeland. She shook it. "How do you light the fire to set it off?"

I reached over, the skin of my forearm grazing the soft warmth of her bare breast, wrapping my hand over hers on the weapon. "Careful. It can be dangerous."

She giggled and leaned over to kiss my cheek. "I know. I saw what it did to Fastello's hand."

I grimaced and took the weapon from her entirely, turning it over with both hands. We both examined it as we lay on the *futon* together. "I need… practice."

She laughed again, a sly smile sticking to her lips. "He might have deserved it, if you ask me."

I stared at her quizzically.

She shrugged and wrapped an arm across my chest, curling her warm body against my side. "I don't mean I wish you'd killed him or anything. But certainly he's sinned enough to deserve the loss of a finger or two."

There were times when she spoke too quickly for me to entirely understand her, but I always recognized the shift in tone, the way the light in her eyes dulled somewhat when it came to Fastello. I never asked what had happened between them—but I knew at the very least she had slept in his bed not too long before she had started sleeping here, and the thought alone burned hot inside me. I hadn't liked all the tender moments I'd seen between Fastello and Cateline, but then I'd have never imagined Cateline could have looked at me with anything but indifference at best, contempt at worst. I would not have deigned to hope for more, to break that image I had of her as one of the silver maidens dancing in the moonlight. But Luana… She did see me. And she danced. How she danced. What did it matter if it was in the firelight? I was from a place that found value in the sun.

It was just a small part of our culture, but I was suddenly eager to embrace it, to roar in the firelight alongside this otherworldly, confident beauty.

I gripped the weapon in my hands as if I were about to fire it, my finger over the trigger as I pointed it at the ceiling. "You put… powder in here." I tapped the chamber with my other hand. "And a… special pellet." I didn't know what else to call it in her language. In my own, we called it something to do with fires and arms. That didn't translate well, I was certain. I closed one eye, as if aiming for a knot in the wood of the ceiling I'd pinpointed. "I pull on this, and inside a weapon, the spark is made. It fires up inside, then send the special pellet flying." I bounced the weapon as if shooting it. I remembered how it buckled when I'd done it. The sound had been deafening, but there was no need for me to reenact my flinch.

"It's that simple?" Nestling her cheek against my shoulder, Luana stared up at the ceiling. "I wonder why the duchy didn't think of such things. We have cannons. It's like a small cannon. Very convenient." She reached up toward the weapon and I handed it to her. There was no powder or pellet in it now, so I was not too concerned for her safety. All the same, I would not have her break it. Last I knew, Father had made only this one.

I wondered what we would do if Mother had thought to commission more from our blacksmiths in the time I'd been gone. How my cousin would fare in a fight with a dozen men all armed with these and she with nothing but her blade to stop them.

We wouldn't even need a dozen men with these weapons. Even one would do. One who fired from the shadows, from where she least expected it.

But Mother had had no interest in this thing. It had been Father's doing and Mother had found it distasteful and loud. She wouldn't have considered it worthy—even Father and Elder Brother Nobutada hadn't taken it with them on their mission to the duchy. She likely would have never searched for it, so Tomiko may have been the only one who knew I'd taken it with me.

I saw the value in it, despite the danger. I would make sure that my country did one day, too.

Luana gripped the weapon above her with both hands and slipped a slender finger over the trigger. She pulled.

There was no pellet inside it, but there must have still been some powder. It made a loud noise and Luana screamed as her hand buckled and the weapon waved above her head.

Nothing crumbled after the weapon fired, but a thin film of dust settled back down on top of us and Luana turned, burying her face against me and coughing.

Grabbing the weapon from her trembling hand, I put it on the table beside me before wrapping my arms around her. I'd forgotten how Elder Brother Nobutada had cleaned it, so I'd done my best by slipping a cloth wrapped around a small stick inside. It must not have worked entirely.

"I am sorry," I said. "It is dangerous. Please be careful."

She kept coughing for a bit, but then the coughs started mixing with laughter even as she shook against me. "You warned me," she said. "It was stupid of me." Her voice quieted. "I'm stupid."

"No," I said, a flash of pain shooting up my chest at all the times Mother had called me that word—in our own language and in barbarian. It was a barbarian word I'd learned quite quickly. "No. I love… your spirit," I said. "Courage."

Smiling at me, Luana pulled away. "For a moment there, I thought a prince had just told me he loved me."

That cold tightness inside me melted as I stared down at her. "I wish I could love you," I said in my own language. I was not foolish enough to think I was entirely in love, even if… Even if the past few nights had been wonderful. Even if there was no one I'd rather be with than her. I had nothing to offer her right now. She thought me a prince, and I supposed I was, but the title was meaningless at the moment. It might not always be. But it was now.

And if I one day had anything at all to offer her, those around me would insist I marry for political reasons instead. No, hoping for more was madness.

"What did you say?" Luana traced a hand down my cheek, like a mother—a different mother than the one I had—might with her child. "Did you tell me you loved me?"

I shifted downward and buried my face against the top of her chest. "You must learn my language to know."

She pinched my arm playfully. "You fiend! You're not the only one who speaks your language around here, you know. I might just go with the nomads heading out to the farmlands tomorrow and find me an outsider farmer to translate for me."

"Not 'outsider,'" I said, my lips grazing her skin. "They live here now."

I could feel her shrug. "True. And they do more for my land than I do, I have to admit." She paused. "Do you think Fastello has noticed I've stayed here the past week instead of going with the others to help build homes at the farmlands?"

It was I who shrugged then. "We have not spoken of this."

She tapped her fingers against my back. I wondered if she was getting any of the soot from the weapon on it. "I can't believe he convinced them to help," she said. "Or to help get that rich bitch's house back for her—even if she had to take in all those nomad boarders." She laughed. "When you have all those meetings, Prince

Jiro, and I'm left all by my lonesome, the tales Gilia and Mina have to tell me about how she whines and cries about helping with the simplest things, like doing the laundry for those who work in the fields and building the homes—"

I leaned back to put a finger over her mouth. It was not a custom we had in Hanaobi, but she had done it to me more than once, and I knew it meant something like, "Stop talking so I can kiss you."

She did and I did.

"Teach me outsi—Hanaobian," she said as she pulled back.

"What means your name?" I asked.

She cocked her head. "What do you mean?"

I put a hand on my chest. "My name means Tiger. Next in Succession. Son." I'd memorized what the characters in my name translated to in barbarian early on.

"That's quite a meaning to live up to." She grinned. "Jiro can mean all that?"

"Kojiro," I said, pronouncing it correctly for her.

She repeated after me, inflection for inflection, and burst into laughter as she repeated it again. She was teasing me, her face so serious, I supposed it was a reflection of what she saw on my own.

"Your name means…?" I said, repeating my question.

She rolled her lip between her front teeth, the whites of her top teeth so bright against the red of her plump mouth. "My mother always told me I was named after the moon," she said. She pointed toward the ceiling and to what we knew lay beyond there.

"She was a Stargazer?" I asked.

She shook her head. "No… Perhaps a little. She didn't go to the Stargazer tower or anything, but she found beauty in the lights among the dark of the sky."

I took a piece of her dark hair in my hand, feeling the soft thickness of it that reminded me of cotton not yet pressed into thread. "Tsuki," I said. "Tsukiko."

"What's that?" she said.

"You." I kissed her on the forehead. "Moon. Moon Child."

"Tsukiko," she repeated. "Kojiro." She nuzzled against my

chest. "Take me with you," she whispered, not for the first time in the past few days.

"I cannot," I said.

"You can," she responded softly.

"Death," I said, struggling to figure out what I wanted to say in her tongue. "Death may be there for me."

"So you would have me never see you again?" She pulled back and looked up at me. "You have been the kindest, most beautiful lover I've ever had." I did not like to think of her having had so many, though I could not blame any man for approaching her before I'd known her. "If you're so certain death awaits you across those waters, at least let me stay with you until then."

I embraced her so she couldn't see my face as I thought it over. Tierny, my cousin, Fastello—they'd see no reason to bring Luana along. I could hardly think of a reason myself, other than for my own selfishness. But no matter what awaited me in that void ahead, I would not be returning here. I could not. And I would never see her again.

For what little it was worth, I *was* a prince. Why did I have to ask the likes of Tierny or anyone for that matter?

There was a knock on the window, a gentle tapping like a single nail trying to claw through the glass.

"What was that?" asked Luana dreamily, pulling her head back from my body.

There was no reason for this. Not this soon before I left. Not when I had company. I got up from the *futon*, not bothering to cover myself as I made my way to the window. I pushed the pane open slightly and snatched the small note tied to the leg of the bird I found there.

"What's that?" I heard Luana ask as the bedding rustled behind me.

"Nothing," I lied, crumpling the paper tightly within my fist.

13

TOMIKO

Every morning, the moment I'd woken, since the day I'd ventured out here among the Hanaobian people, I'd told myself to go home.

Every day, I convinced myself to stay.

I knew Mother would be concerned about my disappearance. I knew delaying my return was selfish. But I truly believed that knowing what our people went through firsthand would make me a better ruler someday if it came to it—or at least could help me convince Mother to be more lenient.

She'd never been angry with me before. I'd been the perfect daughter, the ideal heir.

Only I... I'd done it all for duty first and foremost. I'd done it not to make Mother think less of Elder Brother Kojiro, but to distract her from his foibles. I hadn't meant for it to make her turn on him entirely.

"Wake up!" someone hissed from beside me. It was still dark out —no. I fluttered my eyes open and shut. It must have been dawn because there was an ember glow beyond the paper walls of the small home. It felt sickly somehow.

"Wake up," the voice said again. I shot upward from where I lay on the futon beside Emiko's family. It was Ayako, and she shook both Emiko and me awake. Farther back in the room, I could see several more figures moving. Goro, Bunji, and Emiko's parents— perhaps Ayako and Goro's parents, too.

In the dim light, Ayako's face looked as if drained of all life.

"What is it?" asked Emiko, jumping up beside me.

Ayako pointed over our heads. "Fire. The paddies are burning."

In the bleary haze of waking, I couldn't understand what she meant. There was water beneath the stalks. It didn't seem possible it could be burning. But the stalks themselves could burn well enough.

Emiko jumped up beside me and I realized everyone around me was gathering up belongings, putting on extra *kimono*, as if they planned to wear their small wardrobes out of here.

Finally, the gravity of the situation caught up with me. "What about Yukiko?" I asked.

Ayako shook her head. "We can't get to her family's home from here. Not without going through…" Her voice dropped. "We have to hope they make it out themselves."

I stood quickly, rushing to Emiko's side. "Is there anything I can carry for you?"

She looked at me a moment, hesitating, as if wondering whether or not to ask such a thing of me. But she thrust a *furoshiki* at me, tied tight around some of her family's valuables.

I wrapped my arms around it and made my way for the door, shoving my feet unceremoniously through my sandals. My arms heaved as I held tightly to the parcel in my arms, my already-sore muscles straining to keep it steady. The door was open in front of me, probably thrust open as Ayako's family had made its way inside.

The fields were fire—smoke. They gave birth to a false dawn over the horizon, the real sky blackened, choked by the disaster from below.

"Here."

I turned around to find Goro behind me, his lips tight, his face grim. He grabbed the *furoshiki* from me and slid a long bamboo staff through the knot at the top. "It's easier to carry over your shoulder."

I did as bidden, finding the burden somewhat relieved. He lingered a moment longer. "What could have happened?" I asked. I began coughing, realizing that even at this distance from the fields, the smoke was making its way toward us.

He reached into his pocket and brought out another *furoshiki*, this one coarse cotton and hardly as ornate as the one used to hold Emiko's things. He folded it into a triangle and, without asking, flung it over my mouth and nose, tying it in a knot behind my head. "It'll filter some of the smoke," he said, nodding and staring over my head toward the fire.

I was going to ask more, but he turned, running back toward the others still gathering their things.

Some other farmers ran past the door on the dirt path, shouting and screaming as they carried their own bundles away.

I stepped outside slowly, as if I'd find the world beyond the door hot to the touch, as if it'd send me shirking back inside, burn me by proximity.

More farmers went by, these on a cart led by a panic-stricken and worn-down horse. They didn't stop to acknowledge me, just kept barreling down the path. I watched as they met up with the first group I'd seen. One of the men who was walking started yelling at them to stop, jumping into the path of the horse. The horse reared and the man fell backward. Some women screamed, but the cart wouldn't slow. Once the horse put its hooves back on the ground, that family was on its way, a young man on the cart turning to glance at the fallen man they left behind.

I moved toward the disaster, hoping to check on the man who'd fallen, who lay crumpled on the ground, his limbs up at awkward angles, but I felt a hand on my arm. "Leave them."

It was Goro, his and Emiko's families emerging from the house behind him. Most of the women had *furoshiki* or cloths on their faces like I did, as did Bunji. Goro and the two fathers went without, one of the fathers using his sleeve to cover his mouth instead.

"There isn't time to help everyone," Goro explained. "Come." He gestured to the families behind him. "I know where to go." He pulled on my arm, leading us all in the opposite direction of the other farmers, who'd fled toward the mountains to escape the flames. He led us not down the dirt path, but through an as-yet-untouched field of grass, toward the capital but not in a straight path for it.

"Where are we going?" I asked. I wondered, too, at why we weren't taking the pathway, although with the chaos of the other farmers running to and fro, I supposed that was reason enough.

"I told you," Goro said, clutching my arm tighter. He had a couple of parcels tied to a stick over his shoulder that swung wildly as the tall grasses whipped at our hair and legs.

"The boat," I said, so quietly I wasn't sure he could hear me over the sounds of havoc unfolding around us. I pulled back, hard, straining against the pain in my arm to make him stop.

He did, turning back with wide eyes. He stared at me as the rest of our party caught up to us and gathered around us. He dropped my arm and turned, motioning them onward. "Keep going," he said to his father. "The docks. Take the long way around. Skirt the capital; don't pass through it." His father looked at him and me and simply nodded, putting his arm around his wife and shoving onward, the rest of the party falling in step behind them—except for Emiko and Ayako, who stopped, exchanging an unasked question over their covered noses.

Whether to flee with their families or do their duty and see to my safety.

"Come on," called Emiko's father as he turned around. "Emiko! Come!"

"Go ahead," I said to her. "The both of you. Go—just go."

Emiko nodded and moved on, her extra *kimono* pulling her down somewhat, causing her to stumble as she headed after them. Ayako hesitated.

"Elder Brother," she said to Goro. "She…" She looked at me and I shook my head. I couldn't get on that boat, I knew that. But I didn't want them all to know, didn't want any more of them than need be to overly concern themselves with my own safety when they had their own lives to consider.

"I'll make sure she gets there safely," he said. He put a hand on her shoulder. "Go!"

She locked eyes with me and then left, dragging after the rest of them.

"Did you forget something?" he asked, staring back toward the farm and the flames behind me. "If it's not important, please let it go… I don't know if we could make it back and—"

"No," I said. "Listen."

There was another shriek of a horse from behind me. An image of that poor man being trampled flashed through my mind as we heard a man's voice rage. "What are you doing?" Shirai. "Why have you come here? Why do you burn our crops, our food—?"

"Where is she?" said another man.

"I told you, I don't know what you're talking about!" Shirai shrieked.

Goro tugged again on my arm, but I wouldn't be moved. I turned around to see what had happened—and over the tops of the tall grasses, I could see a battalion. Men on horses. *Guards* on horses.

A *katana* was held aloft in the air, the red glistening off its tip, either from the fire or blood or both.

With a sudden realization, I knew. This had been no accident, no act of nature.

The fire had been set by Mother's men.

"We have to run," Goro hissed. "Before they spot us."

"No, I…" If I leapt out now, could I end this? Could my word alone be enough?

I looked down at my dirt- and soot-covered plain *kimono*, remembered the cloth over my face. Would they even recognize me as their heir?

"Did you know they were here?" I said, finally letting Goro drag me onward.

"Quiet," he hissed.

A moment later, I heard a voice from behind us. "There! Through the field! You, you, and you—after any who escaped!" Horses neighed as the rustling of the field indicated they'd broken through the grasses after us. "But check all the young women!" shouted that guard again. "If I find you've harmed the princess, your guts will spill!"

They were here for me.

They were here for me.

They'd set this place ablaze and attacked the farmers *because of me*.

Because I'd woken up each morning and convinced myself that it was okay to stay.

Because I'd loved the freedom and the movement I'd experienced away from the castle. Because I'd been naïve enough to think it was all for the greater good, that I'd go home shortly.

Goro didn't slow, pulling me, the both of us stumbling forward. He rolled his shoulder and flung his stick off, one of the parcels coming open as it hit the ground, a tea set and some rice cakes spilling forth.

"Drop it," he hissed, and I knew he meant my own parcel. I did, feeling guilty for leaving Emiko's family's treasures behind.

Our pace quickened considerably, but it wasn't enough. The grass rustled on either side of us, but I didn't dare stop to turn and look. The charged breath of the horses grew louder, dominating even over the crackle and roar of the fire behind us.

"Stop," I whispered, out of breath. "Let me go. Keep going; join your family—I can stop them!"

Goro slapped a palm over my mouth, pulling me tightly against him, dragging us both to a crouch near the ground.

I stared up through the tops of the grasses, which bent inward against each other to act like a thatched roof that let in some of the light. I felt hot, dizzy. My throat constricted and I started coughing, and Goro grabbed my head, pushing my face against his chest, making it harder for me to breathe, making the darkness even dimmer—

"Over here!" said one man.

My heart thudded as Goro eased up. I ripped the cloth down off my face, letting it hang limply around my neck. I needed only to stand, to hope they recognized me, to demand they stop what they were doing or at the very least, to provide Goro time to escape—

"Back this way!" said another, and the horses' hooves picked up again, carrying the men away.

Goro and I stood, slowly, still bending our backs slightly as we neared the tops of the grasses.

"No," I whispered. I could see the paths in the grasses now, see them converge on a large party, their heads bobbing visibly through the field.

Goro flinched but gripped on to my arm tighter.

"We have to save them!" I said. His family. Emiko's family. My handmaidens. My poor, patient, indulgent handmaidens. Little Bunji, just a boy…

I'd done this. I'd done this to all of them. My legs wobbled, and I nearly fell, but Goro held tighter, forcing me to stand.

"We can't."

"We must. I can," I said, ready to explain it all. Ready for this foolish excursion of mine to end.

"You can't," he said. He grabbed me by the hand and darted sideways, taking us farther from the capital and more toward the coast. The reflection of dawn from behind us awaited us there—real dawn—and it shot a beam of light at us over the waters. A stream of tears glistened on Goro's cheek as he grit his teeth and led the two of us onward, the distant shrieks of those we both cared about almost deafening in our ears.

❧ 14 ❧

FASTELLO

I didn't have time to see them off to the docks.

It could have been the last time I'd ever see any of them—my hopes for peace were riding on their shoulders—and I couldn't spare time to see them off.

It was just as well, according to Tierny, who thought it best we not make a fuss about him and his skeleton crew launching out, especially since we still didn't know who was spying for the empress.

As I looked out the second-floor mansion window at the ship as it made its way toward the horizon, though, I wasn't sure there was any way of avoiding whoever that person was seeing them leave. There was no way they'd believe it was merely a trading vessel. And even if they did believe that, there was no way they'd find it a detail not worth mentioning to the empress.

No, their hopes now rested on getting there before whatever bird carried the spy's message did. Or maybe Tierny wanted the empress to know they were coming, to think they were merely traders. Frankly, I hadn't been able to keep up with all of the details.

I didn't need to know the details. This adventure was entirely theirs. We all had so much riding on it, but... It was out of my hands.

"Sir... Lord Fas...?"

I turned away from watching the ship grow ever smaller. Agnes had appeared at some point beside me, the dirty rag in her hands at odds with the prettiness of her dress, despite the dirt that dotted her attire.

"Just 'Fastello' is fine," I reminded her. I could actually see the relief flood across her features.

She held the rag up. "I finished cleaning the, uh... guest rooms," she said, grimacing. I'd gotten her family home back from the guards who'd seized it from her, despite their obvious displeasure at the request, but I'd asked—or insisted, really—that she take in some of the nomads and Hanaobians in need of shelter. At least until we were able to build homes for them.

"Yes?" I said, after it was clear she was going to neither say anything more nor remove herself from my presence.

She wrung her cloth between her hands. "I was wondering if... That is... What is Your Grace's stance on religion?"

She couldn't have asked me a more unexpected question if she'd asked me if I would comb her hair for her. "What do you mean?"

"Well, I know you've kept busy, trying to get everything in the duchy up and running again," she said, her hand absentmindedly going to a pendant at her throat. "But have you given any thought to the duke's—the former duke's—decree on... Stargazing?"

I frowned. The first time this woman had appeared before me, she'd been on her way back from the now-burnt Stargazer tower. But the next time I'd seen her—during our secret lives at a tavern and then a farm—she'd just as easily tossed out the religion. I supposed I couldn't blame her, considering the penalty for practicing it at that time was death.

But those were not the first thoughts that jumped to my mind at the thought of Stargazers. Cateline... My fingers ached. "That religion was a falsehood," I said, images of my grandmother rocking in her chair before the fire eroding those of the red-haired young woman in a silver dress. I cradled my hand and swept past Agnes, heading toward the stairs.

"Of course," said Agnes, curtsying meekly, her eyes averted. "And in any case, I... I haven't always been a devoted follower."

Something seemed to catch in her throat. "I turned my back on the faith."

I halted. I didn't want her to think my instinctive reaction was some sort of authoritarian decree. "I don't want the people here to fear any punishment for practicing a faith," I said. The scab over one of my knuckles pinched as I flexed the skin. "So long as that faith doesn't hurt others. But Agnes, the Stargazers… The tower is burned. The mothers are all gone. The children they cared for…" I paused. I hadn't known any, but the news had been bitter to swallow, and to find out it'd been caused by my own grandmother… A jolt slammed down my throat, a mixture of rage and sadness. For that brief moment, I could feel what Cateline might have felt, could understand why she'd done what she'd done to destroy the madwoman who'd been responsible.

"I know," said Agnes quietly. She raised her head once more and started to smile. "But Ytoile never needed all of that, if you ask me." She caressed the pendant again. "I… I lost faith," she said. "And to tell you the truth, I still struggle at times. I've lost so much." She bit her trembling lip and a tear fell down her cheek. I'd have been moved—a part of me was—but I still couldn't forgive how she'd turned on us. Not entirely. But I supposed she'd been a broken woman then, through and through.

She wiped first one cheek and then the other and tossed her head back. "But thanks to Your Grace—"

"Fastello."

"Thanks to you, I've gained so much again, too."

I cocked my head. "Although I've asked you to share it with others?" I gestured around us at the hallway of her mansion. "Though I've put you at the level of those born to a far different life than you?"

"You didn't put me there," she said. "Well, not you alone." She walked toward me and gestured to a woven banner that hung from the wall. "My family's crest," she said. "Did you know that my sister would have helped anyone who asked for assistance—anyone? She volunteered at the doctor's so often to help with patients that my parents and I all worried she'd bring back some communicable disease." Dragging a small hand across the banner, she shuddered.

"The family name was meaningless to her. You people—the nomads, that is, would have looked at her and me and wouldn't have seen the difference. But there was. There was a huge difference." Her hand gripped the banner tightly. "That boy killed the wrong one of us that day."

"Don't say that," I said before I even thought better of it. Who was I to judge her? Didn't I often wish I'd had the fortitude and the foresight to kill my grandmother myself, to rip the choice away from Cateline, even if it meant she were standing here instead of me? And the boy who'd killed Agnes' sister... He'd been my own brother.

My chest seized and I clutched at the front of my shirt with three fingers, crumpling over, kneeling on the floor.

"What's wrong?" asked Agnes. She hovered above me, hesitating a moment, then backed up a few steps. "I'll call for help," she said.

I laughed. She'd just admitted she'd been afraid of her sister bringing home communicable diseases. "No," I said, gesturing my left hand at her. "Just let me breathe a moment."

She took another step back. "Please," I said between breaths. "I'm fine. Don't... Don't tell anyone."

Agnes stood there a moment longer, then gripped her pendant and thrust herself forward, crouching beside me. "Here," she said, putting a nervous hand around my shoulder. "Lean back against the wall." I did. She sat beside me, her eyes closed as she brought the pendant toward her face, her lips moving in what might have been a silent prayer.

"Do you ever... hear Her?" I said after a moment of silence.

She opened one eye. "Who?"

I chuckled. "Your goddess... Ytoile."

"Oh." Agnes lowered her pendant. "Not directly. But I do. I think I do. Sometimes."

"What does She say?"

Agnes' lips pinched as she played with her pendant now, which she held out before her breasts. "It's not what She says so much as what She makes me feel." Dropping the pendant, she rubbed her hands across her face. "But I forget myself. I'm so rusty. Ytoile doesn't appreciate prayer when the sun is in the sky—"

"That's the mothers speaking," I said. "And believe me, they didn't follow someone with a close relationship with your goddess. If Ytoile is as benevolent as they say, She would appreciate a prayer at any time." I stopped myself from saying I wasn't even sure my grandmother—the great Mother Jehanne herself—actually believed in her own faith. In her eyes, it had all been a scheme to get the rich to part with their coin and jewels.

My chest hurt again and I must have clutched at it harder because Agnes' eyes widened.

"What's the matter with you?" she asked.

"I'm not… sure," I said. "I've only felt this way in the past few days." Sweat beaded on my brow and I laughed again to see Agnes' panicked expression. "I've spoken with a doctor. He assures me it's nothing serious."

Agnes frowned. "It might be… That is, my father, before he passed, sometimes he felt a tightness in his chest." She rubbed her thumb on her pendant, staring down at it. "He'd laugh and dismiss it as 'the busy man's burden,' but I wasn't sure what he meant. He said that sometimes people with too much on their minds could just… feel faint sometimes. That it was the body's way of telling you to stop and take a break."

I grimaced. "There's little time for breaks these days."

"You're taking one right now." Agnes smiled at me, and for a moment, I actually felt heat rise up from my abdomen that had little to do with the tightness in my chest. She was hardly a beauty, but she had small moments of attractiveness.

"That I am," I said. "Thank you for sitting with me."

She nodded. We sat in silence for a while.

"Do you think we're all doomed to be like our fathers?" Agnes asked after a moment.

Had she read my thoughts? It was thoughts of my grandmother, my brother, my father—and now even the duke, the grandfather I hadn't even known I'd had—that had put me in such a state. As if my body was rebelling and warning me that I was due to go mad with power, too, that their ghosts would ever haunt me, that they'd drag my memories of Cateline into flames. I cleared my throat. "What do you mean?"

"It's just…" She looked above her shoulder back at the banner with her family crest. "I loved my father. I never once thought of him as a bad man," she explained. "My mother, too. But now that I know… Now that I've seen so much more of the world, and how others live, I wonder… Why did he keep all this to himself?" She gestured around her at the spacious hallway. At the table with a fine vase on it. At the banners that hung throughout the corridor. "Why did we need so much of it? Why couldn't we have been comfortable going without some of these useless trinkets?" She pulled her rag out of her apron pocket. "That do nothing but gather useless dust?"

"When others can hardly afford to eat?" I asked.

She nodded. "Cecily knew. That was why she gave of herself however she could."

"And despite that, she was rewarded with…" Clenching my teeth, I fought back against the tightness, the dizziness. I would not let those ghosts rule over me.

"I know you tried not to lead us to harm," said Agnes, laying a hand on my arm. "Even though you participated. And I doubt we would have arrived home unscathed. Not entirely." She clutched her pendant again. "There are scars you can't see sometimes, you know."

"I know," I said. "I'm sorry, Agnes. I really am." I choked on the words.

A single drop fell from her eye down her face. "I am too."

Without even thinking, I reached over and embraced her. As a friend to a friend. As a way to put the past behind us, where I so often needed reminding it ought to be.

She startled but soon put her arms behind my back and patted me quickly.

I laughed and pulled back. "Apologies," I said, scratching an itch under my nose. A beard was starting to grow there, neglected by a blade the past few days. "My people, we—we're more affectionate than those of you used to life here in the heart of the duchy."

"I've noticed," she said, but she smiled. "I'm so glad you're here. That you're the ruler instead of that… woman."

I grimaced on behalf of poor Rohesia. "Well, I'm glad you're here, too. I'm glad we've come to an understanding and that you're so willing to help."

She brightened at the word "help" and I realized that I might have helped her feel better about herself, just as she had with me.

Leaning against the wall for support, I stood. "Well, I suppose I better actually act like a leader then," I said, stretching. The tightness was still there, but it was a hollow echo of what it'd been just moments earlier. I headed toward the stairs, nodding at Agnes, who bobbed her head back and then turned to look out the window.

"Fastello," said Gilia as I descended the stairs. She looked a bit out of breath.

"Gilia," I said, clutching the banister with my left hand. "Aren't you supposed to be at one of the farms today?" I couldn't remember if she'd been one of the nomads to move in to Agnes' home, but I was sure that her name had been mentioned to help at one of the farms. I'd noticed it because it'd been next to Luana's, and I liked to keep an eye on where she'd be so I could stay as far away as possible. I'd had no idea where she'd ended up in the sleeping reassignments, and I hadn't cared; I was just glad not to see her in the castle foyer anymore.

"Yes," she said, pinching her lips together. "But I was worried…"

"About what?" I stood before her in front of the open mansion door, leaning out of the way as a Hanaobian woman and a nomad man—Nico, I noticed—carried two baskets of food inside. They didn't speak, but I noticed the way they smiled at each other as they made their way to the kitchen.

"Luana," said Gilia. "She never showed at the farm today."

"Why am I not surprised?" I stepped aside, grabbing Gilia by the elbow to guide her out of the way. Some of the other women were carrying linens outside to hang them between the trees in Agnes' yard. It was small but quaint—and offered more grass than most of the residents here ever saw. "Luana wasn't pleased about my idea that we all start to work," I said. "You know that."

"Yes, but she showed up nonetheless," Gilia said. She frowned. "You really don't think highly enough of her. Poor girl."

I rolled my eyes. I wasn't about to debate the virtues of a woman who'd left me for my own father with another one of the women Dad had kept at his bedside. "You think she's in trouble?"

"I don't know," she said. "I just wondered if… She told you where she went?"

I shook my head. "I haven't seen her in days. Did you check wherever she's been reassigned?"

Gilia shrugged. "She'd been reassigned to live here with Mina and me, but she didn't bother moving with us."

Now it was my turn to frown. "What do you mean?"

"She's been spending nights with that prince instead."

"What prince?!" *What kind of sleazy man had she involved herself with now?*

"The outsid—the Hanaobian prince," she said. She seemed puzzled. "Didn't you know?"

"No!" *When the damn had that happened?*

"He wasn't there," said Gilia. "The guards told me he'd left today—gone home on a diplomatic mission! You don't think…?"

She never finished her sentence, but she didn't need to. The aviary beckoned if I hoped to get any answers.

15

ROHESIA

If my green-faced cousin retched one more time, I was certain I would be sick just from the effort of observing him. Despite this being his second voyage—and my first—it was clear which of the two of us had been born with sturdier sea legs.

"There's an entire body of water out there for you to do that in," said Captain Tierny, looking over questioningly at Kojiro from where he sat behind the captain's desk. I'd taken note of the jade lion he had there holding papers in place. It was almost identical to my own. My own felt less slightly less special at the sight of it.

Kojiro, bleary-eyed, simply lolled his head upward from the bucket he clutched to for dear life before rolling it back down again and vomiting some more.

That was it. I tossed down the rag I'd been using to polish my daggers and dropped it all atop the pile beside me where I'd stacked my sword, sheaths, and underarmor. Tierny had assured me my full armor would prove too noisy for any covert mission we'd likely wind up on, and when I'd suggested at least bringing it and storing it on the ship, he'd balked, insisting the ship would be searched thoroughly upon landing, and they'd find such a thing suspicious.

He'd given a similar reason for not allowing me to bring any of the soldiers along.

Wherever they went, they'd look suspicious at a glance.

Even if we'd disguised them as sailors, they wouldn't have been able to go into the capital with us. Only the captain ever did.

Besides, if there was one thing on which I still agreed with my father, there was little point in scorching the earth of a resisting enemy or there'd be nothing left for anyone—ally or foe, ruler or citizen.

So the men had stayed behind.

I blocked out the sound of Kojiro retching again as I ascended the stairs to the deck.

Tierny sailed with a skeleton crew, wanting as few men as possible to know about our mission—and to risk the lives of as small a number as he could. He'd introduced me to the dozen or so sailors before we'd boarded, but their names had flown from my mind as quickly as they'd entered. Still, I'd recognized more than one face, and I'd certainly taken stock of the looks those faces had given me. I wondered if any had been on a crew my men and I had just about wiped out on my father's orders.

Doubtful. We weren't known to leave many alive. Then the look was based on my reputation alone, then.

There was little reason to blame them. I folded my arms and rested them atop the edge of the boat railing, staring at the endless blue water as it merged into the bright blue sky.

I stayed that way for quite some time. Sailors tended to their business on either side of me, their voices buried beneath the clarity in my head.

It'd been a while since I'd felt so at peace. So tranquil. So empty.

Empty is how I used to be. It was how I got through everything Father had asked of me.

A tiny leg kicked out from beneath a blanket out on the water.

I blinked. It wasn't there.

Instead, I saw Father's eyes in the moment before he died.

I sighed and turned away from the water, shaking my head. Images from my past had come to haunt me, taunting me in that short-lived peace.

Two of the sailors glanced my way before one whispered to the other. I glared at them before straightening my shoulders and heading below deck, not back to the captain's quarters, but to the cargo area just to find some space for myself.

It was dark down there. Beams of light flooded in from the few portals high above it all, but it was like walking through the castle at night with nothing but the moonlight to guide my way.

I settled against a wall at the back of the hold, bringing my knees up to my chest. I stared out at the barrels—most stuffed with garbage halfway and only covered with grains at the top to make it seem as if we had anything to offer for one final trade—and wondered.

Laying my head on my knees, I reached to my waist to hold my lion where it sat in my pouch, running my fingers over its surface. My fingers glanced over a vial before they came to a rest on their intended target.

I'd never told anyone—not even Sherrod, certainly not my father—but part of me had always wanted to come here, to see where my mother had come from.

That had been the biggest reason why I'd agreed to join Tierny and Kojiro's foolish plan to liberate this country. I'd wanted to see it. I didn't particularly care what happened to me afterward.

I had little desire to rule a country—either there or at home.

Home. It was odd to think of the duchy as home. Without Sherrod, what did I have? Nothing. No one. My newfound nephew was a good man, but I had no interest in being his long-term companion—and I suspected the feeling was mutual, even though he'd tried to be cordial enough.

I wondered how he was doing with all his schemes and plans to make the duchy a better place. His methods might have been fairer for the majority, but they required so much more work and faith in the individual to do what needed doing without the threat of a sword overhead.

Fastello had been keen that my guards were to be defenders and protectors and nothing more. They hadn't taken to that quietly, expressing their displeasure both behind his back and to his face on more than one occasion, but their gripes had been dismissed time and time again. How else did they expect to fit into the duchy of Fastello's rule? I wasn't sure why they'd expected anything more. I should have felt something for leaving all of them behind—but I didn't know them. They'd been like mirrors. Cold, ruthless—without feeling. I wondered if there was even anything human inside them.

Considering their complaints thus far, I wondered if those cold men could be beholden to a different kind of duke. Their loyalty to my father had never been questioned. But now, with someone sending a secret letter to the empress, with a more peaceful-minded duke, I wasn't sure how far their fealty would stretch.

Gauntlet hands placing a bundle on a river. Gentle, as if the man cared about what was inside.

The little leg kicking up as the infant vanished from view.

A whimper echoed from somewhere across the room.

Instinctively, I pulled my hand out of my pouch and flicked both wrists, but my daggers were in the captain's quarters.

I jumped to my feet at least, taking care to force down the slight feeling of dizziness that took over as the boat swayed beneath the soles of my boots. "Who's there?" I said, loudly. "Show yourself."

I made my way between the barrels, quieting my breaths and slowing my gait to mask my presence. The whimpering had ceased, but there was no mistaking the breathing—not heavy, but loud enough to assure me I wasn't dealing with someone who knew what they were doing.

They weren't even retreating. I came to the corner of the room and found three barrels out of line, almost as if corralling something in the corner. One of the barrel's lids was off, the grain stuffed on the top scattered on the ground, a small portion of it leading like a path to the other side of the barrel.

I clutched my jade lion tightly in one hand, ready to hit someone atop the head if need be.

"Show yourself," I repeated, kicking aside one of the barrels and holding the lion above my head.

A nomad woman cowered in the corner, shivering and shielding her head with her arms.

Lowering the lion and stuffing it back into my pouch, I reached forward to grab her by the arm and pull her into the light.

"Don't," she cried, fighting against me. Her feet slapped the floor over and over as she pulled, but I didn't even budge. "Please don't kill me! Get the prince! Kojiro!" She tilted her head and shouted Kojiro's name, as if he were hiding somewhere over my shoulder.

I frowned, but I didn't let go, watching as she squirmed in vain and dodging backward when she flung her free hand at me, aiming her long nails at my face. "Let me go!" she hissed, suddenly angrier than frightened. "Kojiro will be so mad at you if you try anything. Your hopes for peace will be dashed!"

I continued to stare blankly at this flailing cat woman, trying to appear tougher than she was. Finally, I tossed her to the ground in the beam of sunlight. "What are you doing here?" I asked.

She scowled up at me and cradled her arm. "Kojiro said I could come."

I was surprised at the way she said his name. It sounded more clipped—more like how Kojiro himself said it. She had a suspicious familiarity with the Hanaobian tongue.

But how in the world could a nomad woman be persuaded to be a Hanaobian spy?

Then again, the nomads were known for their greed. Coins or gem stones… Some kind of valuables might be enough.

Fastello might have demonstrated that not all nomads were like-minded, but that certainly didn't mean that this woman was like him.

"What would Kojiro want with a woman like you?" Something caught in my throat. I could tell the woman was beautiful, even familiar… Could my cousin be just as dumb as the rest of the men and have fallen for promises of amorous adventures beneath the sheets? That still didn't mean she wasn't the spy.

"Ask him," she snapped, sliding slightly away from me on her backside. "I don't think you'll believe me anyway."

She wasn't as stupid as I thought. "I want to hear it from you," I said. "Then we'll ask him to see if his story matches yours."

She narrowed her eyes. "We're in love."

There it was. That thing that made all men fall. Sherrod, certainly. Even Father.

"Why are you here?" I asked, ignoring the comment.

"We're in love," she repeated.

I sighed. "So you've said. I repeat: What are you doing here, on this ship, in this very dangerous situation?"

She sniffled and wiped her nose on her sleeve. "Kojiro doesn't plan on coming back," she said, as if it ought to have been obvious. "If I didn't come, I wouldn't see him again."

"Did he agree to this?" I gestured at her. "To you being a stowaway on a secretive mission on which hangs the fate of two countries and thousands of lives?" I narrowed my eyes at her. "Or is that precisely why you wormed your way into his affections?"

"I don't know what you're suggesting," she said.

"I know you," I said. "I've seen you with Fastello. Hanging all over Fastello. Not two weeks ago…"

"Don't talk to me about him."

"I'll talk to you about whatever I please, seeing the position you find yourself in." My voice must have carried the threat I intended adeptly as she scurried back so quickly, she slammed the back of her head against a barrel. She cried out in pain, her hand rushing to rub the sore spot.

"Tell me," I said, inching closer to her, "how are you in love with Kojiro when not two weeks ago you seemed in love with Fastello?"

She pouted. "Fastello never loved me. Kojiro does!"

"And your interest in both men has nothing to do with the fact that they're both privy to this secret mission you find yourself on?"

"I don't even know what you mean," she said, shaking her head.

"I'm telling you, for all intents and purposes, you've acted like a spy!"

Her eyes widened and she scoffed. "A spy for who?"

I strode closer and banged a fist on the top of the barrel. She squeezed her eyes shut and flinched. "Are you the one sending birds?"

"What? No!" She opened one eye and then the other. "No!"

"Who do you know in Hanaobi?"

"No one! I swear!" She held her hands between us above her head. "Kojiro is the only one of his people I've ever even spoken to!" She laughed pitifully. "I can't even write or read my own tongue, let alone his!"

I leaned back, putting some space between us. She was either the idiot she appeared to be or very good at lying. I had no patience to learn the craft of lying. Father had believed in blunt honesty and brute force.

Sherrod… He'd lied by omission, keeping his secrets from me, but he'd never lied to my face.

I reached into my pouch to make sure his two journals were still there. I'd meant to spend the time aboard the ship trying to translate them, not dealing with one annoyance after another.

A murmur of voices rang out overhead and both the woman and I looked up. Footfalls clattered on deck.

"What's going on?" she whispered, as if she suspected she might be the cause of it.

I shot her a look and she gulped, looking down.

I strode across the room and ascended the stairs. She'd have nowhere to run down here.

The sailors gathered around the bottom of the mast, watching one climb down, a bird under his arm.

"Give it here," I said at once, determined to snatch any note the bird carried before these sailors had access to it.

The man carrying the bird jutted his chin at me as his feet touched the deck. "We'll give it to the captain," he said. "This ain't no duchy, no outsider land. His law here."

I pushed through the small crowd and they all gave way. I lunged forward, feigning to grab for the note tied around the creature's leg, anticipating that the man would attempt to stop me, and instead I quickly and decisively twisted his arm away, gripping it hard by the wrist at an angle that made him cry out and loosen his hold on the bird. I used my other hand to rip the note away and then let go of the man, twisting his arm once more to get my meaning across.

"Bitch," he sneered, shaking his arm out, but I strode away, unfolding the note. The wax was embossed with the duke's seal. Fastello.

I cracked it open.

One of my people is missing, it read, too late to be of any use. *And I don't trust her.*

I clenched my hands around the note and made my way to my seasick cousin.

❧ 16 ❧

KOJIRO

Every so often, I attempted to keep my face out of the bucket for more than half a minute, but my head kept lolling forward and my arms squeezed tighter around my wooden savior.

"You're never going to get your sea legs, are you?" asked Tierny from somewhere above my head. He chuckled. "Just as well. I hope there's no more need for you to ferry yourself back and forth after this."

I didn't bother asking him to explain himself. The meaning—and the unintended meaning—was clear enough. He hoped our mission would prove successful and lead to peace. On the other hand, I thought of how if I made one wrong move during this quest, I would be dead.

Tierny went on, unmoved by my silence, repeating the plan we'd gone over at least a hundred times by now. "We'll arrive in the dead of night. Guards at the docks will be alert, but not expectant. Meanwhile, before we approach, you and Lady Rohesia take the rowboat and use the new moon to hide your approach. You can disembark along the shoreline—away from the docks. Liberating the over-worked farmers—convincing them to back Rohesia's claim—is key."

He paced in front of me and I stared up at him. He must have decided I didn't understand him well enough, so he switched to a butchered form of my language, but he stumbled and I held a hand up. "Speak your tongue," I offered. I really didn't need to hear this all again besides.

He clenched his hands together. "With the majority of farmers on your side to act as an army if need be, choose a small band to help you infiltrate the palace. You know the back ways. If all goes as planned, I will be there as a guest"—I let out a small sigh at that, knowing full well Mother would never allow Tierny to step foot in the palace, but having kept my objections entirely to myself; the man was determined and would not be moved regardless—"and I will assist from within. We need only capture the empress, and this will all be over." He nodded, more to himself than to me. "Work quickly and decisively and we will have peace."

I leaned over the bucket again, but the foul stench from its contents made me more likely to retch, so I shoved it aside and settled for cradling my head in one hand, my elbow resting on my knee.

A scurry of sound echoed from above during the blessed silence from Tierny's ramblings—footsteps and voices.

My eyes strayed to the pile of chainmail, daggers, and a sword my cousin had left behind.

"Captain," said a voice as the door to the deck ripped open. He yelped as he stumbled sideways, my cousin instead descending the steps first, a piece of paper in her hand. She strode right past the expectant Tierny and shook it at me. "What were you thinking?" she asked. She scoffed, crossing her arms. "Never mind. I suppose you're no different from every other man, but when you're on a clandestine operation, you have to think with your head, not your—"

"All right, all right," said Tierny, stepping to her side. He reached for the letter and my cousin let him have it, albeit reluctantly. "What's this all about?" He unfurled the paper and his eyes darted back and forth. A frown appeared on his face. "I don't understand."

"The missing nomad woman is in the cargo," snapped Rohesia. "I found her there myself."

Tierny looked over Rohesia's shoulder to the sailor, as if asking for his corroboration. The man shrugged. "That came by bird just now. I meant to give it to you first, but—" Before he could say more, my cousin cut him off with a look, and that was all he had to say on the matter.

"I spoke with her even before the letter came," said Rohesia. "She insisted Kojiro smuggled her on board, that it was all borne of some misbegotten romance, and then that letter arrives." She nodded toward Tierny's hand. "Uncovering her true nature as a liar—and a spy."

Tierny spared a glance at me, but I could hardly move. The dizziness was too overwhelming. "Now hold on," he said, reading the letter once more, "Fastello just cautions to be wary around her. He says he doesn't trust her because of bad blood between them, but that he has no concrete evidence of her acting as a spy—in fact, he's not even sure how she would have become one, or why."

My cousin swallowed visibly, as if this was news to her and she could not admit she hadn't read the letter fully, but she would not stop glaring at me.

Tierny spoke to the sailor. "Find this woman. Bring her here."

I opened my mouth and forced my voice through my dried throat. "Do not... Hurt her."

Tierny nodded. "Be gentle."

The man saluted his captain and left, and Tierny sighed, putting the paper down on his desk and clutching his hands behind his back. Rohesia snapped to attention, walking to her pile of weapons and chainmail and suiting up as if headed to battle.

My heart thumped madly—wildly—but I couldn't summon the energy to stand, to appear regal for when my dear one appeared before me.

I hated myself. I needed to be commanding, to defend my decision. I needed to be stronger than my cousin. I watched her finish tying her wrist sheaths to her forearms and felt disgusted. She seemed entirely unaffected by the sea, steadying herself with each movement of the floor beneath us without even paying attention to what she did. The hair ornament—one from my country, meant for my people—at the back of her head seemed so garishly out of place among her barbarian weapons and chain armor.

I heard Luana before I saw her. She was grunting and saying something like "unhand me," whatever that meant. She was clearly in distress. Swallowing down my fear, I stood on wobbly legs, clutching the wall behind me for support, just as two of the sailors dragged Luana down the steps.

"You're hurting—Kojiro!" Luana's face went from rage-filled to joyful as she set eyes on me. She struggled harder, but the men wouldn't budge.

"Let... go," I said, throwing my shoulders back and standing straighter.

Tierny nodded at his men, but instead of simply letting Luana go, they shoved her forward, causing her to tumble to the floor, her loose dress drooping far too much off her shoulder. I stumbled toward her, crouching beside her and shifting her dress up, glaring at the sailors as I did. Barbaric, filthy cretins.

"Out," said Tierny, but he sounded more exhausted than authoritative. "Thank you," he added as an afterthought, and the men grunted before leaving and shutting the door behind them.

I embraced Luana tightly against me, using her as my anchor as much—or more than—the bucket had been. I wished I'd had the courage to do it earlier. Her warmth beneath my hands, her glorious scent, the softness of her hair against my cheek—it did so much to counteract the wild beating of my heart and the dizziness in my head. She spoke softly, but I did not hear her words. Her need to be held—my need to hold her—was enough for me.

"Prince Kojiro," said Tierny, sighing again. "Why have you brought this woman on board—in secret?"

Rohesia made her way to stand beside him, her hand flexing over her sword at her side, looking for all intents and purposes Tierny's guard instead of the supposed lost empress of Hanaobi.

"I... We... There is love here."

Luana shifted and pulled back, her shining eyes staring up at me. "Oh, Kojiro," she whispered, nuzzling her cheek against mine.

My cousin snorted.

Tierny raised his eyebrows as he turned to look at her.

He cleared his throat, bringing a fist to his mouth. "Well, whatever your affections may be," he said, "you put her—and us—in danger by bringing her here. You must have known that we would disapprove. You hid her, after all."

I clutched Luana tighter. "You would be saying no," I pointed out. "So I did not ask."

Tierny laughed at that. He was difficult to understand. "Fair enough. But still… Why risk her safety?"

"Who cares about her safety?" interrupted Rohesia. "What about the mission? He jeopardized all of us if she turns out to be the spy—"

"I'm not a spy," spat Luana, pulling back from me slightly to sneer at my cousin.

Tierny scratched the hair on his cheek. "All right, ladies," he said. He turned to Rohesia. "It's highly doubtful she's a spy. There were no nomads on the underground that I ever knew of—other than Fastello himself, of course. She'd have had to have met a spy in the duchy during these last few weeks, and what could he have promised her for her services?"

"Jewels," said Rohesia, her hand grazing the ornament at the back of her neck.

Luana laughed and fingered a large shiny necklace at the top of her breasts. "Jewels? Risk upsetting everyone around me, put my clan in danger because of jewels? I have plenty of those. You don't know the nomads at all, outsider."

Rohesia's face twisted and she flicked her wrist, drawing one of her daggers into her hand. I moved to put myself between Luana and my cousin, still a bit stung that Luana had used a word we both knew was meant to be an insult toward Hanaobians among her barbaric people.

"Sorry," said Luana from behind me as she put her hands on both my shoulders. "I wasn't thinking. I have nothing against other out—Hanaobians. Just her."

"She is not Hanaobi," I hissed.

"Everyone, calm yourselves." Tierny walked between Rohesia and me, turning to face my cousin. She was the one being antagonistic, after all. "The nomad woman has a point," he said. "The nomads are notoriously protective of their own people. Some other members of the duchy interpret this as selfishness"—he raised a hand to stop Rohesia from speaking as she opened her mouth—"and that, they very well can be. But they are a family. For her to help in any way, no matter how small, the enemy in a war that could lay waste to the lands her family calls home, could see her family members killed—it doesn't make sense."

Luana crawled out from behind me to stick her tongue out at my cousin. She was surprisingly childish at times, though I found that refreshing compared to all the women of the Hanaobian court, who seemed hard and immobile, hardly alive. Aside from my sister, but only then in secret. And even she carried herself with a stiffness, even when it was just the two of us.

Rohesia used her free hand to slide her dagger back into place and shook her head, retreating behind Tierny's desk. "If you are all determined to trust her implicitly, so be it," she said, "but that still doesn't address the remaining issue. What role is she to play in the task ahead? I will not endanger myself or the secrecy of our mission to ensure her safety." She ran a hand over the papers on Tierny's desk. Most I knew to be trading logs, for when the guards inevitably searched the ship to look for anything out of the ordinary. "You would not let me bring my men," she said, "for fear that they would stand out from the Hanaobian people at a glance." She gestured toward Luana and me. "She will stand out even more so. My men could have been sailors caught improperly wandering the city. A woman from the duchy setting foot in Hanaobi is unheard of."

Running a hand over his chin, Tierny looked at Luana a moment before facing Rohesia. "Who said she need be from the duchy?"

Rohesia scowled. "You speak of the other lands," she said, and I noticed with some pride that her voice somewhat faltered. It was no secret the barbaric, backward people of the duchy had no relations with lands far beyond the Hanaobian mountains. Being an island far from shores other than our own, they had little means to explore these places. She shook her head and began pacing. "I don't like it. It'd be too suspicious, too noticeable still. You said yourself you almost never saw anyone from any of these places there."

I placed my hands on either side of Luana's cheeks, surprising even myself at the boldness of the gesture when there were witnesses to our intimacy. "It will not matter," I said. "We move by darkness. We keep her secret. We find our farmer allies and then we tell them why she is being here."

Luana laughed. Perhaps at my clunky attempt at her language. But her face softened and she leaned her cheek into one of my hands.

"That may be—" began Tierny, but he was interrupted by a clattering of footsteps outside and a knock on the door.

"Captain!"

Tierny glanced at Rohesia and then me, grabbing his blade from where it hung behind his chair. My cousin made to follow, but he gestured for her to stay. "Wait," he hissed, and we listened. The sailors seemed to be in quite a panicked state.

One of the men who'd handled Luana poorly ran down the steps. "A ship!" he cried, the panic evident on his face. "A ship approaches at about fifteen knots, starboard, twenty nautical miles away." He straightened up and saluted. "A Hanaobian ship." As if there could be any other in these waters.

Tierny grunted and gestured to his desk, where some blank paper lay. "Is the bird still here?" he asked, referring to the creature that had brought Fastello's traitorous message about Luana to the deck.

Rohesia seemed to have taken his meaning at once and she sat down at his desk, removing a bottle of ink from a drawer, uncorking it, and dipping a quill inside it, ignoring the splash of ink that spattered across the blank page.

The sailor nodded. "Yes, sir."

"We need to get word ahead," Tierny explained. "Until then, the three of you stay here. Don't let yourselves be seen on deck."

And with that, he followed the sailor out of his quarters.

17

TOMIKO

There were just six of us down here below deck in the cargo area, every one of us unable to stand steady except for Goro. He sat on a step leading up to the deck, his hands clasped between his knees, his head down.

It wasn't seasickness that weighed on his mind, but the separation from his family.

The likely loss of his family.

The tears returned to my eyes, the pounding headache that had begun ever since the chase had ended growing stronger.

My folly had led to their deaths. To the deaths of people who had been kind to me. To the deaths of my poor handmaidens. To the death of a child—probably even more children.

And what had I done? I'd let Goro drag me to the coast, where we'd hidden out in a cave along the seashore for hours, maybe more than a day, and then we'd made our way to the village and the docks. Goro had pulled a small pouch of coins out from his waistband—something I hadn't even known he'd been able to salvage— and the captain of the boat had pointedly looked the other way as we'd snuck on board and joined these other refugees.

A few had skin coated with soot, their eyes exhausted. They'd survived the fire—I might have recognized a few from the fields I'd worked for those few short days—and others had simply made their way here from farms and homes yet unmolested, had planned to take what could be this last chance to set foot in the duchy.

This was the last trade ship to make the journey before Mother was likely to send the full might of her fleet for all-out war. The best I could figure, Mother wanted one last report of the state of things before it all began. The small merchant ship had been but a child in comparison to the overbearing armada gathered around it. Goro and I had had quite a time alternately walking casually and in the shadows to escape the attention of the crowds gathered throughout the area, but none had paid us any heed as food and weapons and other supplies were carried to the ten ships that made up the armada. Even the handful of other merchant ships seemed to be in the midst of being decked out for war. It had been a wonder Goro had been able to identify which ship was the one we were to take, but he'd seemed prepared for this, had even put some coins back into his pouch when he'd pulled them out, as if he'd counted on having to pay for passage for many others.

And he most definitely had.

A child about Bunji's age looked up at me from where her head rested against her mother's chest. I stared back and tried to smile, but whatever expression danced across my face, it did little more than make the girl turn away and bury her face deeper against the front of her mother's *kimono*.

I'd had ample opportunities to out myself to Goro once his determination to get us to the coast had settled down. Ample opportunity to tell him I had to go home. Instead, I'd stayed with him. I'd gotten aboard this ship with him. I'd put my home behind me and had sailed straight for a land about to be engulfed in war.

This was no longer a game, a flight of fancy. If it had ever been.

Leaning my head back against the wall, I fought against the dizziness and stared at Goro across the way. He was filthy—though I fared no better. And he was weary, but there was no mistaking the handsome shape of his face, as if the spirits themselves had molded him out of clay. I would be lying to myself if I didn't admit that he'd made my heart flutter often since I'd met him, but the weariness that had settled into my bones since the fire had made much of that excitement fade away.

My duty was more important than any feelings that may have been growing for a farmer boy. Feelings for a farmer boy would have no place in my life, no matter how and where I lived.

I could never fully escape being the Hanaobian princess and heir. I had never intended to fully escape that.

This had been a foolish venture from start to end—but now, it would be something greater.

Now, I would go to the duchy and I would find Elder Brother Kojiro and together, we would entreat with the new duke and find a way to end this war before it began.

And I would find a way to make things better for the Hanaobian people. To make it so there weren't Hanaobians who paid the last of their meager wealth to huddle amongst barrels and parcels below decks like no more than human cargo.

The new duke had better be a different kind of man than the previous one. If we docked to find ourselves at the tips of swords, I would do whatever it took to stop them from harming these haggard survivors, for blaming them for the things Mother did without regard for her own citizens.

Placing my hands on the wall behind me, I stood on shaky feet.

Goro lifted his head and watched me warily. He nodded toward a bucket in the corner of the room, far from where the small number of us was huddled. "Relieve yourself there." He nodded toward another bucket in another corner. "Water for drinking is there."

The fright and determination coursing through my body had made it so I'd had little time to consider either bodily need, but that was not why I'd stood. I made my way toward him, ignoring how my parched throat ached as I moved on unsteady feet, feeling about to vomit as the boat moved upon the waves.

"I need to speak with you," I said, finally reaching the stairs and sitting beside him. My legs still shook, but the labor I'd experienced since my misbegotten adventure had begun had inured me to this unsteady feeling.

Goro stared at me, the smallest of smiles breaking onto his face.

"I'd planned this for months," he said, without me asking a thing. "Had actually intended to wait just a bit longer—just until Father could be convinced to go, until we could find a way to get Ayako home to join us—but then you, Ayako, and the other handmaidens appeared before us like a sign from the spirits."

Running a hand over his face, he took a deep breath before speaking again. "Father was more amenable then," he said. "We'd heard the empress had executed a nearby farm's owner, had demanded every farm's work production exceed our capacity, and he was just tired. Tired of trying so hard and it never being enough. His family united, I'd convinced him it was time to take our bodies, our spirits, our determination elsewhere."

I nodded and shifted my legs beneath me, tucking them sideways, my palace habits difficult to put behind me, even in such a state as I was.

"And so I traveled to the docks one night after your arrival to find even more dire news—this was the last trading ship allowed to go. Should any duchy ship arrive, there'd be no guarantee it would ever return to its native land. It was this ship or we'd lose our chance forever."

His eyes glistened as he stared at me, taking in my posture, pausing at the strip of bare leg I'd exposed by sitting in a manner more suited for my many layers and my long train. I shifted my thin *kimono* warily, covering up the patch of skin.

Goro cleared his throat and looked away. "It was as if all the signs had aligned. It was time for us to go. We would go. We just needed to work one more day."

"And then the fire," I said, the first words I'd spoken since sitting beside him. "The guards."

Goro cradled his face in his hands. "It wasn't supposed to be this way," he said, his voice muffled.

I could have told him that he'd been wrong, that none of that, starting from our arrival, had been a sign of his family's safety and happiness at last. That it has all been the start of misfortune for everyone he loved—for everyone who'd happened in my way.

Instead, I asked, "Why the duchy?"

"What do you mean?"

The little girl coughed from across the cargo hold and I stared at her, wondering if she was sick, if her parents honestly hoped for a healthier, happier life on the island of our barbaric enemies.

"If you can get away from the village there," said Goro, "you can find work on the farms. That's what they say anyway. Better work."

"How so?"

Shrugging, Goro ran a finger over a knot in the wood of the stair on which we sat. "They expect less of you there. They offer less, but they expect less. And let's be honest—we were never going to earn anything more in Hanaobi. Not with foremen and guards and the empress constantly demanding that we give and give and give without ever getting back."

My heart sank heavily. I'd been so caught up in the novelty of the experience—it had been novel to me at least—that I hadn't thought too hard about what a life of that level of toil might be like. A life without the riches and finery that made existence in the palace seem both grand and shallow in comparison.

"Goro, I need to apolo—" I began, but both our heads whipped up at the sound of an alarm bell ringing overhead.

"Ship spotted!" cried one voice.

"Duchy!" said another.

Goro gestured for me to stay still as he scrambled to the top of the staircase, but I followed, gripping to the walls on either side for dear life. I put my ear to the door just as he had, ignoring the way he frowned to find me at his side.

The voices on the deck were harried and often jumbled, but it all came out clear enough. Ready the cannons—but hold. Send a message to the palace. Full speed ahead—don't stray from the path.

And then they cried out about the white flag.

I looked at Goro, puzzled, but he seemed to know little more about why their cries had suddenly softened. Then I remembered— my studies. "It's a duchy sign of peace," I whispered. "Of surrender."

The only question remaining was whether or not they meant it. My instructors had been keen to let me know that I could never trust the word of a barbarian.

But—if I were to think hard about the strategy my instructors had drilled into me—it mattered not whether or not these barbarians had peace in their hearts. They would have peace with us at this moment. They wanted no quarrel with our ship. And that was probably because they had a greater mission in mind—and they needed to reach the shores of Hanaobi.

"Very well," spoke one voice—probably the captain. "Keep an eye on them and stay the course. We'll have no conflict now if we can avoid it."

We must have been able to, as there were no weapons fired, and at last all the chaos on deck eased back into peace.

෴

It wasn't that long after we passed the duchy ship on its way to Hanaobian shores—perhaps a day—before we heard the cries of "land ahead" from the deck. We'd been closer to the duchy than that ship had been to Hanaobi, for whatever advantage that might offer us.

Snapping up from where he stood drinking from the bucket with a ladle, Goro immediately he took action, walking to the other Hanaobian citizens and gesturing his hands toward the barrels. "Inside," he said. "We have to crawl inside the barrels. We must pass inspection as cargo."

The others wearily stood on their feet as Goro and one of the unsteady men lifted lids off barrels and carefully removed shelves containing rice or dried herbs or vegetables to expose a space at the bottom of the barrel. They helped the others in one at a time, and I watched from where I sat on the stairs, frozen, panic welling inside me as I saw the little girl tucked inside a barrel alongside her mother.

Goro helped the man who had been assisting him into a barrel and then slid on the lid. He motioned for me to come over and pointed at one of the barrels they'd prepared, which stood next to the final such barrel he'd prepared for himself.

"No," I said, shaking my head. I didn't even realize I'd voiced it out loud.

Goro seemed exasperated. "Come on," he said. He pointed to a few small knots in the wood of the barrel. "There are plenty of holes to breathe."

"No," I said again.

I could see blood pouring forth from those holes.

Goro sighed and slapped his feet across the dock as the sounds overhead grew louder, the commands shouted as we got ready for docking. He grabbed me by the arm. "Quickly now. Come on."

"No!" I pulled back as hard as I could, reaching for a post at the bottom of the stairs to anchor myself.

Goro pulled harder and ought to have won, but I twisted and grabbed on to the post with both hands, hooking my arms around it. "I will not," I whispered in a shaky voice. Mother had insisted Elder Brother Kojiro and I be there to see it. Father and Elder Brother Nobutada sent home in barrels—in pieces.

Kojiro had vomited. I had almost fainted, but the tears had poured hard and strong and I had stood on two feet. Mother had mistaken my fortitude for the strength necessary to rule, to seek revenge. But I had only fought that hard because there was no way I could have stood on my shaking legs otherwise.

"Shoko, you must."

I'd almost forgotten the false name I'd provided him. Shaking my head, I swallowed back the tears.

"Shoko, if you don't hide and they find you, they'll tear the entire cargo bay apart. They'll find us all." Goro sighed. "You don't want to put the rest of us in danger, do you?"

I opened one wary eye. The other citizens, risking everything to escape a life that should have been better for them. The little girl. I'd already failed so many of my people. I hiccupped and stood straighter, letting go of the post and moving forward on trembling feet. "So be it," I said, taking Goro by the hand and letting him lead me toward the barrel.

The sight of Father's head, of Elder Brother Nobutada's arm greeted me as I looked down into that barrel. The barbarians had mixed them both together, had filled each barrel to the brim with their parts and pieces.

"Go on," said Goro.

There was nothing in there. Not really.

I put first one and then the other shaking leg inside, keeping my eyes shut tightly. I breathed deeply, trying to think of anything else as Goro lowered the shelf containing rice and then the lid on top of me. I heard rustling as he moved to hide himself, but my strength soon failed me, and I passed out.

I didn't wake again until the glint of a sword shone through one of the holes in my barrel.

18

FASTELLO

The men took to the task of digging through all the barrels in the Hanaobian ship with more glee and vigor than I'd have liked.

"Careful," I said to one who'd just ripped the lid off a barrel and was about to kick it over, "we need those vegetables."

The guard stopped, his foot in the air. "They'd often hide people beneath a small shelf filled with crops," he said, as if I were stupid.

I glared at him and straightened up. Rohesia, Jiro, and Tierny had put some of those very same barrels on their own ship in case their plans went awry and they needed a place to hide the heirs to the country—not that this guard would have been let in on those plans. "I know," I said, with all the confidence I could muster, "but there's no sense in spilling perfectly good food, regardless of how much is in there."

The guard stared down at the dried vegetables and sneered, as if he found it all unappetizing, but he did as bid and dug his hands inside instead. When he was lost up to his shoulder, he frowned and straightened up, pulling out his sword and holding it with both hands above him, about to slice it through the midst of the vegetables.

"Stop!" I called. I didn't care if there was a person in there—or actually, that was precisely why I didn't want him to do that.

He did it anyway, shrugging. "Nothing in here but dried produce," he said, removing his sword, which now resembled a turnstile over a fire pit with all those leafy vegetables on it.

"Sir," said the trembling Hanaobian captain beside me, his voice shaky, "we trade. We just trade. Please."

Rohesia's dashed message—that Luana was on their ship, the supposed lover of that foolish Jiro no less, that they were passing a Hanaobian trading vessel making good time to the duchy—had given me enough time to plan a thorough investigation of the unexpected ship upon arrival. I hadn't counted on the men getting so out of hand, or the captain being able to only speak a few words of our tongue—I considerably missed both Rohesia for her ability to lead these men and Jiro for his ability to translate. And they'd only been gone a few days, might never return, whether successful or not.

Jiro had taken Luana with him? I still couldn't get over that. What was with her and going after men in power? Had my rejections finally made her give up? I'd wanted her to, to be sure. But I was worried she'd smash poor, naïve Jiro's heart to pieces should she discover we'd intended to make Rohesia empress and have Jiro just support her quietly as the next heir.

Then again, if Rohesia was so insistent she never wed, any children Jiro had would have to be the next in line and Luana would be the mother of emperors and empresses... That kind of legacy seemed exactly the type of thing that would strike that devious woman's fancy.

That seemed reason enough for her to be acting so strangely. There was no way she could be the spy feeding information to Hanaobi. She didn't know enough for one—I wasn't even sure she could write. And there was an empress and princess awaiting her in Hanaobi, no man for her to seduce and to sit beside on a throne.

"Your Grace?" said one of the men, and I snapped back to the task at hand.

"Be gentle," I barked, weaving through the barrels myself, my hands behind my back. My deformed hand brushed against my sword sheath as I made the gesture—I still wasn't used to wearing a broadsword. But I needed to look the part of the new duke, and I had a dagger that I could rely on if need be strapped to the leg nearest my good hand. "If there are people inside, I don't want them harmed, do you understand? And taking care with the crops only makes sense. We're nearly in a famine, people."

Some of the men grunted and all went to work. The captain of the ship said, "People? We bring trade!" but there was a sheen on his forehead that meant he was scared of something.

I wondered what reason he could have had to risk coming here—I didn't buy that they were concerned because our own trading ships were late and had come to do business themselves. They'd just had a ship here weeks before. Besides, it was a well-known fact that Hanaobi got little out of our trading arrangement. That all the Hanaobian farmers we had—that many had liked to pretend hadn't existed—had been smuggled in on trading vessels both from the duchy and Hanaobi. And that the previous duke, when the whim had struck him, had had his daughter and his men enforce those "no outsider" laws he'd only enacted after he'd lost his wife to her own brother, who'd pretended to be visiting along with his son and heir on a diplomatic mission.

Everyone knew the duke had gleefully sent Hanaobi's emperor and heir back home in pieces in several of such barrels.

"Clear," said one man after another. Most of these barrels seemed to be filled to the brim with food, food we'd desperately need to keep my people—all my people—fed as we made strides toward fixing the blight on our own lands. I almost wanted to hug the captain, although I still didn't trust his presence here. At the very least, perhaps he'd been sent ahead to get a lay of the land, to send his impressions of the new duke back home, and although I hoped the empress would find me fair and not equate me with my predecessor, Jiro had been convinced she wouldn't be moved to treaty, that she'd exploit any weaknesses. So I kept weaving through the barrels, doing my best to seem stern and intimidating.

"Wait," said one of the guards. He reached a hand into a barrel, and it stopped going in below his elbow. "There's a shelf here."

I froze. I thought I heard something—shallow breathing—from a barrel beside me.

Everyone stood still to watch as the guard removed the shelf on top of the barrel. My uninjured hand flew clumsily to my sword, not sure what I could do with it if the person inside the guard's barrel turned hostile, but certain I should appear wary and ready nonetheless. The blade scraped against the barrel I stood beside as I moved, catching slightly in a knot hole and I actually heard a gasp that turned my head.

"Ha!" said the guard, catching my attention again. A woman spoke in the Hanaobi tongue and hands shot out of the barrel. The guard backed up and kicked the barrel over.

"Hey," I said, my sword down and my hand out, "I said to be gentle."

A woman and a little girl spilled out. They looked up at me with wide eyes, the woman pulling the girl to her chest. The girl reminded me of my little "boss" back when I'd worked at one of the duchy farms.

Guards moved forward to seize both the woman and the girl and the captain at once. "Don't be rough!" I barked. "Put those swords away." I nodded at them and followed suit myself, sliding my own blade back inside. "We're going to take them to the castle," I instructed. "If we can be sure they pose no danger to the duchy, they can find work and join the others in building homes and tending crops—"

"But, Your Grace," said the man nearest me, "they snuck aboard."

I glared at him. "And the other Hanaobians in our lands, you think they had an invite? No. We're a new kind of country now and we're going to do things differently. Keep searching," I said. "There are bound to be more."

I turned to my own suspicious sound-making barrel and removed the lid, carefully taking hold of the upper shelf full of rice grain and lifting it up.

A wide-eyed young Hanaobian woman—probably about my age, if not a tad younger—was crouched inside the barrel staring up at me. Her clothes were filthy, as if she'd been powdered with soot, and her messy, shiny hair clung desperately to the nape of her neck, the dip of the skin at the top of her loose-fitting robe plastered with sweat.

"Out," I said after a moment of her just staring at me. Her eyes grew wider. I struggled to think of the Hanaobian word I might have heard Jiro use, but I was stumped. I reached a hand in, holding it out for her to grab, and she flinched, as if I'd been about to strike her. "Come on," I said, shaking my arm in the air above her. "I'll help you out."

She hesitated but put her palm against mine. I clutched tightly and lifted her to stand, sliding my hands around her waist and hefting her out of the barrel. She seemed so small beneath my grip, so delicate. Her hand had been so smooth, so soft, not at all like the hands of a seasoned farmer.

"Stop!" called one of the men behind me.

I let go of the Hanaobian girl and whipped around to find a Hanaobian guy about my age bolting out from a tipped-over barrel, scrambling to stand, and running straight toward me.

"Whoa!" I called, backing up, my hand instinctively going for my sword hilt. "Get back! I don't want to hurt you!"

The girl I'd helped out of the barrel appeared between us, saying something in her language to the young man, and he halted, the desperation and rage on his face replaced with resignation.

She turned to look at me and said in my language more perfectly than Jiro had ever said anything, "We are here in peace. Please do not hurt us."

My thundering heart—jolted into its rapid pace when the Hanaobian man had started charging at me—slowed down and I realized my hand was still gripping my sword hilt tightly. My damaged hand.

I let it fall and noticed the way her gaze locked on the missing fingers.

One of the Hanaobi people cried out as a guard kicked at him. "Hey!" I snapped, stepping toward him. "Be nice."

"Tried to run," grunted the guard. Oh, how part of me wished Rohesia could have just taken the lot with her and I could have found a more humane bunch of men to take up the ranks.

"I don't care," I said, looking over the small group of Hanaobians and taking inventory of the men. They seemed to be finished checking the barrels. "Is this all of them then?" I said. There were six. Six stowaways. Hardly enough to mount an attack on the duchy.

"Sir, duchy, sir," spoke the captain, probably meaning to call me the "duke" and not the entire "duchy."

The girl I'd helped out of the barrel threw her shoulders back and held a hand out toward the captain, as if telling him she'd be the one to speak.

"The captain did not know of us," she said, and even if it weren't for the slight twitch of her jaw at the statement, I'd have known it was a lie. No trading captain fills several barrels only a quarter full and leaves the spaces beneath empty on a whim. But I had no interest in putting anyone to the death here, no matter how eager the guards seemed to be to do it.

I nodded, playing along. "Then what are you doing here? Who are you?"

She stood even straighter—which was apparently yet possible— and clasped her hands together some distance in front of her chest, as if embracing an invisible ball against her breast. Despite the dirt, the sweat, and her loose robe, she looked a bit… like a goddess.

"I am Princess Tomiko of the empire of Hanaobi," she said, her nose slightly in the air, "and I ask for sanctuary for these citizens of my realm—and I bring as well an offer of peace."

I think I actually laughed.

19

ROHESIA

Although Father had insisted on my basic instruction, he'd always been more concerned with my skills in combat. I could read, naturally, and I had a foundation in politics and the history of our land and our enemy's, but it'd been years since Father had even bothered with tutors in those subjects. Empirical study was the best teacher, he'd said.

Besides, I'd long ago begun to doubt any of the history or politics he'd promoted. I'd just shoved the feelings down, learned to numb myself to stifle any thoughts of my own.

It was difficult, then, to now *have* thoughts of my own when the voices whispering in my ear had all gone quiet.

I stretched my legs out from where I sat on a hammock hanging in the captain's quarters. Infatuated Kojiro and his nomad temptress lay sleeping in the hammock above me. I could see the way their arms wrapped around one another through the holes in the hammock, as if determined to squeeze the life out of one another— to fill any small gap between them—even when asleep.

Tierny and Kojiro may have been right that this nomad girl wouldn't pose a threat, but they were wrong to not care much about the danger her presence could pose. Kojiro was blinded, a fool. She knew nothing of politics, of stealth. To protect her should she make a mistake, Kojiro might make bigger mistakes of his own.

Even Father had fallen in love—really fallen in love, not just taken another woman for a wife. And the loss of her had led to so much hatred, so much more loss of life.

Running my fingers over the jade lion resting against my thigh, I wondered not for the first time how my mother had fallen in love with him, a much older, more bloodthirsty man—a man who'd given no indication that he could be a faithful husband.

But he had been. And from what Sherrod had told me, she'd been happy in the duchy. Of course, when her own brother and nephew had come to kill her… It was clear that the place we sailed to, as beautiful as it might be, hid a festering core beneath it all.

The candle on the stand beside the hammock flickered as the boat swayed, and I rubbed my temples, tired of staring at Sherrod's journals and my mind proving unable to complete the task of deciphering it.

I'd taken him for a fool—and he may have been in many ways—but he'd been smarter than I'd given him credit for.

I must have begun drifting off a bit because I was still hazy when Tierny appeared beside me.

"What's that?" he asked in hushed tones, perhaps not willing to wake the sleeping prince and his folly above us. Yet perfectly content to wake a dozing by-rights empress.

I blinked, struggling to sit straighter in the hammock that seemed intent on swallowing me entirely. The candle had gone out and Tierny bustled beside me, relighting the mess of wax and wick. Jolting awake at the beam of candlelight, I slammed my books shut with a start. I hadn't meant to let anyone see these.

Tierny cocked his head, reaching a hand out. "Let's see here," he said.

I stared at him, wondering if he actually thought it appropriate to ask such a thing of me when it was clear I hadn't meant the books for his eyes at all.

"It's a cipher, isn't it?" he asked. "From the underground? I can give you the code to translate it."

I felt wholeheartedly that Sherrod had intended these journals only for me, but the fact was, I was stuck. Without assistance, they would always mean nothing to me, one journal full of inane observations about Sherrod's meals and routines, the other a mess of numbers, letters, and figures I could never decipher.

Without a word, I reluctantly handed both books to him, swinging my legs over the side of the hammock, trying to fully wake myself up.

Tierny flipped through the books and then walked over to his desk, dipping his quill in ink as he began to scribble in one of them.

A small part of me wanted to scream, to tell him to leave them alone, these last few things I had of Sherrod. I gripped my jade lion and put it back in my pouch, where it clinked against the small vial of poison. Grabbing hold of my jade hair ornament where it had fallen off on the hammock, I twisted my lengthening hair and stuck the ornament through, letting my hand linger on the jade for just a moment.

"There," said Tierny, holding one of the books up to the light of the lamp at his desk. He gestured for me to come closer. "I'll show you."

Readjusting my wrist daggers, I stood. I hadn't planned to sleep, but I was always cautious enough to make sure I didn't fall asleep with them on, especially considering one was often dipped in poison. I had a limited supply of the stuff with me, so neither were coated now, but even after cleaning, it was possible some of the killing agent lingered. Standing beside Tierny and peering over his shoulder at the journals, I studied the man first. His guard was down and I wondered how he could be so wholly trusting of those around him. I could kill him from this vantage point before he even realized I'd moved.

"This book," he said, utterly oblivious to the direction of my thoughts, "tells you where to look in that book. All this nonsense about food and the scent of the ocean and the reddening dawn, that's just to hide the code." He pointed to where he'd marked on both books. "This says that on this page of the journal, you count every four words, then take the third letter of that word." He tapped a symbol. "This just refers to the kind of message you'll find there. This one means underground safe house." He started turning the pages, scribbling in the margins with other notes, denoting what different symbols meant.

I read the translated message Tierny had wrote in the seemingly-innocent journal. "Tavern. Eighth district. Yellow sign. Ask for Meggy."

That name. Malle worked for her, although that tavern was now in a different location.

"I suppose these messages are meaningless now," said Tierny, dipping his quill again. "Now that there's no need for an underground."

He met my eyes and we stared at each other. He did realize that I had been one of the enemies of this network of his, didn't he?

"Not in the duchy anyway," I said, caressing a line of text to try to see the translated message pop out for myself. "Did you… Did you know Sherrod had ties there?"

Tierny's feather quill stopped suddenly. "These are his journals?"

I nodded. Tierny's lips pinched a little, but he turned the page and deciphered another symbol. "There were rumors some of our members had contacts among those closest to the duke, but you have to realize, it would have jeopardized their safety—my safety, as I was one of them—for us to know each other on sight."

As I took the less-cluttered journal from him and read a line, Sherrod's careful message jumped out at me from among the mundane. I could almost hear him speaking those banal lines, see where he might quiver and cower backward as I sent him a look to keep his boring stories to himself.

"Did Sherrod teach you?" asked Tierny. He blew on his ink mark on the cipher journal and then shut the book, handing it to me.

I took it from him, sending him a questioning look.

"I mean, did he encourage you to take arms against your father? Was he trying to get you to our side all along?"

I shut the other journal and then slipped both back into my pouch. As an instructional guide for underground refuges and spies, I doubted I'd find anything of use in either one of them, although a part of me still wished to see the translation through, to find the hidden meaning behind the man's foolish inanity. "No," I answered honestly. "I considered him an idiot. I'd have taken no advice from him."

Tierny grinned. "Ah, but you understand now that there was more to the man than you might have thought?"

"I understand a great many things I didn't before," I said. A snore from across the room started and stopped suddenly, as Kojiro and Luana woke, whispering to each other as they shifted on their hammock.

"Well, we're glad to have you with us now." He took my hand in his and squeezed it, leaving me at an utter loss for words. I slid my hand from his as Kojiro jumped down to the floor and then lifted his arms up to assist Luana.

Tierny laughed. "Without your command over your men, I'm not sure we'd have ever won against the duke, lightning strike or no."

"And yet you made me leave them all behind."

"They don't exactly make for experts in stealth," Tierny reasoned, standing. "It's good that you're awake," he said to Kojiro and Luana as they approached. "We're nearing Hanaobi. We plan to dock by first light, but I want you all off on the rowboat before then." He stared at each one of us in turn and then suddenly embraced Kojiro, patting his back for good measure. My long-lost relative looked as uncomfortable as I had when holding the man's hand. Tierny took him by the shoulders as he pulled away. "May the spirits and Ytoile and whatever else might be up there watch over you all," he said. "It's been a pleasure watching over you, young prince. Now grab your things and prepare. You have quite a—"

But the rest of sentence went unsaid as a thunderous explosion rocked even the waves beneath our feet, a high-pitched whistle permeating the air.

"Cannonball!" said Tierny, and he grabbed both Kojiro and Luana, pulling them down beneath his desk. I followed suit.

The ship rocked, groaning at the impact. Splinters of wood and debris burst through the room, a huge gaping hole appearing in one wall of the captain's quarters. Men screamed from the deck, feet scrambling, muffled orders shouted. I blinked as dust began to settle, looking out at the gaping hole through which trickled silvery moon-light. A huge piece of the deck was missing. The cannonball had landed just outside the captain's quarters.

Water was already flooding into the deck, the boat rocking wildly back and forth.

I turned back to my companions. Kojiro looked pale, sick. Luana's blouse was stained red with blood.

Only it wasn't her own.

Tierny's lips darkened as bubbling blood oozed forth, his hands clutching at a jagged piece of wood that had pierced him just beneath the heart. "Go," he said between clenched teeth. Red liquid dripped from his crimson-stained teeth as he spoke the word. "Go," he said again, his eyes closing, his head lolling backward.

I jumped to my feet, quickly correcting my balance to stay upright. "Grab your things," I commanded, making my way across the room to slip on my mail and tie my sword and sheath around my waist. I turned around to find Kojiro, as silent and still as a statue, and Luana, crying and shrieking, still exactly where I'd left them.

"Grab your things! Now!" I shouted, staggering back across the room and slapping Kojiro for good measure. I held my palm out toward Luana, but she shut up immediately, struggling to stand, tugging on her useless lover beside her.

Satisfied, I made my way out to the deck through the hole, being careful not to lose my balance as I moved. My legs skirted danger-ously close to the gaping hole, the sight of the sea rising up to meet me from beneath the cargo bay below one of the most spectacular, if horrifying, things I'd ever laid eyes on.

"Where's the captain?" shouted one of the sailors as I shook the sight from my eyes and made my way to the rowboat.

"Dead," I answered him, taking hold of one of the ropes keeping the boat in place and nodding toward the other one. "Take that end!" I barked.

The sailor, his face ashen, did as commanded, and we lowered the boat to the rollicking waters below.

"Abandon ship!" he screamed over his shoulder as we finished.

I stepped toward him and withdrew my sword, aiming it toward his chest. "This boat is for me and my companions," I said, looking over his shoulder and urging them silently to make their way here. Quickly. "You'll have to swim for it."

"Are you mad?" he asked as two other sailors moved to join him. An explosion thundered in the air again and I turned just long enough to see a burst of light from the shores cf the Hanaobi capital some knots away as that dreadful whistle permeated the air once more.

Some of the sailors screamed and one jumped overboard into the water, his small splash soon overpowered by the mighty crash of the cannonball just missing our ship and hitting the water on the other side of us. The ship rocked wildly, the rowboat even flying up into the air.

"We have to go," said the sailor, stepping back from my sword to try to climb down. "This stupid plan obviously won't work. They won't let us dock. We'll have to come with you."

I blocked his path, jabbing the sword at him. "Go down with your ship or jump into the water like a coward, but leave this boat at once."

Kojiro and Luana's delay was driving me mad. If I weren't sure I might need Kojiro's assistance even after all the maps and secrets we studied, I might have just left without him. I looked over the deck to find two bodies, two sailors who were either dead or unconscious in the events that had unfolded. Who knew what had become of the rest. The only two left standing seemed to be the ones in front of me.

"You can't stop us both," said the second man, but I flicked my wrist and sent a dagger flying right in front of his feet, grinding him to a halt.

"I won't miss next time," I said, biting my tongue. "That was your last warning."

The sailor at my swordpoint gestured wildly. "You have room for us both," he said, "even with those other two."

Finally, those "other two" made their way out of the captain's quarters—through the door that hung loose over its hinges and not the gaping hole, I might add—and made their way toward us,

Kojiro leaning on Luana the whole way and looking every bit like he was about to retch.

"On the boat," I snapped at them. "Climb down the ladder. Quickly!"

Without a word, they wobbled past the sailors I kept frozen in place. Luana helped Kojiro climb over, then followed suit, her face grim, flecks of blood still staining her cheeks like freckles.

"We can help," said the sailor, but I remembered all of Tierny's warnings about having duchy citizens along with us on our mission, all the reasoning he'd given for not allowing me to take any of my men along. They would stand out—get in our way. There was a movement out of the corner of my eyes and I realized the other sailor had bent to grab my dagger, had turned toward me, his arm pulled back to throw it, but his movements were clunky, elongated, unskilled. I sent the other dagger flying, this one into his throat.

He collapsed.

I'd killed again. But he had meant to kill me. And I had a job to do. I needed to be here or this entire mission was for naught.

"You bitch!" said the sailor still behind my blade. I sheathed the sword and struggled through the lapping water collecting on the deck over to the man who had both of my daggers, plucking one from his limp hand and then the other from where it wedged tightly into this throat. His flesh made a sickening suctioning sound as I pulled.

I swallowed. "Get on," I said.

The sailor hesitated as I slid my daggers back into place at my wrists.

"Climb on the damn boat!" I screamed.

He did and I followed after, quickly taking a dagger to both of the ropes holding us in place. "Row!" I screamed, and the sailor scrambled to grab an oar. "Row!" I said again, to Kojiro, but he looked about to faint. Luana scrunched her face and grabbed for the other oar.

The rowboat began moving, and the farther we got from the boat, the clearer it was that the boat was sinking, its stern already halfway into the water.

"Man overboard!" said the sailor on our boat, pointing some

distance away—toward the Hanaobi capital—at the sailor who'd jumped over earlier.

"Leave him," I barked.

"But—" began the sailor.

"Leave. Him," I said again. I pointed in the opposite direction. "We're going that way."

I could tell the sailor had more to say, but he didn't say it. He and Luana kept rowing and rowing until another explosion and whistle rocked the skies. We watched as it struck the ship and the last of the vessel split into pieces, flying everywhere—some even as far as we were.

I covered my dolt of a cousin with my body as we waited out the blow.

"It's gone," said the sailor quietly however long later.

I sat up again and stared at where our ship had once been.

"Row," was all I said.

20

KOJIRO

I'm dreaming. Every moment since I've woken has been a dream.

Except there was no mistaking the cool touch of the specks of water on my skin as my companions rowed beside me, the scorched scent of the wood burning all around us.

The blood on my palm, the blood on Luana's face.

Tierny.

The captain had always been abrasive, uncouth… But he'd been a good man. He'd been the only one who'd believed in me, the only one who'd looked at me and seen something more lurking beneath the spineless, nervous surface.

He hadn't known me. Not really. He'd projected what he thought a prince should be onto me, had witnessed Mother's cruelties toward me and thought he'd discovered the entire picture of me.

He'd been a good man. I was a terrible one. It should have been me who'd gone down with that ship.

"Your girl is getting tired," snapped Rohesia, ever in charge, ever unmoved by the blood and death around her. "Snap out of it and take over."

But it felt like she was floating somewhere outside of me, somewhere far beyond reach.

"It's okay," panted Luana. Beautiful, caring, kind Luana. I would give her everything she wanted and more.

A palm struck against my cheek, my eyes drawn to how dangerously close the tip of a dagger got to my skin as it did. My cousin gripped my cheeks tightly, pulling my head toward her, boring her eyes into mine. "Wake. Up." She said the words commandingly, but there was something like a glimmer of light as her gaze roved over my face.

But it could have just been the approaching light of the breaking dawn.

I snapped up, rolling out of her hands. I checked to make sure the box was there—Luana had grabbed it, had been more of use than I'd been when our ship had been sinking around us—and sighed in relief. "That way." I pointed to a patch of land far enough away from the capital so as not to draw attention to our landing. I'd spent virtually no time outside of the palace and capital, but I had been with Father and Elder Brother Nobutada on some trips through the farming fields, and I knew we'd find some behind the hills that crested in that direction.

I bent down to take the oars from Luana, who rewarded me with a fluttering smile before collapsing backward into the boat, her breaths shallow.

Rohesia nodded, seemingly satisfied, and relieved the barbarian sailor we'd taken with us for some reason.

We rowed in silence after that, only exchanging words when we hit land and I instructed my companions to bury the boat beneath the cover of the reeds so no Hanaobian guards would find it.

Two days had passed and no guards had descended. No one had seemed to guess we were anything but what we'd said we were —haggard Hanaobians looking for work.

At my cousin's insistence, we had left Luana and the sailor in the bamboo forest at the edge of the farm. I didn't like leaving her alone with such a barbaric-looking man, but I'd visited her since and she claimed he hadn't put a hand on her. She cradled the box containing Elder Brother Nobutada's weapon and in hushed tones, I'd instructed her to use it on the man should it come to that—though to not ever let him see it until it became necessary. I didn't trust him not to run off with it and I needed it. It would be my salvation this time, not a useless tool that caused nothing but the wrong kind of destruction in its path.

I'd wanted to have Luana pose as my wife from another country—not the duchy, of course—but Rohesia had said it would be too odd, too noticeable right after a duchy ship had sunk in the sea.

Although it wasn't that topic that occupied the minds of these farmers. The farm to the east, the most prominent one that sat between them and the capital, had been burnt to ashes by Mother's guards the previous week.

They'd taken all the young women and had left no one else alive.

I couldn't begin to think what had angered Mother, what had driven her actions, but the whispering tongues of these peasants had put two and two together well enough. Princess Tomiko was missing.

My sister—my genial, benevolent sister—had disappeared from under Mother's grasp.

I hadn't known. And while voices whispered she'd been kidnapped by someone at the farm—thus the need for the cruelty—I wondered. It was Tomiko, along with Tierny, who had seen to it that I had escaped before Mother's wrath could catch up with me. Although she had never left the palace to my knowledge, I did not think it impossible that she could organize a similar escape for herself.

The question was: Why? Mother loved her. Took pride in her. Had groomed her to be empress next.

Still, although I worried it'd meant she might have come to harm, part of me was relieved that she would not be here to witness this—this mad plan to knock Mother off her seat.

To give the old bag—the pretender—what she deserved.

"That's a very pretty ornament you have, dear," said the elderly farmer woman, one half of the couple who'd invited Rohesia and me into their small hut when the foreman had agreed to give us work.

My cousin blinked and nodded at Kimi, a horrible imitation of a smile at her lips as she stabbed at her bowl of rice with her chopsticks, making the older couple laugh. I really should have thought to teach Rohesia about the cultural differences in my homeland. She really should have thought to ask.

"It was our mother's," I lied, keeping up the pretence that we were siblings. I lifted my own chopsticks and got Rohesia's attention with a few words, showing her again how to pick up a small cluster of rice with the tools between just two fingers. My cousin stumbled to follow suit, the discomfort evident on her face. I smiled and turned to the couple. "You have to forgive her manners," I said. "The accident that left her mute—it made her a touch stupid, too."

Rohesia didn't know enough of the language to make me feel afraid of calling her dumb. In fact, it felt rather good to be the one in charge here, to see my cousin stumble and falter. She probably felt so vulnerable since she'd had to leave her chainmail and sword behind with Luana and the sailor. I'd managed to explain her barbarian attire—the shirt and pants that men wore beneath their armor—by explaining she'd taken to untying her *kimono* and our mother had worried about her showing off her naked flesh while traveling. But that she could handle a *kimono* now if they'd any to spare—and Kimi and her husband, Kento, had.

"You know, it's been so long since we've had a young woman here," Kimi had said as she'd helped Rohesia into the coarse material of a proper peasant *kimono*. I'd grinned as she'd changed in the hut behind me, proud of myself for explaining my cousin as stupid and lascivious with her being none the wiser. Kimi continued, "It was why the guards left our farm alone, I'm sure of it. They had no young women to take."

Thinking about it now, I wondered if it wouldn't have been better to have Rohesia pose as a man. Her face was delicate—beautiful even, if you could forget about everything else associated with her—but she carried herself as a man even in her barbaric country. But it was too late now. And I hadn't known about the edict ensuring all women Tomiko's age were to be taken back to the palace. But besides, Rohesia had grown her hair longer since I'd first met her, tying it back with that fine hair ornament I'd tried to explain to her had no place on a farmer girl's head.

She fancied herself the leader of this mission, laughably assumed she could rule a country whose tongue she did not speak, and she'd made such a simple error as that.

She couldn't have done this without me. No question.

The old couple smiled and nodded as they averted their eyes from my cousin, forgiving of her bad manners but likely unable to witness them. I'd seen much coarser behavior in the duchy, so it didn't attack my sensibilities quite so much. It simply put a smug smile on my face.

Rohesia used the opportunity to tuck her rice bowl beneath her *kimono*. Food for Luana and the sailor. I nodded toward the plate of roasted peppers and she grabbed some of those as well, grimacing as she did. She hardly ate herself, but the old couple certainly thought she had quite the appetite.

"There's something different about her... face," said Kimi, and Rohesia snapped to attention, laying her chopsticks down on their rest and smiling broadly like the fool I'd claimed her to be. She had no idea what the old woman had said.

I frowned. Rohesia did have a touch of... There was something about her barbaric blood about her. But I'd always been stricken by the fact that she looked more Hanaobian than anything—a lost Hanaobian princess taken to running around in barbaric armor.

Still, I supposed that touch of barbaric blood—which colored her strongly from the inside, even if it didn't from the outside— might be more noticeable the first time you met her.

"The accident," I said again, nodding, helping myself to a sweet potato.

Oh, how I'd missed Hanaobian food. Even this peasant meal was divine... So gentle on the stomach compared to that barbaric garbage. They didn't even prepare the Hanaobian foods we'd traded to them properly. I couldn't wait until I could show Luana what a full royal feast could be.

"Poor girl," said Kento, not for the first time. "Poor, poor girl."

I rested my chopsticks and put my hands together, bowing

slightly in apology. "Thank you for your hospitality despite my wretched, clumsy sister."

Kimi laughed and stood, gathering her and her husband's dishes. "You speak so politely. Your parents must have had jobs in the palace."

"My grandparents," I lied, wincing at the fact that I'd forgotten how roughly peasants spoke to one another, my own tongue stumbling over the less formal words. "But let me," I said, grabbing my own dish and taking the dishes from Kimi before she noticed Rohesia's was nowhere to be found. "You two rest," I said. "It's been a long day."

And it had been. To my utter distaste, Rohesia had taken to the work better than I had, the hard labor causing barely a sweat on her brow. I remembered what I'd learned during my brief stay on the farm in the duchy, could tackle the task with skill enough, but my strength failed me.

I didn't like that my cousin had more strength than I did, even when posing as the fool.

"Thank you, dear," said Kimi, and she helped her husband stand. They took their futon out of the closet as well as the one they'd offered for Rohesia and me to share and set them up some distance from the fire pit as I shoved the dishes at Rohesia and gestured for her to take them to the wash basin before putting out the couple's fire.

"Oh, you could have left the light to work with," said Kimi, but I shook my head, my eyes adjusting to the moonlight trailing through the thin paper walls.

"Get your rest," I said. "My sister and I can work by the light of the moon." I opened the door widely, a warm breeze wafting in. I could hear Rohesia get to work scrubbing the dishes as I gathered the rest, scooping any scraps onto a single plate. Once we heard the snoring of the others in the small space, we nodded at one another, gathered the leftover food, and made our way on light feet toward the bamboo forest a short distance away.

"They're too old," snapped Rohesia in her barbaric tongue the moment we stepped inside the cover of the trees. "Have you been speaking to the younger workers as I asked while we're out in the fields?"

I hadn't been whispering words of treason and revolt to strangers, no. My cousin had no idea how dangerous such a thing would be. She ought to have. Had not her father ruled his lands tyrannically?

I shook my head. "I must know who might join. I cannot ask boldly. We must be slow. Patient."

Her lips twitched. "We don't have time to be patient. The empress is going to send her warships any moment—she might have already. That trading vessel was likely meant to scout ahead." She grunted. The sight of a Hanaobian woman walking boldly through a forest in a *kimono*, her legs showing every step between the folds of the fabric, one hand unceremoniously clutching a bowl of rice and vegetables, was such a bizarre sight. She looked beautiful enough—could have been a princess like her birthright allowed her to be—but she walked and composed herself with all the propriety of a hairy, barbaric man twice her age.

"Destroying a duchy trade ship is an act of war," continued Rohesia. "There will be no diplomacy."

Her intent was clear, even if some of the words didn't connect with my mind.

We reached the clearing where we'd left our companions.

"Kojiro," said Luana sweetly, keeping her voice down but not disguising the delight in her tone. She waddled toward me, my box between both hands, and gently put it on the ground at my feet before embracing me.

I wanted to embrace her back, but I had the other plate of food in my hands.

Rohesia handed her bowl to the sailor, her nose wrinkling as he dug in with his hands. As if she had any right to think someone else uncouth.

I handed Luana my plate and she kissed my cheek, taking it from me. She didn't pull back yet, though, whispering in my ear, "He's getting restless." I tensed. "He hasn't laid a hand on me, but... Please hurry. I don't like being out here with him."

Stepping back with her plate, she copied the sailor, grabbing morsels by hand. She grinned as she ate a fried sweet potato and sat on the ground, and I knew she appreciated how much better everything tasted here.

Still. That was two people now who had entreated me to hurry. But how did one hurry asking for laymen to become soldiers?

Rohesia sat on a rock most impolitely, bending over and splaying her legs out, clutching her hands together tightly between her knees. She looked at the sailor and Luana and me in turn.

"Do we need soldiers?" she asked. She gestured back toward the farm. "How much use could they be?"

I sat beside Luana on the ground, taking care to sit on my calves like a decent person. None of the people around me—even beautiful Luana—took note or followed my example.

The sailor nodded at Rohesia, his mouth full even as he spoke. "Whatever you do, do it fast." He itched the back of his neck and made a grotesque face. "I'm getting tired of just hiding here with nothing to do."

Lifting an eyebrow at him, Rohesia said nothing. She probably wondered what he was doing here with us in the first place. The sailors had been meant to dock with Tierny, to stay with Tierny and not interfere with our plans.

"What mean you?" I asked, my brain feeling dusty. It was an adjustment to hear nothing but the glorious Hanaobian language during the day and to go back to this monstrosity at night.

My cousin looked amused. "I mean, why don't we sneak into the palace ourselves? Just the two—three—four of us." Her lips soured as she looked at Luana and the sailor, but she was mad if she thought I was leaving Luana behind.

"For doing what?" I asked.

"Take the empress," said Rohesia. "We only need to capture her for this all to be over."

I laughed. Most impolitely perhaps, but I'd spent quite some time among the coarsest people who'd ever lived, so it could be forgiven. "Capture Mother? She will simply order her guards to kill us all."

"And risk her own life?" asked Rohesia.

"Perhaps it will be so," I said. "Instead of giving throne to you… or me."

It was Rohesia's turn to laugh. "Then who would rule?"

"Tomiko," I whispered.

"The lost princess," said Rohesia. She sighed and stared off into the bamboo. Luana had gasped at their beauty when she'd first seem them. She'd been even more surprised when I'd told her we used them not only to build, but that they could be edible too—if prepared properly. She'd frowned at being unable to pluck a piece off to taste it.

"Then we kill her," said Rohesia flatly, her eyes meeting mine. She was studying me, waiting for my reaction. "Before she has time to issue any orders."

A short, sharp stab of something ripped at my throat. She was, despite it all, my mother. But this was not the first moment I'd contemplated ending her, forever ensuring that horror that had dominated me was out of my life.

"I do it," I said, straightening my shoulders with a boldness I only partially felt. "I will end her. I will make her feel no hope and I will make her cry."

Rohesia raised her eyebrows but said nothing more. Luana stared up at me, cocking her head puzzlingly.

"Damn," said the sailor, munching on a chunk of rice he'd grabbed with his fingers. "This country is barbaric."

❧

We needed rest as much as a strategy, so my cousin and I couldn't stay long. I kissed Luana before leaving, holding her possessively and glaring at the sailor across the small clearing to make things very clear. He hadn't paid attention at all, simply talked to Rohesia, who refused to acknowledge more than a quarter of what he said. I grabbed the plate and the bowl so the old couple wouldn't miss the dishes.

We broke the clearing and made our way back to the path that ran along the workers' houses just as the moon was covered ominously with a swath of clouds.

"Hey," said a voice, and I turned around, slipping the plate and bowl inside my *kimono*. "What are you up to?"

It was Kazu, the foreman. What was he doing strolling through the farm at this time of night?

As if to answer my question, he readjusted the sash on his *kimono* as he approached. There were no young women on this farm for him to visit, but there were plenty of older ones who could serve him well enough, I supposed. Although I was certain they'd all been married.

"Walking," I said, bowing my head. Rohesia studied me a moment but bowed too.

Kazu stared at her, a lascivious grin spreading on his face. "They're looking for young women, you know," he said.

"Who?" I asked, although I knew he meant the palace guards.

"Our lord has been quite put out by the dearth of young women around here." He snatched at Rohesia's wrist, but she pulled her arm out of his grasp.

I shook my head at her, cautioning her against flicking those daggers out just yet, and stood between Kazu and my cousin. "She's dumb," I said. "And she can't speak."

Kazu laughed. "But she's pretty enough. Yesterday I told our lord about her arrival and he thought we might keep her from being taken to the palace if she stopped by and paid him a visit."

I winced. A visit could only mean one thing.

"She doesn't understand—" I started.

"I go," said Rohesia, stepping forward. She'd spoken Hanao-bian. Poorly. But she knew a word at least.

I stared at her, dumbfounded.

Kazu laughed and snatched at Rohesia's hand. She watched me as he dragged her after him, and I had no idea what plan her eyes tried communicating to me.

I only knew that without her, I'd never have the fortitude to make it close enough to Mother to see our objective through.

My reception was unlike what I'd expected. When I'd made my bold declaration, I'd hoped that my position might lead my countrymen to be spared. I'd regretted it almost immediately, images of how my father and eldest brother had been received here still strong in my mind. But I'd been scared of seeing my people hurt more, willing to bargain myself for their safety.

Not even considering that it might not guarantee anything for my people. That it might even make their fates worse.

The last thing I'd expected was for us all to be welcomed, for us all to be put to work.

"We're here." The new duke—Fastello—laughed. My eyes were shut so tightly, my thoughts so meandering, I hadn't even noticed the horse on which we'd ridden had stopped.

"You can let go now," he said again. "In fact, maybe it's best you do before I pass out from lack of air."

He spoke so quickly, this barbarian leader, but it didn't take long for my mind to catch up. "I apologize!" I said, releasing the grip I had around his abdomen.

He maneuvered free and removed his feet from the stirrups, jumping down. He held a hand back up to me and I took it hesitatingly. My leg got caught in the barbaric dress he'd had a woman provide for me and I stumbled, falling sideways.

"Whoa!" he said, catching me. His hand went to my back, his other beneath my knees.

I'd never been touched in these places by anyone, let alone a barbaric duke.

I could feel my cheeks burning and Fastello grinned. He bent over to settle my feet on the ground. "There you go."

Just as I regained my balance, the dark creature next to us snorted and scraped its hoof in the dirt.

I screamed.

Fastello laughed again and grabbed the horse's reins, murmuring soothing words to it, and it settled into near silence.

"They don't have horses in Hanaobi?"

It took me a moment to realize it was a question, not a statement.

"We do," I said, straightening my back and doing my best to appear regal. I didn't know whether or not to tell him about the other nations we traded with, like the one that had introduced horses to us long, long ago—Mother liked that the duchy seemed clueless about the extent of the world around them. "But a princess need never ride them."

"Oh?" asked Fastello, turning back to his horse and calling it a "sunset." "And how do princesses go from one place to the next?"

"We walk," I said. "Inside the palace. There has been no need for princesses to travel anywhere else."

Fastello nodded, patting the dark creature's neck. "The nomads pretty much just walk, too," he said. "But I got used to riding the horse. You can cover so much ground with the beast's help."

He held his hand out toward me and I had no clue what the gesture meant.

"Here," he said, reaching for my palm. He guided it to the horse's long mane, which was soft, silky. I was surprised.

Fastello's teeth glistened. He sure liked to smile. It was hard for me to imagine him suited to the position of a country's ruler. Evidently as hard as it was for him to imagine me as one.

"I was gifted this horse by my… aunt," he said. "Sunset. She sure stands out among the other beasts, I can tell you."

My lips pursed as I caressed the creature's fine strands between my fingertips. "Rohesia," I said. It wasn't a question.

"Right," said Fastello, stepping back and rubbing a hand over his face. He was missing fingers on that hand. It was the only thing about him that made it seem like he'd known roughness, that he'd known pain. He otherwise seemed so at ease, so charming.

So difficult to fully trust.

A pale barbarian man approached from the foundation of a small cottage that stood beside several others of its ilk on freshly-upturned soil. They reminded me of the homes the farmers back home kept, although their design was sturdier, if also coarser somehow.

They spoke some distance away for a moment and I couldn't pick up all of what they said. The pale barbarian wiped his reddened brow with a cloth a few times, his face covered in sweat. Hanaobian citizens and barbarians worked side by side, constructing the next home.

Fastello had taught me so much about his land in the days since I'd been his guest, after I'd been given a room in his palace to sleep in. He clearly didn't believe that I was the princess of his sworn enemy country, but he did want me by his side—as a translator. My language skills surpassed even those of his last translator's, he'd said, and when I'd asked, he'd gone quiet and hadn't explained who that had been and where that person currently was.

I could think of only a few answers to both.

For Elder Brother Kojiro was nowhere to be found, and unless he was in hiding, mounting some kind of resistance, there was that barbaric ship we'd passed at sea…

And there was Lady Rohesia, too. Unaccounted for and not a topic Fastello liked to dwell on.

Although he'd explained his claim to the duchy throne—a grandson of the previous duke's, he'd said, although he hadn't even known the man, and his grandmother had been forsaken as a duke's wife after the devious duke had married my own aunt, Princess

Momoko—he refused to explain why Rohesia, daughter of the duke, long-lost heir to Hanaobi, had not claimed the seat in his place.

That could mean only one thing. She was on her way to my home—perhaps there by now, assuming Mother had even let her get near land—and she had my brother along with her, as an ally or a hostage.

I'd left the palace to seek a greater understanding of the world, to do some good for my country. Yet my decision had done nothing but the opposite at every turn. Not even seeking my brother out had turned out as I had hoped. I was wise enough now to know how foolish I'd been. And to worry about my brother's fate without me there to stay Mother's hand.

Fastello had refused to let the Hanaobian ship return just yet. He'd insisted the sailors were not his prisoners, but he'd also insisted some of his guards stay along with them in the castle. We were all waiting, he'd said. They'd be free to go once he knew what the empress' next move would be.

He was probably afraid of any of them sending word back to Mother.

Which was precisely, I thought, what Mother had hoped they'd do. Why else had she let one last trading ship scout ahead of her fleet?

"Shoko!" called a familiar voice. I did not fail to notice Fastello's raised eyebrow at the name as Goro put down the piece of lumber he carried and made his way over toward me. I met him halfway, scooping a ladle of water from the bucket the workers had set aside for breaks, and offering it to him as he approached.

"Thank you," he said, accepting it. He sipped the water carefully so it wouldn't spill, then dipped the ladle again and dumped its contents over his head.

I shouted a little in alarm and jumped out of the way of the splash.

"Sorry," he said, and he smiled—just a little. His smiles had been so rare in the past few days.

"It is fine," I said, remembering again how he teased me for my formal speech. I surveyed the house behind him and spotted a few more familiar faces. Even the little girl who'd traveled with us was with other children—Hanaobian and barbarian alike—some distance from the construction, shucking a yellow, pimpled vegetable —corn, I remembered, from the traded products—into baskets. And laughing.

"Are you doing all right?" I asked. "All of you?" I added, to be sure.

"Yes," said Goro, heartily. His smile faltered.

"What is it?" I demanded. "Are they working you too hard?"

He shook his head. "No, it isn't that. It's just… I miss them. I wish they could have made it here with me." He dropped the ladle unceremoniously into the bucket, sending a little more splashing toward our feet. I didn't move this time. "It's my fault they're…" He didn't finish his sentence.

"No," I said. "It's mine."

Goro studied me, looking back over my head, possibly at Fastello behind me. I peeked. No, it was one of Fastello's guards—one of the men in barbaric armor who'd been rough with us in the ship's cargo hold—who had his attention.

Goro's voice grew quiet. "Why did you tell those men you're the princess?"

I'd debated what to say the next time we were alone. I owed him the truth after all we'd been through. After all he and his family had sacrificed for me. But he hadn't seemed to have taken my admission as an actual possibility, hadn't done more than stare dumbstruck at me since. True, he'd agreed to work at this farm to help build homes almost as soon as Fastello had offered it—and I'd been asked to stay behind, to serve as the new duke's translator—but when he'd pulled me aside before we'd parted, he'd only wished me the best.

To tell the truth, I'd been disappointed. After what we'd been through—from even before then, I'd… I'd thought there might be a little something more to us. Just a little. But with the loss of those he loved, of those who'd been so kind to me… I could never hope for more. I didn't deserve to hope for more.

I had grown since I'd taken back my mantle.

I straightened myself up, standing properly with my hands clasped in front of me. "I *am* Princess Tomiko."

Goro blinked.

"How much did you know about"—I grimaced as I thought of poor Ayako—"your sister's job at the palace?" I asked.

Thinking about his abandoned sibling, probably dead at the hands of the palace guards, drained what touch of life had appeared on his face. "She's a handmaiden. She was a handmaiden. To the…" He stared at me. "The princess. I thought you were, too, like the other girls."

My shoulders sagged. "They were *my* handmaidens. I… I left the palace. And they accompanied me."

Goro's jaw opened and he crossed his arms, studying me. "But the princess can't leave the palace."

"I wasn't supposed to."

His eyes widened as he grabbed me by both shoulders—something a Hanaobian gentleman would never think to do. "But the empress," he said, his voice raising. He attracted the attention of some of the people around us, strangers and even the mother and girl who'd traveled with us looking up from their work. "The fire!"

From behind me, a sound like the clank of metal against metal rang out above the murmuring from all around us. "Lower your voice," I said. Fastello stepped away from the barbarian farmer, patting his shoulder as he did.

"No!" Goro screamed. "The guards—they were looking for young women. They were looking for…" He was shaking me now. "They must have been looking for you! And if I hadn't hidden—if I'd shown you to them, they would have left my family alone! When were you going to tell me?"

Almost everyone around us had stopped what they'd been doing now, some merely curious, others scurrying to put some distance between us.

They needn't have been frightened of him. He was upset—with good reason. I deserved all his anger and more.

"I apologize," I croaked.

He threw his hands in the air. "And on top of it all, you have the gall to speak to me so formally—to say you're sorry in such a cold, uncaring—"

Before he could say more, before I could even blink, the barbaric guard appeared between us, striking Goro on the head with the steely hilt of his blade.

22

FASTELLO

"Stop!" I cried, almost tripping over the Hanaobians who stood between me and the guards. "Don't—"

But my words went unheeded as one of the men hit the Hanaobian who'd gone hysterical on the back of the head with the hilt of his sword.

At least he didn't use the blade.

I arrived beside them, my new translator's face stricken. I followed her eyes to find the young man bleeding from a bump on the back of his head.

"Get help!" I snapped at the guard as I fell to my knees beside the man. "Ride back to town and get a doctor!"

"It's just an outsi—"

"Now!" I shouted. A Hanaobian woman crouched beside me at the same time Brenner, the farmer I'd been talking to, appeared, already tearing a towel he'd grabbed into strips before heading over. "Hollis," he said to the Hanaobian woman. "Get Hollis. She has better cloth for wrapping injuries."

The woman stared as Tomiko—or Shoko, whatever her real name was—swooped in to convey Brenner's message. The Hanaobian woman stood and left for the main house, still some distance away.

"Use this to staunch the bleeding," Brenner said, patting the injured man's head with the towel. He gestured for Tomiko to take it from him. "Hold tight. With both hands."

I turned around to see if the guard had left yet, but he simply stood there, staring down. Jumping up, I grabbed him by the arm, not entirely surprised that his first reaction was to lift his sword slightly in my direction.

"I gave you an order," I barked. I stared down at the sword in his hand. It shook slightly, but the guard slipped it back into his sheath. "You shouldn't have hurt him," I hissed.

The man's hand lingered on his sword hilt. "I didn't intend to kill."

I gestured toward the fallen man. "Does that look like a man who might survive?" I regretted the words almost as soon as I said them. Tomiko paled as she stared up at me, her lips quivering. Tears overtook her eyes and her hands fell, but Brenner shouted at her to keep still as he slapped the Hanaobian man's cheeks and forced open his eyes one at a time. "I'm trying to broker peace here," I said, turning back to the guard.

His eyes had narrowed. "You don't know what it takes to lead," he spat. His gaze focused on my hand clutching his forearm with three fingers. "And you're a fool for not doing more to prepare for what awaits us. If you had any sense in your body, you'd know that one less outsider isn't a bad thing."

Tomiko shrieked from behind me.

I let the man go. "Get the doctor. Quickly."

He turned and made his way to his horse. I regretted having no other guards with to accompany him, to make sure he did as asked. Not that there was a single one among them I could truly count on, despite the prospect of war with Hanaobi.

Rohesia ought to be here in my place.

The Hanaobian woman returned with Brenner's wife, who gently pushed Tomiko aside. "Stand back," she said, not unkindly. She pulled back the rag slightly and grimaced.

Tomiko seemed lost as she looked on, so I went to her side and helped her up, guiding her to a stump so she'd give the others some space to tend to him.

"I'm… sorry," I said. "My man… He overstepped."

I didn't know if she hadn't heard me or she simply didn't understand, but she grew still, clasping her hands together and closing her eyes.

If this was some kind of Hanaobian prayer, I didn't know it. Jiro had never prayed. And I supposed I didn't spend enough time with any others to know. I looked around. Some were standing or sitting in imitation of Tomiko's pose. Others simply looked on, fear clear on their faces.

Standing, I cleared my throat and projected my voice as loudly as it would go.

"Please," I said, "do not fear. This was a mistake. A horrible mistake. And I will not let it happen again." When I was met with blank faces, I turned back to Tomiko. She'd opened her eyes and stood, wiping her cheeks with her sleeve. Composed and elegant, she straightened her back and translated.

"He reacted to what seemed like a woman in danger"—I looked at Tomiko, as if to confirm my assessment, but she simply shook her head as she spoke, her voice shaking—"and tried to end the danger without… without lethal force." I swallowed as Brenner stood up and wiped his brow, his hands smeared with red. I stared at my own hand, the image of its red-stained skin from the day I'd first lost my fingers seared into my mind. Although Jiro had assured me it wasn't the case, the idea of more of those weapons he'd carried in the hands of Hanaobian soldiers… We needed peace here if we stood any chance against the dangers that could be approaching.

"I don't want you to think you need to go into hiding again or that—" My voice caught in my throat as Brenner approached, his face grim. "Is he…?"

He shook his head.

Tomiko cried out and collapsed to her knees beside me.

Even when I solved problems, when everything seemed to be going right, things could still go so wrong.

I didn't want a single death on my conscience—ever again. Not like this.

My hands gripping the reins were stained with blood, the image of my dad's face before he fell… Of Cateline rushing into the fire. I should have saved her. I could have saved her.

Tomiko sniffled quietly from behind me. I didn't know what that man had been to her—or if she'd have mourned the same for any of her people—but I wanted to let her know it was okay to sob. It was okay to spill your anguish openly into the wide world.

I didn't realize I was crying, that a gasp had escaped my lips, until that moment.

"I'm… sorry," I said again, as much to Cateline as to Tomiko.

Tomiko loosened her grip around my waist somewhat to wipe her face with her arm. "He believed this land was a better place," she said. "Even before he knew the previous duke had fallen… He dreamed of freedom here."

I'd never understood why so many Hanaobians had fled here, how they had pictured this place as a better alternative to their homeland. I was trying to build a peaceful place where there was room and purpose for everyone, but we had a long way to go. And before, with the duke's edict to execute an "outsider" on sight… Besides, both Tierny and Jiro had claimed Hanaobi was such a beautiful place. Their food was more plentiful, that was for certain. I'd once thought of running away there myself.

"Why did you come here?" I asked. "You said he—"

"Goro."

"Goro wanted freedom. Is that what you sought as well?"

She took a deep breath and I felt her rest her cheek against my back. "I wanted to know," she said. "I wanted to meet my people, to see what life was like outside of the palace. I suppose in a small way… I wanted freedom, too. However, I never meant to travel this far. I never meant to be gone so long."

I chewed the bottom of my lip, not sure how to proceed. She was still, even in the midst of her grief, committed to pretending to be a princess? Was it… possible? If Jiro had made his way here, and I'd believed him to be the prince… But I'd had Tierny's word to trust as well. If only she'd arrived before Jiro had left, I could have known for certain.

"War is said to be coming to these shores," I said. "From your people."

"I know," she said quietly. "I know. I hoped to find Elder Brother Kojiro here. Mother does not know for certain where his loyalties lie. I suppose I don't either at this point."

"Where do *your* loyalties lie?" I asked, deciding she was either the princess or she must have had good reason to pretend. Either way, I could learn much from her.

Sunset shifted her back with a dip in the road and Tomiko squeezed my waist tighter to hang on. "With my people."

"Is it really so wretched for them there that so many make their way here for refuge?"

She laughed. "Your land houses but a small number of my people." That didn't give me much confidence for the war that might be ahead. "But... I suppose so. I've seen so little of how my people live." She straightened up, pulling herself away from my back. "The palace is beautiful. The landscape is lovely. The food is more bountiful than it is here. But it's never enough for Mother."

"Why not?" I asked, thinking of all the thought and strategy that had to be put into feeding the population here. How happy I'd been with even the smallest bit of progress.

"She knows," she said quietly. "She knows she's not the rightful empress. That as soon as Father... died... Elder Brother Kojiro should have been made ruler."

"And what of Rohesia?"

"In absentia," she said, using words I didn't even know belonged to my tongue, "Prince Kojiro was heir."

"Jiro told me his mother wanted him dead."

Tomiko's grip flinched somewhat at that. "That is true."

"And you?"

"Of course I didn't want him dead!" She sounded offended I'd ask, even if I'd only known her a few days and hadn't even been sure I believed she was who she'd said she was.

She sighed.

"Jiro told me his sister helped him escape."

"He told you that?" she asked, something like pride coating her voice. "I… I am glad. I did my best."

I stared down at my scarred knuckles. "He said she was the one who told him to bring something with him for his journey, something that once belonged…" I let my voice die, waiting for her to finish.

"To our eldest brother, Nobutada," she finished. "The firearm," she said.

"The what?"

She paused. "Father and Elder Brother Nobutada said the blacksmith who'd made it for them called it a 'firearm.' It's a weapon that bursts into sound and light, a small cannon in your hand."

She knew of it. So either these things were really more common in Hanaobi than Jiro had claimed or… I shook my head. No, she knew too much. She had to be who she said she was.

I lifted my hand. "We were allies, Jiro and me. He panicked, though, in the midst of a fight. His… firearm… did this to me."

I heard her gasp. "You were fortunate it didn't pierce you elsewhere."

"Yes, fortunate." I flexed my remaining fingers and slid the hand back through the reins. The sun was setting, the ember glow of twilight bathing the fields all around us in a quiet kind of beauty. We passed the spot where I'd first met Cateline, where my friends and family had taken her Stargazing mothers from her.

My clan was no less bloodthirsty than the duke's guards… Even if they'd acclimated better to the new world I was trying to build.

"Were you… Were you really my brother's ally?"

I nodded. "I met him on the underground when he first arrived, and we stuck together all the way through the duke's end."

"Why were you hiding?"

"It's a long story." Something got caught in my throat and I pushed away the image of the girl with the fiery, red hair sitting in front of me, my arms around her waist.

It was my turn to ask questions. "The man—Goro—called you 'Shoko.'"

"It was a false name I gave him," she said. "Everyone knows the name of the princess. It would have been too strange to have shown up with the same label."

I nodded, not really sure I understood or needed to understand.

Her voice cracked. "He only was upset back there because I told him the truth, I told him what I'd said to you was genuine. He… We got separated from his family because of a raid on the farm where we'd been working, a raid Mother had made looking for me. They're… They're all dead."

Something like ice shot through my blood at her words as the heart of the duchy came into view after we crested another small hill. "How did she know where you'd gone?" I found myself believing her, believing Ytoile and whatever other goddesses were out there must have plunked this princess into my lap. For what purpose remained to be seen.

"I do not know," she admitted. "I have thought about that in the days since, and I suppose she might have followed the trail to my handmaidens' families since they had gone missing with me."

A bird flew overhead, its great big wings soaring broadly, making it seem like a monster in the sky.

"Why did the empress let that single trade ship through," I started, referring to the vessel on which she'd arrived, "if you also believe she intends war?"

Before Tomiko could answer my question, the very skies shook with an explosion. The bird ahead shrieked and dipped, flapping its wings quickly to get to the mountains behind us. Sunset jostled in place and I had to work to keep her steady, the reins slipping through the gap in my fingers.

"A cannon," I said as I wrapped the reins tighter, not sure if I was hearing fire from approaching ships or from our own ships in the harbor and the turrets and cannons in the defense structures among the docks. Who had I left in charge in my absence to answer to such a threat? I could hardly even remember their names, the men who'd once served the duke in his tyranny and slaughter.

"They have come," whispered Tomiko. "The war has begun."

Although blocked largely by the heart of the duchy in front of us, there was no mistaking the dark dots that poked out from the horizon on the waters. Ten, twenty, fifty…

Cannon fire shook the air again.

We had no hope.

❦ 23 ❦

ROHESIA

Two old women who lived in the lord's household—servants, I
supposed—dressed me the day after my arrival there in the
finest, silkiest outfit I'd ever seen. It was bright red with long sleeves
and a larger sash than most of the poorer folk wore here, which they
went to great lengths to wrap and wrap around me and tie together
at the small of my back. Then they added another smaller rope to
make it even tighter. The bright patterns woven into the silk of the
fabric must have taken an artisan months, if not years, to create. I
wondered at how they could afford to waste someone's labor on
such a thing for so long, but then again, this land was bountiful,
marred only by the scorched land between here and the bustling
capital. They smoothed my hair with a cold stone comb, pulled and
tugged at it and added several other long hair ornaments to the one
I'd received from Malle. They'd run sponges over my dirt-caked skin
before all of this, too, their noses wrinkling as they barked at me in
their own tongue. I obliged as often as I was able, willing to paint
myself like a doll to get a chance to observe the person with the
most power in the area, see if there was any chance of Tierny's
stupid plan being worthwhile.

The one thing I didn't cooperate with was their desire to remove
my belt and the pouch that hung on it. I held it firmly, saying the

word for "no" that I knew, for "important," until finally they gave up and slipped the first clean, white, silken robe over it. I wondered at how women could move with all these layers.

I was made up to shine brightly when all I'd ever known was to hide beneath the grime.

The old women got up to leave, one rapping my knees with a comb. She said something and pointed to my legs, which I'd stretched out in front of me, her face colored with distaste.

I picked up the word for "sit"—Kojiro was not the only Hanaobian in the duchy, and there were records of the language Mother spoke, written in our own letters instead of the ideograms the Hanaobians used—but I had to admit I had a long way to go before I could manage for long without Kojiro or another translator.

The woman sighed and I remembered how I'd sat with Kojiro and the old couple who'd offered us shelter, so I shifted my legs carefully so as not to undo all the work the women had done to wrap the robes tightly around me and put my shins on the smooth mat floor, tucking them beneath me.

The woman grunted, satisfied, and she and the other one left.

My hand caressed the flooring. Just like that in Mother's room in the castle. I wondered not for the first time how she'd had it imported, how long her family had pretended to be on good terms with her, only to turn a visit from her brother and nephew into a bloodbath.

I may have had conflicted feelings about Father, but that he'd sent the Hanaobi emperor and heir home in pieces for killing Mother was not a thing with which I disagreed.

Minutes passed and it became clear I was not to immediately have this meeting with the lord, so I reached up the skirt of the robe at my thigh, trying not to loosen it too much, to dig through my pouch. I felt the cold comfort of the lion but left it there, pulling out the two small journals instead. I had no quills with me, nothing to take notes, but there was no need to transcribe what I found written inside. Secrets for another time led by another ruler. Secrets about the man who'd seemed to me so spineless, so placid, but who'd done what he could.

I wished I could remember how Father and Sherrod had met. He'd always just been there.

Turning to a random page, I searched for its corresponding page in the cipher journal. I had to keep flipping back and forth to match up symbols with the notes Tierny had scribbled for me—mere moments before his death—but I started to see an extra meaning beneath Sherrod's account of the view of the sea from his room.

Rosie in Momo's room today. Going to practice cipher. She likes her mama's things. He can't know.

I blinked. Rosie? Was that supposed to be me? He'd called me "Rosie"?

Perhaps it was just for the convenience of the cipher to shorten my name. I checked the date. I'd have only been five. But even then, I didn't remember him ever shortening my name.

I did remember him smiling more, though.

There was one time I'd been running around in Mother's room. I hadn't known Sherrod was nearby at first, but in truth, he always had been. He was like my nurse, even though those were typically women. Why Father had trusted the man so much, I'd never know. It clearly, in the end, hadn't been warranted.

"What is she doing?"

The cold, harsh voice sucked all the joy right out of me.

"Your Grace," said Sherrod, rising from where he sat scribbling in his books in the corner. "She was just playing."

"In here?" Father looked around the room, at the small piece of Mother's world he kept locked away behind a great big door.

I hugged the lion to my chest tightly. Father stepped forward and snatched it away, slamming it back on the table in the middle of the room. "This place isn't for children," he said, more to Sherrod than to me. But I felt as if he'd struck me regardless.

"Yes, Your Grace," said Sherrod, standing, dropping his book to the ground behind him.

Looking down, Father studied me. "But perhaps she's ready to stop being a child."

"Your Grace?"

Father stiffened, then grabbed me by the wrist and tugged me after him. "Come, Rohesia," he said, his voice growing quieter. "Come see what it is becomes of those who live amongst things like these." He turned to look at the room, something that might have been sadness flashing briefly through his eyes before he marched us out into the hallway.

Perhaps his wounds over losing my mother had been too fresh at that time. He'd taken me to see an infant drown after that. I'd stayed out of the room during the daytime—or whenever I'd thought I might attract his notice. Each time I'd snuck in thereafter, it'd been alone, a new layer of dust spread all over the woven mats that covered the floor. Until that night after the fire in the Stargazing tower when he'd caught me there—and had had a much different kind of reaction. A kinder reaction. A more thoughtful reaction.

The fact that I was rarely again caught that room before then hadn't spared me from going on more raids thereafter. But I'd always remembered the last time he'd seen me laughing and what it had led to. I'd always remembered to shove those feelings down whenever they'd surface. Which grew to be less and less frequently as I'd matured.

The door opened and I slammed the journals shut.

One of the old women had reappeared. She spoke and gestured, curving her hand downward. I didn't know what else it could mean but to come. I stood, slipping my books through a slit in the robe into my pouch.

The woman walked across the room and smacked my arm as I did, muttering and tugging again at my sash to tighten it. The books were safely secure in my pouch, though, along with the daggers I'd hidden there. I surprised myself by not immediately backhanding the woman for striking me.

Then again, I had ruined the arduous work she'd done to dress me.

And I had a role to play. I'd be meek—meeker than any of the women I'd seen in the duchy. Even Kojiro was meek. The Hanaobians seemed to cherish quiet and compliance. Something I found innately comforting.

When she finished fussing, she led me through the open door and down a wide hallway. I'd been kept in this house for a night and a day and it was twilight now, the sun casting its last light on the sky. Despite the slow, careful walk of the woman in front of me, I tried to set a more normal pace, but it was hopeless with the confinement of this robe. Even duchy dresses—which I hadn't worn for the majority of my years—were less cumbersome than this nonsense, as beautiful as it might have been. At least in those, your legs could actually move. Instead, my feet merely shuffled, the raised sandals beneath my soles clopping quietly like a soft-footed horse.

The old woman stopped in front of a door and took to her knees. She spoke to that door, then looked up at me, her eyes wide. She gestured toward me, pantomiming for me to join her on the mat.

Part of me wondered if the Hanaobians valued cleanliness so much because they spent so much time crawling on the floor.

Still, it was clear what I had to do. Carefully, trying not to upset her work for the second time, I followed suit, just as someone with a deep, harsh voice spoke from within the room and the door slid open.

A man in clothes almost as fine—if not quite as resplendent—as my own sat on a cushion toward the back of the room, a small saucer in his hand. He was middle-aged, a touch plump with wiry hair and a satisfied smirk on his face. He locked eyes with me and raised an eyebrow, sipping from his saucer. The woman in front of me spoke, and at the lord's command, she stood, bending slightly to bow and snapped at me, gesturing her hands again.

I stood and shuffled toward her. She gestured toward the lord.

For such a big room, it was mostly empty, reminding me too of how Mother's room had been furnished. The lord didn't even have a table at which he sat, although there was a small tray beside him with a miniature jug and a plate with what appeared to be dry, dark bark on it. Behind him was something that nearly took my breath away: a thin, long sheath resting on two small pillars only a few inches off the ground. A blade was inside it, given a place of honor in this lord's welcoming chambers. I'd call it a throne room, but there was only the cushion. Still, Father had had little use for his, had had little interest in meeting with his people. Had had no interest in meeting with foreign visitors, not after what my uncle and cousin had done.

The lord spoke, and his tone conveyed that he'd spoken before and I hadn't taken note of it or otherwise something was expected of me and I hadn't acted in accordance.

The old woman repeated his words, gesturing to the tray. She bowed toward the lord and said something more, pointing to her ears and mouth and shaking her head.

She can't speak or hear, the movement seemed to say. Or perhaps simply that I didn't understand.

The lord looked puzzled, but as I picked up on the cue and sat beside the tray, he laughed. He waved a hand at the woman and barked something. She bowed again and retreated from the room, leaving only the lord and me and two of his guards on either side of the door. I looked to their sides and saw the thin sheaths there, fascinated by the potential advantage of a weapon that brought with it so little weight.

The lord spoke again and I turned to face him. He shook the hand holding the saucer out in the air toward me. When I moved to grab it from him, he snatched his hand away, out of reach.

He stared at me incredulously. Then he laughed, launching into words that felt less harsh and clipped than before. Shaking his head, he pointed to the small clay pitcher on the tray.

I picked it up with one hand. He shook his head at that, almost revolted by my action. I lowered the pitcher toward the tray again, its clear contents nearly sloshing out of the lip. The lord moved forward, grabbing my wrist with his free hand, then sighing. He put his saucer on the tray and grabbed the pitcher from me, taking it in both hands instead of one and clearly trying to make me take note of that. Then he tilted it gently toward the saucer, letting no more than a few sips' worth fill it. Putting the pitcher back, he took up the saucer again, drinking it in one go.

Smacking his lips, he held the saucer out toward me again, his eyes watching me sharply.

This time I picked up the pitcher with both hands and poured a little into his saucer.

He grinned, downing the sip, and laughing. Putting the saucer back on the tray, he clapped his hands together. Then he stared and pointed at the pitcher, gesturing toward the tray. I put it down.

Turning toward the doorway, he shouted something at the

guards there, causing both to incline their hands and retreat out the door, pulling it shut behind them. I could see their shadows through the paper-thin walls as they took up their posts on the other side.

The lord spoke softly and cupped his hand downward. Exasperated, he motioned more widely and I stood carefully, shuffling to his side.

He sighed as I sat, but still, his eyes lingered over my form, settling on my face with something akin to hunger there. He took my head in both hands, turning first one cheek and then the other toward him.

He said something, then licked his lips.

The sight made me think briefly of Sherrod's annoying habit, although I didn't think this lord did it because his mouth was dry. He didn't have those protruding teeth and gaping-open lips that had made it a necessity for my constant companion.

Constant companion.

His loss stung hard in that moment. He'd have never have let me get into a position such as this, where a lascivious lord handled my face like a piece of flesh for sale at the market.

Even if he'd been no different, procuring his own flesh from such a market.

As the lord leaned in, his lips headed toward mine, his eyes closed, my left hand grabbed hold of the hilt of the fine sword he kept on a pedestal and I lifted it above us, bringing the hard hilt down on his head.

❧ 24 ☙

KOJIRO

"She went willingly?" Luana asked, not for the first time.

I paced back and forth in the clearing in the bamboo forest, wringing my hands. I'd gone back to the old couple after Rohesia had left, had waited for them to rise to ask them everything I could about the lord and why Rohesia might have been called there. Their faces had been a bit grim, but they went about their business preparing breakfast and getting ready for the day.

"She will be treated well. Not unkindly," the old woman had said. Her lips had twisted slightly. "I just worry because she's so…" She left the rest unsaid. "I hope she understands enough to do what's bidden of her."

What was bidden of her… I couldn't picture Rohesia cooperating with such a thing.

I stopped. "Perhaps… This is being for the best," I said.

The sailor slapped his knees and scoffed. "Sure. Stranded in a foreign land of outsiders—"

"We're the outsiders here, you know," added Luana.

The man kept talking. "Hardly closer to the palace here than we were back in the duchy, a horde of guards between us and that palace, and the cold-hearted bitch who can slaughter them all without blinking isn't here to help?"

172

"Watch yourself," spat Luana, her eyes sparkling even as her face clouded with anger. I hadn't known she'd had any feelings toward my cousin, but it was clear as day she didn't like this sailor and hadn't appreciated continuously being left alone with him.

Well, I wasn't leaving her alone again. There was no point fanning out among the farmers in the fields, trying to speak to them of rebellion and treason.

We would not lead an army to Mother's doorstep, with or without Rohesia. There had never been any hope of success in such a plan.

We wouldn't get close enough to Mother for my hopes to see fruition if we came with a crowd to her door.

"I'm not even supposed to be here," said the sailor, drinking from the bottle of *sake* I'd snatched from the elderly couple in my last raid of their home for food. His face practically pruned as he pulled the bottle away.

"Give it here," snapped Luana. "Don't hog it all for yourself." She walked across the clearing toward him, never letting go of the box with which I'd entrusted her. She took her own swig and plopped on the ground beside him, heedless of the dirt that would cake up on her skirts.

She was already filthy, her clothes wrinkled and stained from our adventure at sea and the days since.

This isn't what I'd promised her when I'd brought her with. Yes, I'd wanted to keep her safe, but more importantly, I'd wanted to offer her more. She deserved more.

"Tsukiko," I said, using my pet name for her.

She looked up and put the bottle down between her and the sailor. "Come here, love," she said quietly.

The sailor rolled his eyes and folded his arms. "Yes, this is the perfect time for lovemaking."

"Shut it," said Luana as I sat beside her, wincing at the thought of my *kimono* coated in dirt. She stuck her long, lovely legs in front of her, her shins poking out from beneath her skirts. Placing the box down behind her, she patted her lap.

Dirt and mud or not, I needed to feel the warmth of her

beneath me. I lay my head where indicated, closing my eyes as Luana's fingers wove through my hair.

"Very helpful," sniffed the sailor. A rustling of clothing and a crackle of forest debris made it clear he'd assumed my post at pacing. "Leave it to a nomad to think of nothing but debauchery at a time like this."

"Excuse me?" began Luana.

I shot up. I wasn't certain what the man had said, but I could feel the way Luana's body had tensed.

"You heard me," he said.

I stood, my eye spotting Rohesia's sword where she'd left it on the ground in Luana's care.

As if I could wield it.

Luana jumped to her feet and pushed the sailor back. "Apologize."

"No."

There was the box behind where she'd been sitting.

"You scum." Luana spat at the sailor, and he jumped back. "You know nothing of my people."

"I know they're raunchy, murdering whores."

I ran to the box, fumbling with the lid. The special pellets remaining—only a few left—lay enticingly in the corner of the box.

If I wasted too many now, I wouldn't have many when it came time to face Mother. But Luana needed me. If he were to attempt to hurt her…

"You vile—" started Luana.

"Quiet!"

A voice from the edge of the clearing drew our attention and the argument instantly faded.

"Oh, at last," said the sailor, the tension releasing visibly from his body.

A Hanaobian girl dressed in finery stepped out from the trees, a sword drawn at her side.

Oh. Of course. My cousin.

"Where have you been?" asked Luana as I stood beside her. She shifted to lean against me, one arm wrapped behind me and the other placed on my chest.

"To chat with this farm's lord." Rohesia shook her newfound blade and blood I hadn't noticed before flicked vividly onto the ground.

"How much chatting did you get done when you don't seem to speak more of this outsider tongue than I do?" asked the sailor.

Rohesia wiped the sword against the trunk of a bamboo tree. "I listened with my eyes," she said, "and spoke with my sword."

"Your sword is there," I said, pointing.

She stared at the sheath, almost contemplating. "Leave it."

"What?" asked the sailor.

"Or one of you take it. I don't care." She held her new sword up, catching the moonlight as she examined it. "I found this one more agreeable."

I shuddered to think of how she had come to that conclusion. I had a sudden pang of regret at her return, even if she would undoubtedly prove useful should the guards present an obstacle. Which they undoubtedly would.

"Kojiro," she said, sliding the blade into a thin sheath at her waist, "we need to talk."

Luana studied me, and I tried my best to will the dread out of my expression. My first thought... But no. There was no way my cousin had spoken to anyone who could have told her. No one here would know. Besides, she could not speak to anyone here, period. Not more than a short phrase.

"Speak," I said, wrapping an arm around Luana's waist.

Rohesia's lips soured. "Without the burdens."

"Burden?" echoed Luana, and I knew whatever the word was, it was an insult.

I hadn't decided yet when I would tell Luana. Or if I would tell her at all. There were all sorts of ways I could explain what I hoped to happen should it all go as I'd conceived. And she'd had no love left for her homeland anyway.

I kissed Luana's forehead and slipped free, falling in step behind my cousin.

The sailor approached. "Whatever you're planning, we're a part of this, too. You can't—"

Rohesia cut him short with a look.

He scoffed and went back to where he'd been sitting, spotting the bottle of *sake* and swiping it before he sat down. "So what's this?" he said, peering down at the black, engraved box. "I was wondering what she clutched so tightly to her bosom."

"I'll thank you not to stare at my bosom," snapped Luana, stomping across the clearing to grab for the box.

"Lower your voices," said Rohesia sternly, her hand gripping at her hilt. As the long sleeve fell down her arm, I caught sight of one of her daggers there strapped back into place. She'd put them in her pouch when she'd been dressed at the elderly couple's, and I'd been hoping she'd keep them there.

A sudden thought gripped me. "Luana, be…" The word escaped me. Careful. How to say "careful"?

She snatched the weapon out from the box and gripped it in front of her with both hands. "Call me a whore now, you wretched beast."

"What is she doing?" hissed Rohesia.

"Luana!" I called, taking a step toward them, my hands out.

The sailor licked his lips, holding the bottle out to the side of him. He clearly seemed inebriated. "Why else would you be hanging all over this outsider?"

"Stop calling him an 'outsider' or Ytoile help me…"

Just as I was about reach her side, the man laughed and said the word "outsider" again.

And with a crack that echoed throughout the forest, the sailor slumped over, dead.

🙠🙡

"I didn't mean to," whispered Luana again from beside me. Her clammy hand shook in mine.

I shushed her, gently, whispering back as I'd done before, "I know."

"I only meant to scare him," she said again. "I thought it wasn't loaded."

I let her keep speaking, the cursed weapon tucked under my

other arm. It was I who'd loaded it earlier, when she hadn't noticed, when I thought I might have to defend her against that boisterous, unpleasant man. He'd made Tierny—spirits watch over him in death—seem downright meek in comparison. And I hadn't even cared about him enough to remember his name—assuming any of us had even asked for it.

To tell the truth, I was glad he was gone. I straightened my back at that thought, Rohesia's old sword tied around my waist whacking hard against my shin as I did as if in rebuke. I still didn't care. He would have been a burden.

And now Rohesia had thought of a plan to get us into the palace without an army, without a dozen and a half chances for the citizens to report us for treason.

The palace had been collecting all the young women about Tomiko's age. So we would blend in.

I'd told Rohesia during our many planning sessions about the crack between posts in the fence of the garden. Small, likely impossible for a full-grown man to slip through, but not for Rohesia. If I squeezed myself, probably not for me. Luana could wait in hiding outside of it.

There was the soft jingle of my cousin's chainmail I'd insisted Luana wear rather than abandon behind with the sailor's body. I just needed her to stay put and stay quiet and I could count on her to stay safe.

"You're certain they won't find anything amiss about their long-lost prince wandering around the palace?" asked Rohesia as we skirted the edge of the bamboo forest past the wreckage of a burnt-out farm just beyond the capital.

Grunting, I paused as Luana stumbled and wiped her nose with the back of her arm. On instinct, I flinched, but I reminded myself that she was filthy and in a state of disrepair at the moment, that eventually, I'd give her everything she deserved, and she would live like a beautiful, pristine flower. My Tsukiko—royalty like Hanaobi had never seen before. "These clothes," I said, jutting my chin downward, "for peasants. Also, no one at this palace liked me muchly."

Luana giggled behind me. She sounded drunk or delirious. "Muchly," she whispered and I felt my face flush.

As if either of these women could speak more than a few words of my language. And we were in *my* country, if I might point out.

My cousin didn't smile, though. She simply looked Luana up and down and shook her head. "We should leave her here."

"No," I said.

"It's as much for her own safety as ours." She pointed to the palace now and the numerous buildings that stood between us and it. "Before we can get to that hole in the fence, we'll have to walk through the village. She'll stand out."

I regarded my cousin, the sword at her hip at odds with the finery of her clothing. The clothing alone would be enough to turn heads, especially with a missing princess.

My heart panged suddenly at the thought of my missing sister. I prayed nothing nefarious was the cause, although I didn't figure that Mother would have turned on her, her last remaining heir. Especially if she was sending the guards out to search for her.

"No," I said again, pointing to Rohesia. "You will find being noticed too." I pointed to the edge of the burnt fields, where the grasses remained intact. If the fire had blazed much farther, it'd have reached the capital. I wondered what Mother would have thought at that.

"We go this way," I said, "all the way back through the grasses. Then we go through quiet alleys." I thought about one of the rare times I'd left the palace and all the back ways I'd taken to get from there to the dock. Yes, I was certain I could find the way.

"We go quietly," I said. "We go together."

"We go muchly," said Luana, laughing again as if she could not stop, even when she slammed one shaky palm over her mouth.

My cousin glared at her and then at me, as if to tell me that proved her point.

"We go muchly," I repeated, lifting the hand that cradled Luana's, as if to show my cousin that I would not be parted from her.

Sighing, Rohesia gestured for me to pass her. "Lead the way," she said. "Wait." She stared out at the coastline, which was only somewhat visible from where we stood. "The fleet is gone," she said. "The war has begun."

Luana hiccupped and belched before giggling and stepping into place behind me.

25

TOMIKO

As we approached the gates leading to the bustling village that Duke Fastello had called the "heart of the duchy," Fastello slowed his horse's pace down to a trot. From where I sat behind him, my head craned around his shoulder to look ahead at the smoke that towered over a portion of the buildings, I could hear the gasp that escaped his lips.

"Where are the men?" he asked, and there was no one at the gate to greet us curtly as there had been during previous trips to and from the village. The door was open, and the reason soon became clear as groups of barbarians, belongings stuffed into baskets and blankets and carried over their backs, streamed out of the village.

Fastello bent over to grab at the top of a man's arm as he passed. "What's going on?" he barked.

The man stopped and looked up at him as if he'd gone mad. "We're under attack!"

"I know that. Where are you going? Where are my men?"

Realization washed over the poor, distraught creature. "The new duke," he said, but he did not bow. Mother would have had his head for not groveling on the ground. "The guards are all headed toward the dock," he said. "They told us all to hide in our homes, but some of us got it into our minds to flee." He watched as more barbarians rushed by. "We're headed toward the farms or the forest—what's left of it."

Fastello grunted and let the man go. He lifted the reins of his horse and we galloped on again, straight through the open gate.

Crowds were shifting every which way throughout the already-tight paths that wove their way between buildings. The closer we got to the smoke, the more damage I saw.

At one charred building, an ashen body lay on the doorstep, his head at an awkward angle, his eyes wide open, blood and soot all over him.

I leaned over the side of the horse and nearly retched.

"Out of the way!" shouted Fastello. "Forget your things—just get out of the city!" he said. "Follow the people running into the farms and forests."

I thought about that for a moment, about the way the duchy was an island, about how Mother's spies had mapped the entire lower portion, where you'd find the village, the forest—although I'd noticed it'd been largely burnt—and the farmlands. "Wait!" I shouted at the top of my lungs. "Head for the mountains!" I screamed. "It is the only safe place."

I'd just told my country's enemies where to find succor.

But looking at their panicked, dirty faces, I'd known I had to. Even if these barbarians had killed Goro despite claiming to have turned over a new leaf. I was as much to blame for Goro's death as these brutes.

Fastello glanced over his shoulder. "There's nothing at the mountains but the ruins of a tower."

"Then they should hide there," I said, summoning all the authority I could into my voice. "Mother plans an attack from south, east, and west of the island. She knows the mountains are too dense, that no one lives among them in the north. It's the only safe place for them."

Fastello swallowed as his eyes widened, but he cleared his throat. "To the mountains!" he shouted. "And tell everyone you meet along the way—to the fallen tower of Ytoile. To the tower!"

His horse maneuvered skillfully through the crowds and the debris now, almost as if it sensed his purpose. As we rounded the corner and came upon a tavern, he tugged the reins to slow the creature to a stop, then shifted himself off to dismount. He turned back with raised arms, his eyes almost pleading. I leaned into his grasp. "What is this place? Why have we stopped?"

He led me by the hand inside, dodging a slightly wobbling old man who came out with a mug held aloft. "I think I know the woman who runs this place," he said. "She'll get you to safety."

I tugged backward on his grip, pulling us both to a stop in front of a counter. The place was filthy, likely coated in grime long before it'd been coated in the ashes of nearby buildings. "And where will you be?"

"Here," he said, clearly exasperated. "Trying to save my city." Even though half the candles were snuffed out inside this place, I could see the tears glistening in his eyes. Although he carried himself so differently, he reminded me of Elder Brother Kojiro in that moment, so daunted by the prospect of responsibility.

There was no point in my cowering in the mountains. I'd have doomed my handmaidens, their families, Goro… For nothing. It all had to mean something. It all had to mean *something* in the end. I would not let my poor, foolish choice to leave the palace lead to nothing.

"I'm staying with you," I said, squeezing tightly on the hand that still clutched mine.

"Look, princess or not, there's no sense in you putting yourself in more danger—"

The sky cracked as another cannon must have fired somewhere nearby—shaking the ground as it crashed. I screamed and before I knew what was happening, I found myself flush against the new duke's chest, his heart hammering like thunder in my ear.

"Who are you?" barked a woman.

"Looking for Meggy," said Fastello, his hands pushing tighter against my back. "Didn't she set up shop here?"

"She's gone," said the woman. I pulled away from Fastello so I could see what was going on. Dust and ash hung clearly in the air and I choked, lifting my sleeve to my face.

The young woman who'd been speaking to us did the same. "She tried to help those who'd been injured, and I don't know what came of her after that. Fastello…?" She stood straighter, examining him.

Fastello nodded, coughing, and shoved me toward her, both hands on my shoulders. Even now, in this moment of insanity, I couldn't help but stare at his deformed hand. "You work with Meggy? Can you please get her to the mountains?"

"The mountains?"

"The tower," said Fastello. "What remains of it. It's the only place that's safe."

"But what are you doing here?" she asked. "Why aren't you leading the men into fighting back?"

Almost as if on command, the sky rung out again with a crack, this one louder, closer. But nothing shook. Instead, the sound of a wave—a wave magnified times a thousand—roared out moments later.

"Retaliatory fire," said Fastello, and it took my mind a moment to translate the words. He turned back to the woman. "I'm on my way. I was out in the fields when this started. I just need to see this Hanaobian to safety."

The woman clutched his arm. "Don't go," she said. "Be careful."

He looked horrified. "What are you talking about?"

"Meggy heard some whispers about the men turning on you," she said. "The guards. And tonight, before the attack even started, she was warned that some of the guards were leading an insurrection."

I couldn't follow everything she was saying as quickly as she was saying it, but I knew. I remembered how the guard who'd killed Goro—intending to or not—had never come back with a doctor. Not that he would have been able to come back in time to help. Even so, we hadn't met them along the way—by then, the attack had started, but…

Fastello seemed to lose his footing as he let go of me entirely. He stumbled toward the counter, leaning back against it to stay upright. "No," he said. "No… Not now of all times. Not when I'm alone." He stared up at me and the other woman, almost pleading. "I need them. I need the guards to save this city!"

The woman stepped forward and gripped his arm. "You have those of us left on the underground," she said. "Besides, I don't think the guards are aiming to take over a ruined city. It sounds like they're fighting back. They may protect the city all on their own. You just need to stay away from them."

"I can't," he said, almost crying. "I won't. I can't abandon this land now to save myself." He held his injured hand out in front of him, staring at it as it shook. "I won't hide from this. Or any challenge. Even if it means my life."

She shook her head. "Then you're a fool."

"Maybe." He bit his lip. "So will you get her to the tower?"

"I am not going," I said, striding toward them.

The woman met my gaze. "Neither am I," she said.

"Tomiko," I said, introducing myself.

"Malle," she replied.

"Malle…?" said Fastello, almost as if asking a question. "I've met you before."

"Of course you have," snapped Malle. "Cateline was one of my dearest friends."

"The farm!" said Fastello, whatever that meant. "You married that… Rohesia's manservant."

She grimaced. "Yes, yes, and became a widow shortly thereafter. But now's not the time to belabor any of that." She nodded at me. "We're not running. None of us." She turned back to him. "So what do you want to do? Meggy might have run for another underground post."

"There's a house," Fastello said, "assuming it's still standing. An aristocratic house with a woman who'd once been on the underground. There are nomads and Hanaobians there, assuming they were able to return from work before it all started, assuming they didn't run once it did—although I don't know whether to wish for that or not. I don't know if I can mold any of them into an army."

"That's a lot of assuming," said Malle, her hands on her hips. The air shook out again with another boom, but this one was farther and didn't cause the floor to shake beneath us.

"She's attacking other parts of the island," I explained, and Fastello's face went almost as pale as moonlight.

He rubbed that broken hand over his forehead, massaging his temples. "What if the guards couldn't be trusted to protect the city?" he asked. "What if they've been working with Hanaobi this whole time?"

"Why would they even—?" started Malle.

But I shook my head. "No. They're not. They wouldn't. Mother would never—"

"Enough, Tomiko—Shoko—whatever your name is! Enough." Fastello looked tired as he crossed his arms tightly against his chest.

"You still don't believe I'm the princess."

"The princess?" echoed Malle. "Of Hanaobi? How did you get here?"

"It doesn't matter," barked Fastello. "Lives are on the line and I can't just trust you and hope that you're telling the truth."

"You believed me when I said the mountains were the safest place."

"Because that makes sense," he said.

"And when I tell you that Mother would never work with duchy guards, that does not make sense to you?"

Fastello sighed and looked away. "Someone was communicating with Hanaobi," he said. "Someone told them that the previous duke had fallen before I could send an official message."

I thought back to when Mother had received the news. Her demeanor... She hadn't been joyous enough. In fact, she'd been almost angry, more determined. "We did receive a message," I said. "But it was written in our own language. Could any of your guards manage that?"

Fastello let out a deep breath. "No," he said. "It'd have to be... One of the Hanaobians."

"Farmers cannot often read and write," I said. "Mother thinks it a waste of their time and efforts. She wants their children to start working as soon as they are able."

"Couldn't a nobleman outsider have snuck in among the farmers?" asked Malle.

"And spend his life toiling the land while in wait to tell my mother news?" I asked. I shook my head. "You cannot know, but the lords of my land do not take their positions lightly. They would not sacrifice so much for their country, nor would Mother think to ask them to. She needs *some* people to support her rule."

Someone screamed outside the tavern and Fastello jumped up, running toward the door.

Malle and I followed suit.

Fastello was helping a woman to her feet, grabbing a child who cried nearby and pushing them together. "The mountains," he said. "The tower. Get there quickly." He shifted an overstuffed blanket that had been tied tightly around the woman's neck up over her head. "Leave it," he said. "For now, just leave it all behind. You'll move faster without it."

The woman gazed at him, fear in her eyes, and nodded, lifting her small child and running away.

"Come on then," he said, grimacing as he faced us. "If you won't go, come with me."

"Wait, Fastello!" I said, running to catch up with him. "I know how you can win this—without relying on the soldiers." He searched my face, seeming to look for a lie, a contradiction, an inevitable dash of his hopes.

But I knew it would work. It had to.

Malle coughed some more as she caught up with us. "That's great," she said, "but can we get somewhere away from this dust and debris?"

Fastello looked over his shoulder. His muscles relaxed visibly. "To Agnes'," he said.

"Agnes?" asked Malle. Her nose wrinkled. "Are you sure? Isn't that the woman who betrayed—"

"I'm certain," he said.

And because I wanted him to trust wholly in me, I decided to trust wholly in him.

❧ 26 ☙

FASTELLO

I banged on the door leading to Agnes' home, and it creaked open at my touch. A woman—Gilia—practically ripped the door off its hinges and jumped back to find me standing there, Tomiko and Malle behind me.

"Fastello." Gasping, she heaved the basket she carried over one arm higher. Mina, Nico, and several other men and women appeared behind her. "We were just about to get out of here, head for the forest. What do we do?"

I turned around to survey the damage. The city looked tarnished, injured—but not entirely lost. A lot like the hand I kept obsessing over.

I shook my head. "Not the forest," I said. "If you're going to run, head for the tower at the mountains."

"It's rubble," said Mina.

I pushed past the group to step inside, Tomiko and Malle trailing behind me.

"It is the safest place," said Tomiko.

The group just studied her.

"If you're going to go, go," I said, "but be careful. Stick to the middle of the island as much as possible, out of the cannonballs' reach."

187

A few of my people, along with some Hanaobians, headed out the door. Nico left with a curt nod my way, his arm wrapped around a Hanaobian woman. Gilia and Mina exchanged a look. "But why are you here?"

"I need help," I said. "I need to get a message to the aviary." I exchanged a look with Tomiko to confirm our plan. She nodded. "But I need to stay out of sight of the guards along the docks." The more I spoke, the more helpless I felt. "I was hoping to find…" I looked around. The place was empty. "Some help," I finished.

"Fastello?" Agnes descended the stairs, clutching tightly to the handrail as the skies rung out again. Another retaliatory cannon. I didn't know how many had been fired, how many there were left.

"I need to take advantage of your hospitality once more," I told her. For a moment, she visibly flinched, but she straightened herself as she reached the bottom. I turned around to find Tomiko huddled with a small group of Hanaobians, who'd either requested work in the heart of the duchy or who'd come back here from the farms before we'd left to rest.

"I need paper and a quill to start," I said. "And then I need a team of brave souls to take it to the aviary and attach it to a bird used to flying the short distance to a boat."

Agnes laughed. "The paper and quill I have, but…" She pointed at herself. "Do you see bravery?"

"I do," I said, grabbing her by the arms. "Ytoile does. Or She never would have asked all this of you. She never would have found a woman who'd lost so much willing to give of herself to so many."

Her eyelashes batted, perhaps in an attempt to stave away tears. "You had to force me to help—"

"But I'm asking you now. I'm begging you."

Gilia stepped up from behind me. "We'll go with you," she said, nodding at Mina.

"And I," said Malle. "Have any of you sent messages via bird? My husband did," she said, reminding me again of the rumors about the duke's most trusted servant not being so trustworthy after all, "and I can tell which birds will go the short distance."

"It's settled, then," I said before Agnes could object. She studied Malle, seeming to recognize her and perhaps remembering what she'd done to her when she'd told the duke's men about Malle's secret marriage. But neither woman brought it up, as there was no time for such worries now. She seemed resolved, albeit grimly, as she turned to get my paper and quill.

I gestured for Tomiko to come, to write her letter.

She'd be writing it in her own language, so I'd be trusting her wholeheartedly not to write something terrible that would seal my country's fate.

It looked as sealed and hopeless as ever right now, though.

"And what will you do?" asked Mina.

"Tomiko and I head for the castle," I said, "to speak with the crew of the ship that brought her here."

Malle didn't look pleased, but she'd been over her objections with us already. It was Gilia's turn to worry.

"Son," she said, although I wasn't her child. I supposed she was the closest thing I'd had to a mother after mine had died. "Be careful."

She didn't know about the guards and how they might stop me.

That was where the letter would come in. A failsafe. But we'd try to get the word of as many reliable witnesses to Tomiko's presence as we could. Even if it meant my death.

I caught Tomiko's eyes and we both nodded at once. "You be careful too."

❧

I borrowed a cloak at Agnes' to hang the hood over my face. I looked more suspicious than ever—especially considering most anyone else on the streets was screaming and running for their lives —but there was no other way. We needed to get into the palace and up the stairs to the room decorated in Hanaobian style, where I'd housed the Hanaobian captain and his crew.

I didn't know how many guards awaited us between here and there. We'd already dodged a few of them as we'd woven through the streets. But they'd been running, shouting at each other—most headed to the docks.

I felt sick to my stomach at the thought of what awaited the ladies I'd sent there. But then again, being a band of women, if they were caught, I hoped they could feign ignorance and panic and simply be guided on their way without the men searching them and finding the letter.

But I needed them to succeed. I needed them to get that letter to any of those boats out there.

The ground shook again with cannon fire, but it didn't seem to land anywhere in the heart of the duchy this time. Still, I steeled myself. We had no time to waste. Even in success, if we didn't hurry, there'd be little of the duchy left to save.

We rounded the corner and came to the palace doors. There was still a single guard there.

Could I overpower him? Was it possible he wasn't coordinating with the others and would recognize me and let me be on my way? Or even join me? I didn't know who to trust, but I could use all the might and muscle possible. Could I risk showing myself?

Before I'd made a decision, Tomiko strode forward and walked toward the guard. When I hissed out her name, she gestured behind her for me to stay put. I did, bending my knees and ready to pounce after her should things go poorly.

"Get out of here," spat the guard. "Can't you tell the skies are raining cannonballs, outsider? Get!"

"I need to get inside," she said.

He narrowed his eyes at her. "You'll find no shelter here. It's your people who're showering those cannonballs at us, you know! You're lucky I don't strike you down where you stand." He gripped his sword hilt and I made to move, but Tomiko gestured behind her again.

He didn't pull the sword out. My heart rate slowed. I supposed Tomiko was right that the duchy guards and Hanaobi would never work together. Even if they hated me, they hated Hanaobi more. Or they probably hated me because I hadn't hated Hanaobi more.

"My family is in there," said Tomiko.

"The only outsiders left in there are the captain and his crew from that suspiciously-timed arrival…" This time he did pull his sword out and Tomiko took a step back.

Gestures or not, I wasn't letting her face this alone. "Halt," I said stepping forward and tossing down my hood.

The guard looked at me and laughed. "We thought you were dead maybe," he said. "Caught up in a blast. Either that or you turned tail like the soft coward you are and went hiding with the rest of your people back to the charred-out forest you came from."

I gripped my own sword hilt and pulled it out. "As you can see, neither is the case." I gave him a slightly theatrical bow, my sword now in my left hand, my cloak acting like a cape. "Let us pass," I said, straightening. "We need to see the captain and his men. It's a matter of life and death."

The guard laughed. "You're with her?" He took a step toward me, abandoning his slow pursuit of Tomiko. Good. At least she was safe for now. If it came to blows with me, I had little confidence I would succeed. The sword shook in my hand, my grip loose and unsteady on the heavy thing considering I'd never taken the time to practice and train even before I'd lost fingers on my hand.

I'd been so concerned with forcing peace among three groups of people that I hadn't thought to—hadn't wanted to—prepare for what would be necessary if that peace wasn't well received.

At times like this, I wasn't so sure the duke's method of fear and brutality was the wrong way to keep some semblance of peace.

But I was the duke now. And I was tired of doubting myself.

I couldn't have prevented the Hanaobian attack—that was what Rohesia, Jiro, and Tierny were trying to do.

I couldn't have won over the guards in such a short amount of time. Perhaps I never would have.

But cajoling the nomads and the Hanaobians and everyone else in the duchy to work together for the benefit of us all—that had been the right thing to do.

My gaze flicked as Tomiko opened the door as quietly as she could and slipped inside.

I prayed she didn't encounter any more guards along the way, or that they mistook her for a frightened farmer girl and sent her on her way.

But there'd be guards outside the door holding the captain and his crew captive, and I needed to be there to see this through. That meant I'd need to settle things with this guard first.

"Stay your hand," I tried, "and get to the docks to help with the counterattack."

The man scoffed. "You mean the counterattack that we're leading—without the assistance of a spineless, deformed excuse for a man?"

His eyes went pointedly to the hand not gripping my sword at my side.

"I am your duke," I said, "and I need you to stand down."

"You're no duke of mine," said the guard, his sword raised overhead.

I went to lift my own, but it was simply too heavy and I had no idea how I'd guard against the blow. So I pulled my arm back and just tossed it at him, rolling out of the way to escape his thrust, which staggered off its course as he jumped back slightly to avoid my haphazardly-thrown blade.

"Looks like you're a coward, after all," sneered the man, but I had already sprung for the open door.

"Hey!" he started, but I was inside, shoving the door shut, and slamming the door hold into place just as he jostled at the handle on the other side. "Open up, you bloody coward!" He pounded on the door.

"I'm not the one with blood on my..." I'd been about to say "hands," but as I held mine out before me, I could see it. Not truly still there, but the stain of memory. My father's blood. And perhaps in less direct fashion, Cateline's.

Voices carried through the empty palace from somewhere up above.

I gripped both hands tightly. Blood or no blood, I would do what needed to be done for peace—but never to the innocents. Never to those who didn't deserve it.

I took the stairs up two flights two and three at a time. The landing was empty. Most of the guards probably had gone to the docks. Most of the other citizens had escaped.

When I passed the room I'd been using as my own—whenever I could spare a short while for sleep—a thought struck me. I could see the room where two guards stood, hear them exchanging harsh words with Tomiko already. But I would have to spare a minute to go inside and strap on something beneath my cloak, something I hadn't used in ages. Something that had struck me as blood-soaked, that I'd left behind with my people, only to find that Gilia and Mina had managed to salvage it among their jewels and some other weapons from the forest fire.

I strapped in my false blade and made it look as if it'd struck me just inches from my heart.

"Help!" I gasped, putting extra volume into my voice as I shuffled out of the door and toward Tomiko. "Help! I've been struck!"

A guard shoved Tomiko aside and they both approached me, their hands on their hilts. "Who goes—?" one started. And then he laughed. "The false duke?"

The other chuckled as well, not bothering to withdraw his sword. "He's been stabbed. By a dagger. A fitting end for a spineless man. What happened? Did a little girl stab you?"

Tomiko tugged the door open, but she wasn't so quiet this time. That, or the guard thought to look at her as if to confirm she might have been the one to stab me. "Hey!" he barked, withdrawing his own blade.

But I tackled him from behind, screaming as loud as I could to get the other one's attention.

"What the—?" the second man said as I wrapped my legs around the first man's torso entirely, clutching his neck tightly, knocking off his helmet with my grasping fingers, and then biting his ear.

"You're mad!" said the second man, pointing his sword at me even as Tomiko slipped inside the room.

I spit the blood and perhaps flesh in my mouth to the ground, sickened at my own veracity. Then I grinned, quite sure my lips were soaked red. "No," I said, "I'm just a different kind of fighter than you." I squeezed harder on the man's neck. "Now get to the docks and help with the attack," I said, "or I squeeze the breath out of him."

The second man lowered his sword, laughing. "We have our

orders," he said. "We have this whole counterattack under control. No thanks to you."

"So I see," I said, grunting as the man beneath me stumbled toward the wall, slamming me into it. The false dagger's hilt kind of hurt when squeezed so tightly into my chest, blade or no. "And I'd commend you all for it if it weren't for the fact that you committed treason by keeping me out of it."

Another explosion heralded out across the sky, causing us all to shake and the man in my grip to slip down against the wall, landing on his butt. He thrashed, but I kept my grip, squeezing harder.

"Stop!" said the second. "Just stop!" He tossed his sword down, sending it scattering across the floor.

Loosening my grip slightly, I allowed the man to breathe but didn't let him go.

The second guard grinned. "So you're not entirely a coward after all," he said.

"No," I said matter-of-factly. "I do what needs to be done when it needs to be done." I swallowed, not sure whether to lie about my intentions or let it all go unsaid. But I said it anyway. "I killed my father when I saw his ways were leading my people down a path of wickedness." I eyed the standing guard. "And I'll kill anyone else who tries something similar."

The man nodded, something like resolution passing over his face. "So be it. We'll help with the counterattack. Let him go."

I did, but not before kicking the other man's sword more out of the way.

On shaking feet, I stood. The man I'd choked was red-faced and equally unsteady. There was a dark mark on his throat, which he cradled as he stared at me.

I pointed behind me. "Speaking to these men may help put an end to the attack," I said. "If the ships out there fly the white flag… I need you to get the message to the others that we're to enter a ceasefire."

"How?" choked the red-faced guard, but the other put a hand out to silence him.

"The others might not listen to us."

"Make them listen then," I said, standing straighter. "We can't win this war with firepower. We can't. There are ships on three sides of the island, and there's no room for our own fleet to get out. Even if the ships stop firing, we can't hope to overpower them for long and firing despite a ceasefire will just put an end to all hopes of peaceful resolution." I nodded. "Do whatever you need to do to put an end to this war. I'll do what I must," I said, and I left them, sending half of my hopes with them.

Tomiko was already speaking in her language to the men inside and the captain's pale face was grim as he walked back and forth.

"You know, then," I said, striding into the room. I grabbed hold of Tomiko by the arm—I hoped not too roughly. I hoped she would forgive me. This had been her idea. "I have the Princess Tomiko, heir to the throne of Hanaobi, as my hostage. Send a letter to the other captains and tell them to put an end to the hostilities if they hope for her release." That was what had been in the contents of the letter I'd entrusted to Agnes and the rest. We'd just thought that in case the other captains hadn't believed it, it would be best to hear the same from the captain we'd had here.

Tomiko translated for me and the man nodded, resigned.

"Get him some paper and a quill," I snapped at another of the Hanaobian sailors. At Tomiko's word, he went to a desk in the corner of the room—perhaps the one piece of furniture in here that didn't look like it was from another country, and rifled through the desk's contents to bring out the paper. He stopped suddenly and said something in his language.

Tomiko's brow furrowed as she responded.

He spoke again and held up a letter—an already-written letter —with their ideograms on them.

Tomiko nodded at me and I guided her toward it, letting her go as she snatched the letter from the man and read it, her eyes moving up and down desperately.

"What is it?" I asked, realization dawning on me that it had to have been written by Jiro—unless it was so old it was from the duke's Hanaobian wife. Who else had spent time in this room and could write their strange language on paper?

"It is from my elder brother," she said, confirming one of my theories. "He writes to Mother—it looks like this was a practice letter; he made a few mistakes in the calligraphy." Her accent made each word sound so strange, but she still spoke with more grace than I'd ever heard from a native speaker. "He writes of the duke's fall. He explains how it happened. He…" She stopped.

"He what?" I asked.

She clutched the paper to her chest, her eyes widened. "He asks for clemency because he sails there with our cousin in tow." She bowed her head slightly. "He promises to kill her if Mother lets him take his place as heir once more."

That little bastard! Impossible… My throat went dry. But there was no way to reach them. No way to warn Rohesia in time. And besides, we had our own crisis to worry about.

"Write the letter," I snapped to the Hanaobian sailor who stood near us, even if he couldn't understand me. I locked eyes with Tomiko and my voice caught in my throat for a moment. "We have a war to stop here first and foremost."

$$\text{27}$$

ROHESIA

To have gotten all this way unaccosted—it was like Ytoile herself guided our way.

Not that I'd ever believed in such things.

Still, considering everything we'd lost, how far we'd come, there was no turning back.

I needed to see the seat my mother had given up.

I almost didn't care if I wound up taking it for myself.

But Kojiro was asking something of me I wasn't sure I was comfortable with. Not when we were so close to facing our objective.

"Leave this," he said, pointing again to the sword I'd purloined from the lord. The lord who had surely been found dead or injured by now, along with the two guards I'd encountered on my way out. I didn't stop to see what state they'd been in, only knew that they were no longer a threat and I had no need for further bloodshed.

Even if part of me had thought the lord had deserved death after how he'd looked at me—what he must have done to other girls—I remembered Sherrod and his pleasure girl wife. Compared to Father, who never looked at another woman that way—not in my lifetime at least, not since he had fallen for and lost my mother. No. The act of looking at a girl like that wasn't enough alone to condemn a man. I didn't strike with intentional killing blows, the threat of dying from blood loss aside. I would not kill if I did not need to. Not anymore.

Although a lot of good going out of our way to save that sailor had done in the end.

The question now was if anyone had been dispatched to the palace, had warned them of the mute girl who might have unleashed this danger upon their lord's home.

Luana had stopped giggling for some time, but she looked about to pass out right here at the edge of the palace gardens. She did not strike me as a good guard for this new blade I'd grown so fond of in such a short amount of time, but I had to concede that a Hanaobian girl of my age wouldn't be wandering around the royal palace with a blade at her hip. Likely neither would a Hanaobian woman of any age.

"What of yours then?" I asked, removing the sheath and tossing it at the ground at Luana's feet. She was slumped against the outside of the garden wall, hidden by wild-growing shrubbery.

"I will be guard," he said, his back straightening at the words. Still, he looked down at his sword and removed it nonetheless. "I cannot use this sword."

My blade, which had served me well for so many years… Clearly duchy-made in comparison. Heavy, sturdy, out of place.

Luana, wearing my chainmail… I still couldn't believe he'd hoped to keep her safe with it.

"Take the other one, then," I said, pointing to the blade I'd discarded. All the better. I could always take it from him when I needed it.

I ran my fingers across the blade that hadn't been dipped in poison at my wrist. I had these. They would have to do. The other, now soaked with the last of the poison that I'd ensconced in my bottle, I would save for the empress.

Kojiro nodded, but before he retrieved the sword, he crouched beside Luana, running a careful hand across her brow as she slept. I couldn't believe she'd been that drunk or exhausted to fall asleep so suddenly like that. When we'd reached the end of our journey at last.

I turned to give them privacy, peering through the gap in the garden fence to watch for patterns and get a clearer image of what we'd be up against.

Almost no one appeared—none in the garden, and only two men with swords walked along the palace walkways at the edge of the garden. Guards. And they were outfitted fairly differently from Kojiro. I turned to look at him just as he was tying the sheath on. How did he expect them to believe he was a guard?

I still didn't believe they wouldn't recognize him as their long-lost prince, poor man's outfit or not.

If he got caught—either for looking out of place or looking like an imperial—I wouldn't get far if I was standing there beside him.

Without a word, I reached through the gap and squeezed my entire body through, the pouch at my waist beneath all these layers of clothing digging tightly into my shin.

Sherrod's words, his careful, desperate message that never had a reader beside me, never had a purpose—other than to show me how much more of a person he could be, despite the despicable things he'd done on my orders—echoed in my mind.

They were words from the man I'd cared about without even realizing what those feelings were.

And I would get through this to finish transcribing his messages at least, pointless as they might be.

I heard Kojiro call my name, but I moved quickly through the strange stone garden and shuffled down the hall, my head slightly bowed, in my best imitation of the old women who'd dressed me.

❦

I WAS GOOD AT MAKING MY FOOTFALLS NEAR-SILENT, HAVING remembered to kick off those worn sandals before I'd climbed onto the walkway. Even guards walked around the palace in socks—I'd have to remember that weakness should I ever need to stomp a foot or fling a dagger at one to make my escape. The guards here, though quieter in spades than the men I'd left behind in the duchy, were still noisier than I was. I'd managed to duck around corners and pull back into shadows at virtually every moment until now—

when I heard a crowd of at least four or five guards speaking to one another, their paces quickening.

Had Kojiro been found? I'd known he couldn't have been far behind me, but I'd gone quickly anyway, determined to put some distance between us.

I'd known he wouldn't agree, so I hadn't asked.

If he'd been clever and kept his head down, there'd been a chance he wouldn't have been found out so quickly. Besides, he should have some authority here if it came down to that.

I grabbed hold of one of those strange sideways-opening doors and stepped inside, pulling it closed just as the parade of guards passed by.

After the halls went silent, I went to open the door again, but someone spoke from behind me.

I recognized the word for "who."

I turned around to find a roomful of young women in the dark, a small candle their only light. They looked to be in an array of clothing—finery and pauper's—but all seemed slightly disheveled and in disarray. A portion even had soot on their faces.

They'd been so quiet, I hadn't even thought to turn around and inspect the room behind me.

The missing girls, taken when the guards had been looking for the vanished Princess Tomiko. So they hadn't been killed, just rounded up. This would have worked out perfectly, except I had no intention of biding my time and waiting around here.

I approached, bowing my head slightly, and said the word for "empress," emphasizing that it was a question by raising my voice at the end.

The girls nearest me all turned to look at one another, the confusion clear on their faces. One spoke quickly to me, but I shook my head, pointing to my ears.

They spoke amongst themselves again and I heard footsteps approaching—another group of soldiers. I slipped among the girls, sitting in the middle of the group as the door slid open. It didn't stop most of them from staring at me, but their attention was soon caught by the man who stepped through, barking harshly in his language.

All around me the girls rose, so I did, too. Their heads lowered, they stood in a line as the man walked amongst them. He stopped in front of some of the girls—the ones wearing finery, I noticed, the ones in red robes—and said something, and each girl stepped forward.

Of course he did the same to me, and I obliged, my fingers twitching to let loose the dagger beneath my sleeves.

Not yet, I told myself.

He stepped back and said another word, and then the other three girls and I were led into the hallway.

They wouldn't have known to look for a girl in a red robe dress if someone from the lord's household hadn't come to warn them.

Or if…

The other girls moved slowly in front of me, their hands clutched together. I didn't like how that would add one more moment to the movement I'd have to make if I had to fling my daggers, but I did it anyway. I couldn't act now. There'd be no point in acting now.

I had to stand over the empress' body before I could show any aspect of my true self.

After that… My hands brushed against that pouch. After that, I hadn't even been sure I could hold on to the throne. That I cared if I could. But now, I wanted to… And it was too late. We'd failed to arouse the rebellion that would support us through a transition in power, as Tierny had hoped we would. But then again, I'd never seen success in that path. We never would have gotten close enough to the empress for it to succeed.

It was this path or nothing. And I could do this much for Fastello and Malle and the men back home at least.

This is what Sherrod had seen in me. In a way, I was glad he was gone so he wouldn't try to stop me.

The guards and the girls came to a stop in front of another screen. The guard spoke and there was a response before he opened the doors.

Inside, toward the back of the room, sat a woman in the finest robes I'd ever seen. There was no throne. She sat on the floor like the rest of these people seemed to.

Two other women sat behind her in fine clothing that was not quite so eye-catching. Men flanked the room on either side, some with weapons, others without. And near the back of the room, mere steps from his mother, was Kojiro, two guards on either side of him.

His eyes diverted to the ground as soon as I caught them.

So it'd been him, not a messenger, who'd told them how to find me?

He truly was a coward, always concerned more for his own safety than anything larger than himself.

Or maybe he'd had an idea? I took one last look at all the people gathered in the room. Perhaps there was no way I'd have gotten so close to the empress otherwise. The other girls stood in a horizontal line in front of the empress at something the guard said, and I followed suit.

She leaned to the side, where Kojiro stood, and said something, though her eyes faced forward, traveling over each of us in line.

He said nothing.

"So," said the empress in my own tongue, "I hear we have a visitor today." Her diction was near perfect, although there was a cadence to how she spoke that revealed her origin, even if her finery and poise already did. "Which of you is my dear niece, Rohesia?"

The other girls shifted slightly beside me, exchanging a look without lifting their heads. They probably didn't even understand her, though it was clear enough she was expecting something. I hoped my own movements matched the same.

"My son"—she gestured to Kojiro—"could tell me and spare me all this trouble, but…" She nodded at the guard who'd led us into the room and he removed his sword from his hip, slicing through one of the girls' backs. She crumpled to the floor in a heap, the blood that pooled around her red robe staining the pale brown of the soft mats beneath our feet.

The empress raised an eyebrow and turned to Kojiro, though his head hung low. "All right. I can spare a few innocent Hanaobian girls if it means I put an end to this madness." She nodded at the guard again.

Before he could take his swing, though, I flicked my wrist with the poison dagger, sending it straight toward the empress.

Only before it could reach its mark, Kojiro appeared in its path, somehow free of his captors.

It struck him in the shoulder. And he gasped, the pain already distorting his face.

What had he done…?

"Thank you, son," said the empress, and Kojiro stumbled a few steps to the side. She laughed. "Welcome, my dear Rohesia."

She flung a hand at the guard and they dragged the two remaining red-robed girls away. The fallen one's robe continued to darken and a thin trail of blood now reached my white-socked feet.

Kojiro struggled to stand, but he did, his hand trembling as it ripped the dagger out. He screamed as he flung it to the floor.

He couldn't have known it was poisoned. Or would he still have stepped between me and her? What was he thinking? Had he been on her side all along, despite everything he'd shared about her hatred for him?

Someone had sent word, had been spying on our country for the empress.

It had been him. It had to have been.

But why?

I practically growled at Kojiro as I stared him down, and his shaking hand reached for the hilt of the sword at his waist, red running down the sleeve of his other arm.

"Why?" I asked. Kojiro's eyes darted to the floor.

"She speaks at last!" said the empress. "You did not expect my son—my heir—to betray his country, did you?" She looked at Kojiro fondly then, but there was a note of falseness in her manners and how she'd spoken.

Without the princess, I supposed she had no other heir to speak of regardless.

Little did either realize she'd have no heir in her son within minutes.

Part of me hurt—actually, physically hurt—at what I'd done, even if it was entirely, unequivocally his fault. Even if I shouldn't have spared one more thought to his inevitable death.

Still, I'd thought we were in this together. That we were… If not friends, at least family.

I got ready to flick my other wrist. My aim would have to be true.

"Oh. Do you have another one of those?" The empress seemed genuinely curious as she covered the bottom half of her face with her long, voluminous sleeve. She nodded at a guard and he stepped toward me, leaving me no choice but to dodge, lest I waste my last remaining weapon. I tripped on the accursed long robe and spun again, shrugging out of the outer red layer, leaving nothing but the white robe I wore beneath and the pouch on my waist.

Two men came at me from behind and I turned, flinging forth the dagger on instinct and striking one of them in the neck, causing him to crumble.

But that was it, my last dagger with which to strike the empress. I rolled again, dodging first one blade and then another, the empress' laughter echoing throughout the hall.

I couldn't take them all on by myself. All right, then, this was it —but I would take the empress down with me.

I rolled on the ground, knocking into Kojiro's feet, and he shook, almost falling. His face had grown hot and was covered in sweat. I jumped to my knees to pull that sword off of him, sheath and all, and just as I tore it away, I looked up to find that strange thing Luana had held in her hand when she'd struck the sailor pointed down at me.

"I am sorry," he said through gritted teeth, just before a crackling explosion rung in my ears.

❦ 28 ❦

KOJIRO

I missed.

Even I didn't know if it'd been on purpose.

But the weapon had hit its mark nonetheless—right on the shoulder.

A mirror image of my own wound.

My wound throbbed. No, not just my wound. I felt shaky everywhere.

My legs gave out beneath me as I slunk to the floor.

"I see you have not lost your flair for the dramatic," snapped Mother, speaking once more in our own tongue. She pursed her lips as she studied me. Once, her words, her look, might have hurt me.

But I hadn't saved her for her approval.

I stared at the weapon in my hand, its final little pellet discharged. I'd left the box with Luana; there'd be no hope of adding more powder and a pellet now.

I slunk to my knees. In front of me, my cousin's blood stained her white inner *kimono*; her body lay still.

Perhaps I'd hit a vital part after all.

My vision clouded the longer I stared at her.

"Get the physician," barked Mother, and I thought there was

something like anxiety in her voice. But that was impossible. "And make sure that pretender is dead."

There was movement all around me, but I stared instead at Rohesia.

Was this what I'd wanted? It was only halfway there, I knew. The part I'd struggled with, even after Luana and others had told me of my cousin's deeds among her own people.

I'd told myself she'd deserve it for what she'd done, the people she'd killed—both from Hanaobi and her own barbaric land. And that she couldn't hope to lead a country without even speaking its language.

She and Tierny had hoped I'd stay by her side—as her husband or her advisor. Translating for her, guiding her through our customs. No. I would not be an emperor in the shadows for an empress who led only by name.

I would not trust her to be a better leader than her father, than my mother.

I didn't care if she never had children and my own would then be next in line. It wasn't enough. I couldn't be sure there'd be a Hanaobi for them to lead come then if Rohesia had sat on the throne.

My head raged with fire and I slunk harder against the *tatami*, my arms suddenly like weights. I stared at the weapon still in my hand.

I had to do this. Before I drifted off into unconsciousness. I had to kill Mother.

But with so many witnesses, could I trust they wouldn't put an end to me while I slept?

As the hot, burning feeling overtook me, I thought to myself, *What does it matter?*

"And who is this?" asked Mother.

I looked up again. The physician made his way toward me, tugging at my *kimono* to expose my shoulder. Guards surrounded Rohesia on the ground beside me.

But it wasn't they who caught my attention, even as the physician prodded at my wound and made me growl.

"Kojiro!" said Luana, kicking her legs. Rohesia's chainmail

jingled and clanked as she swung, held aloft by two guards. My vision swam, but I focused on her face. Her soft, beautiful face was darkened by worry.

I had to save her. I had to protect her. I had to show her what I wanted to offer her, what I could be…

My hand reached out toward her—the pain excruciating—and the physician gently pushed it down.

"Your Majesty," he said. "A word…"

Mother stared at him but said only, "Inspect the girl. Make sure she is dead."

The man padded my wound with cloth and nodded.

"You know this barbarian, Kojiro?" asked Mother.

"Kojiro!" shouted Luana. "Kojiro! What happened to him? You monsters! He's dying!"

The word slapped me across the face. I looked to the physician to correct her, but his lips were tight, his face grim as he turned around to inspect Rohesia.

But it was only a wound in the shoulder. Like Rohesia's… But my blood loss was far less egregious.

"Let her go," said Mother, and at first I thought she referred to Rohesia. But soon Luana pounded across the *tatami* mats.

"Kojiro." Hands cupped my face, wiped my brow. "What happened to you?" Her voice shook.

I looked over her shoulder at Rohesia and the physician crouched over her. She'd been aiming at Mother. I had no one but myself to blame for this. But why? It was just my shoulder. I stared at the weapon in my hand.

"Kojiro," Luana whispered, bringing her forehead against mine, "talk to me."

"Tsuki…ko," I said.

She embraced me and through my hazy vision, I stared at Mother. She stared back.

"Where is your sister?" she asked.

I shook my head. It felt like tiny daggers were rattling around in it.

"I thought she might have gone to you. She always did have a soft spot for you." Her nose wrinkled. "All the same, I'll need an heir. I have faith she is out there somewhere. Her recovered hand-maidens promised me they saw her alive but days ago." She looked at the red-stained place where she'd had that innocent woman slaughtered, perhaps remembering. "And who is this?" she asked. "Why have you brought a filthy barbarian here?"

"I'm sorry," said Luana. "I got worried after they caught you in the garden and I…" She didn't need to finish.

Mother must have been looking at us because she laughed. "If you thought for one second I would let you sully our bloodline by marrying a barbarian like your foolish aunt did—"

"Your Grace," said the physician, "she's still—"

Luana jumped back as a flurry of movement sounded from behind her. My cousin leapt to her feet, gritting her teeth and clutching at her wound, as alert as if she'd never been shot at all.

Everyone's attention turned to her as she pushed the physician onto his back and lunged for the sword I'd carried, which she'd managed to knock off me before I'd fired the weapon at her.

A raging course of energy shot through me. I gripped the still-warm weapon as hard as I could and slammed it against the ground, splintering it.

Luana looked from Rohesia to me and back again.

"Run," I said through gritted teeth. I launched to my feet, pushing away all the dizziness that threatened to send me back down. Guards drew their swords, clashing with Rohesia, the clank of metal on metal ringing wildly in my ears.

"Stop her!" shouted Mother, as if her men weren't already attempting to do just that.

I staggered over to her, letting my unsteady footsteps launch me into a run.

"Kojiro, what are you—?" Luana's voice drew Mother's attention from my cousin's plight.

Our eyes locked just as I raised the splintered weapon above my head.

"You—" said Mother.

But I brought a jagged edge of the wood down right into her throat.

Her eyes widened as red mixed with the white painted at her

neck, trickling down her collar into the depths of the unpainted skin hidden deep beneath her violet *kimono*.

She slunk to the ground almost immediately and I did too, my hand still clutching the shattered weapon even as it dug into her throat.

"Kojiro!"

"Stop!" said my cousin in the Hanaobian tongue. "Stop now! Look!"

I didn't know if the people gathered bothered to look where she was pointing, but the sounds of metal and footsteps stilled. No one came to see if their empress was still breathing. Only Luana appeared beside me. She turned me over, practically peeling my fingers away from my mother's throat.

My hand was tinged with purple.

She pulled me into her lap and I stared upright at her lovely face, her full bosom. "What's happened to him?" shrieked Luana. "Rohesia, what happened?! Tell me!" She was shaking and crying, though her words were tinged more with anger than sadness.

My cousin approached. Evidently, the men let her do so unaccosted. She stood over me, staring down, the blood still trickling from her shoulder.

"He sacrificed himself," she said, staring into my eyes, "so the imposter empress would lower her guard and could be defeated."

She was lying. This had never been our plan—although yes, I'd wanted to be the one to put an end to Mother. I'd thought defeating my cousin in front of her would indeed get her to trust me, provide me with a chance to put an end to her as well.

"Translate," barked Rohesia, swinging the tip of her red-streaked blade toward me.

I licked my lips and did my best to speak her words aloud to the room. I owed her that much… And I supposed there was no hope for me now. No chance I would ever sit on that throne.

"I am Rohesia, daughter of the rightful Empress Momoko," said my cousin. "I am, and should have been, your empress. You follow me now."

I translated her words, my breaths growing shallower and shallower. I choked at the end and felt a wet, warm liquid pool over my chin.

"Doctor!" barked Rohesia, but I didn't translate. She pointed her sword outward and then back at me. The physician crawled back to my side.

"There is no saving him," he said in Hanaobian.

I nodded and pushed him away. "Tend to the empress," I said.

"She's dead."

"The empress!" I barked, and I must have made my meaning clear as he stood beside my cousin.

"Thank you," she said, staring down at me as the doctor pulled her *kimono* down to look at her wound. "You were brave."

There was so much more she could have said. So much more that would never be said between us, but she walked away, the physician trailing after her, leaving me to close my eyes and drift off in the lap of my beautiful Tsukiko.

"Don't," she whispered. "Don't die. Don't leave me."

"You… strong woman," I said, my mind losing grasp of her clunky barbaric tongue. But I strove to think harder, I strove to convey my words to my beautiful barbarian—my beautiful nomad.

"But what will I do without you?" she asked. "I can't live without you."

"You can. You will."

"No," she said, sniffling. "I've never lived without a strong man at my side."

I felt my lips grin at being called "strong" in turn. Even if she'd only loved me because she'd thought I could provide for her. Because she'd thought I'd make her a princess or an empress. "You find another one who… value you."

"I don't want another one!" She launched herself over me, nestling her head beneath my chin and sobbing into my chest. "I love you." Her words were quiet, but heavy. True.

My heart leapt as I struggled to run a hand through her hair. "I… love you," I said in her tongue. Then I repeated it in my own. "I love you, Tsukiko."

The last sound I heard were her cries echoing out my name.

29

TOMIKO

As the duchy's hostage, I put an end to the assault on the barbarian's island nation. Fastello had been fraught with worry the entire time—my supposed captor pacing back and forth in the Hanaobian-decorated room of his castle, leaving me entirely unguarded because it'd been I who'd offered myself as his saving grace—because he didn't know if the duchy guards and ships would respect the white flag we'd told the ships to wave.

But they had.

It had taken a while for the firing to cease around all three sides of the island—for the duchy to cease firing too—but once it had, Fastello had turned to the Hanaobian merchant captain and his men and me and said, "Let's go. To the docks."

He did not arm himself or us, the only thing in his hand that hilt of a dagger he'd used to cause a distraction.

I was most intrigued. I would have to ask him about that sometime.

He trusted the sailors not to run. Not to attack him as he led the way.

He trusted his own men to meet us there and not strike him down where he stood.

Or perhaps he didn't firmly believe in that. Perhaps he just knew that even armed, he'd have no hope of overpowering them if they turned against him. He marched on regardless.

"What's going on?" asked a dark-skinned woman—a nomad, I'd learned—huddling in the doorway of a building with two children as we passed. "Is it over?"

"We negotiated a cease-fire," said Fastello, who didn't stop. "But be wary. Stay in your homes."

The woman whispered to another light-skinned barbarian who walked nearby, who turned to his neighbor—a Hanaobian, I noticed—who turned to hers. People were pouring out through the cracks and alleyways of the streets as we passed, coming out of doors, asking questions, speaking amongst themselves. By the time we reached the mansion Fastello had taken me to earlier, a large crowd had formed behind us.

The citizens of the duchy were following us.

"Fastello!" cried the blonde, fair barbarian woman who'd met us at the large house previously. She and the other three women approached from the direction of the docks. "We did it! We got the message out."

Fastello smiled and despite everything—despite how torn every little bit of me felt—a pang of something like awe shot its way through my chest. "We saw," he said. He shot forward and embraced her and she startled, jumping back a little, eyes widening. "Thank you," he said.

She hugged him back, grinning.

He let go and hugged the two nomad women who looked more like him and then Malle, too. He pointed back at me and the Hanaobian sailors, his brow furrowing slightly as he took in the large crowd behind us, as if noticing them for the first time. "We have another message to send. This man's account that this is indeed Princess Tomiko and we request a treatise."

Malle stepped forward, her hand out, and I handed her the letter the captain and I had drafted. "I'll see to it. The guards paid us no mind."

She ran off.

"We'll catch up!" shouted Fastello after her before he turned back to us. "Please," he said, raising his voice, "return to your homes. This peace is shaky and I cannot guarantee it will last. You might retreat to the mountains—"

"We'll stay with you," said a pale woman, stepping forward and curtseying. "And we've sent word that those who retreated toward the mountains should join us."

Fastello frowned. "I don't think that's wise."

"We're on your side," said a nomad man, who kissed a Hanaobian woman atop her head and then got to his knees, with her soon echoing his stance. "You won't let us call you our king, but at least let us call you the duke."

Man after man, woman after woman, and child after child followed suit, all getting to their knees, until eventually, only the Hanaobian sailors and I were left standing. Even the Hanaobians among the crowd and the three women Fastello had entrusted with his mission took to their knees.

"You don't have to… Don't trouble yourself." Fastello's voice grew quieter and he ran his injured hand under his nose. "I don't deserve this."

"You do," said the blonde woman, raising her head and smiling. "You brought us all together. For the good of the isle." She touched a pendant at her the base of her throat. "You gave us all freedom to be who we would be."

"You gave us purpose," said one of the nomad women he'd hugged. Her eyes shone with tears and resolve. "You gave us hope."

"We stand with you," said a stranger from the crowd. As if on cue, everyone did stand. "We face this together."

"I can't let you put yourself in danger like that," said Fastello. "It's not just the Hanaobian ships that are a threat."

"We stand with you," said a man, repeating himself with determination in his eyes.

Fastello swallowed, his gaze meeting my own. I did not know what he was trying to say with his earnest eyes, but I said it too. "I stand with you. I want peace. You can deliver it."

"Only with your help," he said, taking my hand in his. The grip of the few fingers left didn't feel any less weak. He stepped back and bowed slightly. "Princess."

I nodded and we picked up our feet again, hand in hand.

The sounds of shuffling feet from behind me—endless, endless shuffling feet—gave me strength even when we passed ruin and rubble. Even when I caught sight of a body here or there, an expression of horror on the poor person's face. I gripped Tomiko's hand tighter every time that happened, though I kept moving forward; I didn't dare linger.

As we approached the docks, I found them upended at several points along the coastline. Most of the duchy's ships, too, were impaled, broken, sinking—it looked like none of them had gotten far from the harbor. The wall with the cannons and the tower that housed the aviary was largely intact, our land's last hope for peace still possible.

Except that Malle wasn't in the aviary. She was just before it, a guard clutching her arm tightly as she struggled to break free.

"Let me go!" she cried. "I must send this letter!"

The man's eyes lifted as I approached, the citizens of the duchy behind me.

"What…?" he said, his grip loosening, his eyes on me as if I were some shepherd straight out of the tales of the age of Ytoile.

Malle broke free and nodded at me, running back toward the aviary.

"Halt!" called the man, pulling out his sword. Other guards soon joined him.

"Stop!" I said. "Let her go. She's on a mission from me."

The guards exchanged a look. "We thought she could be a spy," he said.

"She's not," I said, coming to a stop in front of him. I let go of Tomiko's hand and stood straight, feeling stronger than I had in ages thanks to the wave of support at my back. "She's sending another letter to bring about peace."

"Another?" asked a guard. He looked over his shoulder at the fleet, its white flags flying high. "Is that how you got them to stop?"

I nodded. "And this letter asks for an envoy to be sent to negotiate for peace."

Another group of guards approached from behind me, their own gazes traveling over the crowd. "We told them to stop when the flags flew," said one—I recognized his reddish face from when I'd choked him in the hall. "They didn't believe it would happen, but we said we were just telling them what you told us." He looked out at the ships as if to marvel at my words coming to pass. He nodded at his companion. "He thought to send word to the remaining duchy ships as well."

A bird fluttered out from the aviary window, spreading its wings and gliding toward the nearest Hanaobian ship.

"Peace," I began, moving toward the group of guards, "is possible. With minimal bloodshed. If you'll let it be possible."

"You're still soft," said a man, pushing the other guards aside to stand in front. I recognized him as the one who'd killed that Hanaobian Tomiko had been fond of—even if it had perhaps been on accident. His eyes flicked to Tomiko and the merchants behind me. "And your softness will get people killed."

"Your cruelty, your carelessness is what causes death," said Tomiko, stepping forward. Her eyes blazed with anger, even though there were tears. "It is the same for the empress of my people. No more. We will have peace."

The man laughed, peering again at the ships behind him. "There is never peace. Especially without might."

I moved closer to him and his hand twitched at his hilt, although he didn't pull out his sword, his gaze flickering to the crowd behind me. They were unarmed. But the guards were outnumbered.

"What's your name?" I asked, perhaps not for the first time. But I'd gotten so used to them being there in the background, had initially counted on Rohesia to handle them, had filled my head with so many strategies and ideas for bringing the farms back to life and integrating the nomads with the rest of the duchy—that I'd let these men go overlooked.

Despite their violent past. Despite their loss of a leader to whom they truly felt they could swear fealty.

"Lysander," he said.

I embraced him—but not before his hand swept quickly to grab his sword and fell just as quickly to his side as he accepted my touch, even if he didn't embrace me back. "I need you." I stepped back, my eyes darting to all the guards gathered around us, stopping apologetically on the man I'd choked. "All of you. Please. Protect the duchy with me. Trust me."

Out on the waters, a rowboat descended from one of the ships and tiny figures climbed down into it, one carrying a white flag.

"Let's prepare to greet our guests," I said. Lysander grunted and nodded toward the other men. They formed a line flush against the wall, at attention in case needed, but out of the way just enough to prove our intentions were for peace.

Looking over the crowd of people spilling into the alleyways behind the docks, I smiled. I moved toward Tomiko and took her hand in mine again. A thought struck me then, perhaps because of how hopeful I felt at that moment when I looked at her, how I was suddenly struck with the loveliness of her face, the strength in her demeanor.

I didn't know if I could ever love another like I had Cateline.

But I could trust this woman by my side, see what she could offer my country. What I could offer hers. Love might come later, and if it never did, well… I respected her. I believed in her.

"Princess, will you become my duchess?" I asked.

It was as if I'd asked her to pull Ytoile down from the skies.

Although I didn't think she found the idea entirely unflattering.

EPILOGUE: ROHESIA

Although I found the clothing of my country beautiful to look at, the heft and volume of a ceremonial robe—*kimono*—was something I would never learn to love. I usually stuck to the simpler cloth *kimono* of the lower classes whenever possible; I kept a sword at my hip or at least at my side, despite my advisor's objections.

But today, one year after I'd claimed the throne that should have been mine since I'd been a toddler, Sougo was quite insistent I dress in the full regalia.

"You will receive your people today," he'd said. "Many will lay eyes upon you for the first time. You must look like a spirit on earth. You are their equal by blood, even if…"

He probably said something like "that blood is diluted," but I still struggled on occasion to grasp the every word of my new tongue.

Fortunately, there had been instructors skilled enough in my native tongue to teach me.

I'd almost felt hopeless for a moment when we'd lost Kojiro. Despite what he'd done—and I might never know entirely why, even if his sister had her theories—I felt a great pang at his loss. But most of all, I pictured myself adrift in this country, trying to wrest control with no one to convey my words to them.

Kojiro had always been in my plans. He was supposed to have been at my side, making heirs for his country with his coquettish nomad bride, teaching me how to adjust to his country's customs while guiding them to a better future, teaching them to let go of anything that held them back.

"This one," I said to my handmaiden, a young woman about Tomiko's age named Ayako. She'd told me about Tomiko's spontaneous adventure to explore her lands and what had become of it. Ayako had lost her family, her friends—and when Tomiko had visited some months later, Ayako had learned she'd also lost her brother in the duchy.

I had seen enough of the pain caused by tyrannical rule. Although I felt my rule would be the best option for peace for both Hanaobi and the duchy, I'd vowed I wouldn't shed any more blood to keep it. If the people had rejected me, I would have gone on my way—or let them put me to the blade as they saw fit.

I didn't need to live for myself, for the empty shell I felt I was. I could live for them.

Ayako wove the jade ornament Sherrod had intended for me through my hair. I stared at Mother's jade lion, which sat on a small, short-legged table in my chambers. I could hardly remember her, but I hoped she would be proud of me. She'd seen decay here beneath the country's beautiful, impeccable surface, and she had abandoned it for the filth and decay of the duchy. I could only imagine what she'd seen in Father to entice her—or if she carried a darkness in her heart that better explained the union. I shook my head. That was in the past. I could leave that all behind me, buried. I had watched it all turn to dust and ashes, and I had risen above it all to find new hope.

I and Fastello and Tomiko—duke and duchess of the land I'd once called home.

We were at peace. Our countries traded—fairly and without conflict. Our people were free to move between the lands as they pleased, although we'd found that few had made the move yet. Life had improved in both places.

"You look beautiful, Your Majesty." Ayako smiled. My heart pounded quickly at that smile, a strange feeling most out of place.

But she had become a friend over this past year—and her presence made me happy. Something I could hardly ever say for anyone in my old life.

"Thank you," I said, swallowing back my feelings. I didn't always want to, but I still felt more comfortable keeping such things at bay. "May I have a moment?"

"Of course," she said, bowing, and shuffling out of the room, her back never toward me. A gesture of respect.

Once she slid the door shut behind her, I fell forward just a bit, letting out a breath I'd held tightly in her presence. My insides did that sometimes. The barriers I'd long ago erected in my heart to deal with the horror and terror and loss—they'd started melting. I needed them to stay strong, if pliable. I could recognize the need to empathize, to eschew cruelty, but I still needed the strength they lent me.

I was still just a little afraid to feel.

Grabbing Sherrod's journals off the shelf, where they sat beside Mother's jade lion, I flipped to a random page. I'd translated the entire book—and I'd been right, there wasn't anything of use in it, especially since an underground against the duke's reign no longer needed to exist. But I'd been comforted by the messages nonetheless.

Rosie thinks I didn't notice, read the message I'd transcribed. *But she smiled today. At Sunset. She brushed the horse's mane and when it rubbed its nose against her forehead, she laughed, though it was quiet. Her smile gives me strength to keep up this fight, to set her free.*

He had. Though his own efforts hadn't led directly to who I was today, his ceaseless support had. His sacrifice had meant more to me than the death of my own family, of my own blood.

"Rohesia?" called a voice from behind the door. I slapped the journal shut. Only one person in the palace dared to address me by my given name without a title.

"Come in," I said to Luana.

The nomad woman slid the door open and shut it behind her, staring at a parchment in her hand. Her absentminded stride was so at odds with how the Hanaobians entered a room, particularly in my presence.

"It's from Fastello," she said, her lips pursed. His sole visit to my country so far—his new wife, my cousin, at his side—had been unpleasant for her. She hadn't done more than nod at him as he'd passed her in the hallway, retreating back to her rooms at the palace or venturing out into the capital, where she danced at a tavern not because she had to to earn her keep, but because she took delight in it, the way the Hanaobians stared slack-jawed at her and her wild moves. I could not say if she ever took another lover, but there were none she brought home to the palace, none she introduced to me. I often caught her, her eyes closed, in front of the small shrine my teachers had shown me was the proper way to memorialize the fallen prince who'd sacrificed his life to restore my empire to me.

She opened and read the letter without handing it to me, no doubt having snatched it out of a messenger's hand in the hall, beguiling him into confusion by twirling around him even in the constricting *kimono* she wore. "She had the baby," Luana read aloud. "And mother and child are both healthy and happy."

"Boy or girl?" I asked, wondering if this cousin-niece or nephew would grow up to rule over the duchy or come across the waters to take my place here.

"A girl," she said, nodding at the letter. "He says she's as beautiful as her mother and twice as strong as her great-aunt."

I scoffed at that. What a confusing family tree... But I was happy to have the two of them—three of them—on it, the new buds giving life to the scorched and hollowed-out tree.

"They named her Kotoko," she said. Her eyes began welling up and she shoved the letter at me rather unceremoniously. I took it from her, brow raised. *Ah.* The ideograms in the child's name... They were naming her after Kojiro in their own way.

"We shall write our congratulations," I said, setting the letter aside. "Perhaps send a gift."

Luana nodded and plopped down beside me on the floor. Although she'd tried to learn more of the language here, she would certainly never fit in.

She leaned against me—another friend I'd made, perhaps, although I still found myself at a distance from her—and clutched her legs to her chest. "Fastello is a good man," she said, somewhat wistfully.

"Yes. He and Tomiko both—they're both good people. If they hadn't stalled Hanaobi's assault on the duchy long enough for me to send word to put an end to it once and for all, there might have been little left for them to rule."

"Does he love her?" she asked, completely oblivious to the more important issues at hand. But that was Luana, one of the last little reminders I had of my former home.

"His child?" I asked.

"No, of course not." She tossed her head and shifted again so her shoulder dug against mine. I winced at the phantom pain the movement brought, the wound Kojiro had left me with. "His wife."

I laughed. "Does it matter?"

"Yes!" Luana leaned back and stared at me. After a moment, she reached behind my head, straightening my hair ornament.

"Did you love Fastello's father?" I asked, not completely forgetting what Fastello had once told me about her, though I'd cared little at the time.

"No," she said, grimacing. "Well, I mean... He could be fun..." Her eyes went wild. "But I never loved anyone like I loved Kojiro. He made me feel... special."

"If you seek love, if you give it, you will perhaps find it." My lips drew into a thin line as I thought of Sherrod and Malle, and how my poor besotted father figure had never quite earned her love, even if she'd respected what he could offer her. "But that is not all life has to offer. That kind of love isn't even the only kind of love you'll find."

"Your Majesty," said a voice at the door, "it is time."

"Come in," I said, standing. Ayako's lips upturned slightly in a graceful smile as she passed me and my heart beat faster while the procession of handmaidens came in through the open door, shifting into place behind me and picking up the train on my long *kimono*. I could not easily grab for a sword today. I would not easily dodge an attack.

But for the first time in my entire life, I felt so at peace, I was certain I wouldn't need to.

ABOUT THE AUTHOR

Amy McNulty is an editor and author of books that run the gamut from YA speculative fiction to contemporary romance. A lifelong fiction fanatic, she fangirls over books, anime, manga, comics, movies, games, and TV shows from her home state of Wisconsin. When not editing her clients' novels, she's busy fulfilling her dream by crafting fantastical worlds of her own.

Sign up for Amy's newsletter to receive news and exclusive information about her current and upcoming projects. Get a free YA romantic sci-fi novelette when you do!

READ MORE FROM AMY MCNULTY

THE NEVER VEIL SERIES

"The story is fun and engaging, featuring a female protagonist who will resonate with young teens." ~School Library Journal

"...A whirlwind of time-bending adventures that immerse readers in a maelstrom of plot twists and allusions to "Beauty and the Beast" and other fairy tale love stories, while Noll's understanding of gender-based social and cultural dynamics develops." ~Publishers Weekly

Nobody's Goddess (Book One in The Never Veil Series), winner of The Romance Reviews Summer 2016 Readers' Choice Award for Young Adult Romance:

> In a village of masked men, each man is compelled to love only one woman and to follow the commands of his "goddess" without question. A woman may reject the only man who will love her if she pleases, but she will be alone forever. A man must stay masked until his goddess returns his love—and if she can't or won't, he remains masked forever.

> Seventeen-year-old Noll's childhood friends have paired off and her closest companion, Jurij, found his goddess in Noll's own sister. Desperate to find a way to break this ancient spell, Noll instead discovers why no man has ever chosen her. She is in fact the goddess of the mysterious lord of the village, a man who refuses to let Noll have her right as a woman to spurn him.

> Thus begins a dangerous game between the choice of woman and the magic of man. The stakes are no less than freedom and happiness, life and death—and neither Noll nor the veiled lord is willing to lose.

FANGS & FINS (BLOOD, BLOOM, & WATER SERIES)

A dapper vampire. A sullen merman. Two heirs to a great conflict—and each needs to claim a beloved to become his kindred's champion.

High school senior Ember Goodwin never had a sister, but after her mom's remarriage, she now has two. The eldest is no stranger to her—Ivy is a witty girl in her grade who's almost never spoken to the shy bookworm before—but she's surprised to find the popular girl quite amiable. Their burgeoning friendship is tested, however, when Dean Horne, a pale, besuited charmer, shows interest in them both and plans to reveal his appetite for blood to the one who'll stand by his side.

Seventeen-year-old Ivy Sheppard is tired of splitting her time between her dad's and her mom's, particularly when her dad uproots their lives to move them in with his new wife and step-daughter. Used to rolling with her parents' whims, she tries to make the best of it and befriend her nerdy new step-sister. Her hectic life grows more unwieldy when she catches the eye of junior Calder Poole, whom she swears she sees swap well-toned legs for a pair of fins during a dip in a lake. Now she's fending off suitors left and right, all while trying to get to the bottom of the strange happenings in her town.

The first book in the Blood, Bloom, & Water series sets family against family and friend against friend as an epic, ancient war comes to a head in a supposedly sleepy suburb.

BALLAD OF THE BEANSTALK

A Library Journal Self-e Selection.

As her fingers move across the strings of her family's heirloom harp, sixteen-year-old Clarion can forget. She doesn't dwell on the recent passing of her beloved father or the fact that her mother has just sold everything they owned, including that very same instrument that gives Clarion life. She doesn't think about how her friends treat her like a feeble, brittle thing to be protected. She doesn't worry about how to tell the elegant Elena, her best friend and first love, that she doesn't want to be her sweetheart anymore. She becomes the melody and loses herself in the song.

When Mack, a lord's dashing young son, rides into town so his father and Elena's can arrange a marriage between the two youth, Clarion finds herself falling in love with a boy for the first time. Drawn to Clarion's music, Mack puts Clarion and Elena's relationship to the test, but he soon vanishes by climbing up a giant beanstalk that only Clarion has seen. When even the town witch won't help, Clarion is determined to rescue Mack herself and prove once and for all that she doesn't need protecting. But while she fancied herself a savior, she couldn't have imagined the enormous world of danger that awaits her in the kingdom of the clouds.

A prequel to the fairy tale *Jack and the Beanstalk* that reveals the true story behind the magical singing harp.

Ballad of the Beanstalk is available now in e-book, paperback, and audiobook.

www.ingramcontent.com/pod-product-compliance
Lightning Source LLC
Chambersburg PA
CBHW071255190726
48292CB00007B/2541